Dead Summit

By
Daniel Loubier

Sera,
Thank you so much for the
support! Hope you enjoy!
Dan

www.AuthorMikeInk.com

ISBN: 0-9845801-6-6
ISBN-13: 978-0-9845801-6-3
Library of Congress Control Number: 2011910880

First Published by *AuthorMike Dark Ink*, 10/15/2011

www.AuthorMikeInk.com

AuthorMike Ink and its logo are trademarked by *AuthorMike Ink Publishing*.

Printed in the United States of America

For Bailey,
My favorite little zombie.
Without all those sleep-deprived nights,
I may have never found the inspiration
or the stamina.

There is a place in the woods occupied by things far more dangerous than wild animals. A place where bears, snakes, and mountain lions would be considered welcome guests by comparison. A place where evil endures only because the living continue to visit. A place so calamitous and so damnable nobody would go if they knew what awaited them.

A centuries-old secret lies there, beneath the earth. A secret that, when the time is right, rises to wreak havoc and chaos on those who pass through. A secret, ready to unleash hell and anguish once again upon those who return...

1959

There was a chill in the air that night. The moon, concealed by the clouds that canvassed the campground with a cold, dark gray blanket, offered no light. Low temperatures were typical in the mountains, even during the summer months, but especially at night. It was perfectly normal to have eighty-degree days and forty-degree nights. This particular night, Sam could see his own breath escaping from his mouth even as he sat by the fire.

A Boy Scout as a child, Sam enjoyed campfires. He loved listening to the popping, snapping, and crackling of the little pockets of sap that would burst as the wood heated up, and the *whoosh* of the flame when it grew too high. For him, even as an adult, there was a sense of excitement, and pride, in being able to create a red-hot blaze from nothing more than a tiny spark and a stack of logs. Of course, he enjoyed building fires for her too—for Linda.

Linda Ashley and Sam Campbell were high

school sweethearts. The All-American Boy and Girl, the Homecoming King and Queen, the Yin and Yang—inseparable. They attended the same college; their families vacationed together in Cape Cod each summer. Although they were only dating, Sam called Linda's parents "Mom" and "Dad." Most people would say they had a "fairy-tale" relationship.

Linda sat in a chair, away from the fire, watching Sam's concentration as he stoked the flame.

"Are you going to teach your son how to build a fire someday?" she asked.

Sam looked up. After all these years, she was still a vision. Her tattered and faded blue Yale sweater and sweatpants, unflattering by most accounts, still managed to hug all the right curves of her body. A runner in college, she hadn't lost her athletic figure since graduation. Her dark, flowing hair only enhanced her intense brown eyes, which seemed to pierce right through his, probing his thoughts, perhaps. Sam loved the way she would rub her delicate little nose against the stubble of his face when they were in bed. The way her feet would seek his under the sheets on winter nights. Amid these thoughts, he almost forgot what she had said only moments ago.

"Who says it's going to be a boy?" Sam smiled. He knew Linda had dreamed of having kids ever since high school. He also knew she dreamed of having a son.

"Why does it have to be Daddy's little girl? Can't it be Mommy's little angel?" she pouted, playfully.

Sam stood from where he knelt by the fire. He couldn't tell if the sweat on his forehead was from the heat of the flame or just his nerves—all he could think about was his travel bag inside their tent. Inside the bag was a little box with a little ring with a not-so-little diamond in its setting. Sam planned to propose while they were on vacation.

It made sense to propose while they were out here. They vacationed in the woods often. They even made love for the first time while camping in a tent as teenagers. Because they lived at home, they had never been able to find enough privacy until then, and they were more than ready for each other. Through college and even after, they still enjoyed the same intense affection for one another. They also shared the same passion for the outdoors. They loved the fresh air, the peace and quiet, the simpler way of life synonymous with the northeast.

Sam walked over to where Linda was sitting and looked down. His eyes met hers. He stared for a moment, at the reflection of the fire in her eyes, and then reached out for her hand.

"It's getting late," he said.

"Are you saying you want to go to bed?" Linda asked.

Sam nodded. She gave him her hand, and he didn't let go as he led her into the tent. She turned toward the fire.

"Isn't it dangerous to leave it like that?" she asked.

"I thought it would be romantic," he said.

Linda smiled and followed Sam into the tent.

Linda awoke with a start. It was late. Very late. And there had been a noise.

What the hell was that?

She sat up and waited in silence, waited for the noise to come again. She listened to the sounds of the night: the occasional chirp of a cricket nearby, the hoot of a night owl, the rustling of leaves and sticks off to her left.

There it is again.

She nudged Sam. He snorted and shifted, and his eyes eventually fluttered open.

"What is it?"

"I just heard something," she whispered.

"What did you hear?" he asked.

"I don't know. It sounded like....*shuffling.*"

"Probably just a raccoon or something."

The sound came again.

This time it was much louder.

"Okay, that sounds close!" Linda said, a bit of panic in her voice. Sam was now sitting up too, immediately more alert than he had been only a half-second ago. Linda was sure that it was something big. Definitely not a raccoon or a squirrel. More like a deer or a bear.

In that instant, Linda thought about the security of their bear bag. She was fairly certain that Sam had tied it high and far enough away from the site. In addition to building fires, Boy Scouts had also taught Sam that the safest place to store "smellables" (food, deodorant, toothpaste, etc.) outdoors is up high, about fifteen feet above the ground between two trees.

"All right," he said. "I'll go check it out."

He quietly got dressed and unzipped the door to the tent. He found his shoes just outside and, after putting them on, stood up to take a look around.

It was dark. The clouds overhead remained; there would be no moonlight. He scanned their site and tried rubbing the sleep from his eyes. He looked behind the tent, by the car, even into the site next to theirs. It was then that he saw the man standing among the trees.

WHAT THE FUCK?

As his eyes adjusted, Sam could see that the man was facing away from their tent, unmoving, as if staring at something in the darkness. He turned back to Linda and asked her for a flashlight. Linda hurriedly looked around the floor of the tent—no flashlight. She began to search through Sam's travel bag with her hands. She recognized a few items; a hair brush, shaving kit, and then she touched what she thought felt like a jewelry box. Ignoring it, she found the flashlight and handed it to him. Sam turned it on and aimed it in the direction of where the man was standing.

He was gone.

How is that possible?

He scanned the area surrounding their site but saw nothing. The only sound he could hear was that of his own pulse thumping in his ears. The sound grew more intense as he walked away from the tent and toward the camp road, searching for the man in the woods.

In the tent, Linda got dressed and looked for another flashlight. She was concerned about Sam, but she also began to wonder what was in the jewelry box in his bag. After putting on a shirt, she found a second flashlight and sifted through his bag again. She knew she shouldn't, but her curiosity had gotten the best of her. When her hand finally rested upon the little box, she pulled it out of the bag and opened it. She saw the ring.

OH MY GOD!

She finally knew Sam's intentions. He had been very secretive about their vacation plans; he hadn't given her any details other than that they would be camping in the woods. She began to imagine herself wearing a white dress with a veil over her face, surrounded by a dozen bridesmaids all wearing Yale blue bridesmaid dresses. In her mind, she was walking down the aisle. She could see Sam wearing his tuxedo. The priest was there too. They were standing at the altar, waiting for her. Her parents were in the front row, turning toward her, watching proudly as their daughter walked toward her future. There was an organist too, and he was playing—

She was roused from her fantasy by the sound of Sam's screams.

"*SAM!*" she yelled, snapping out of her wedding fantasy and back to reality. She climbed out of the tent and shouted his name again as she left the site and began to run down the camp road, pointing the flashlight in the direction of Sam's screams. She desperately needed to hear his voice.

"*SAM!*" Still nothing. She expected to be joined by other campers awoken by Sam's screams, but to her surprise, she was alone, searching through the shadows and led only by phantom screams somewhere far off in the night.

After running for a while, she finally saw a figure up ahead, but she was unable to tell who it was as her flashlight danced around like a butterfly in the darkness.

"Sam? Is that you, baby?"

He didn't move. He just stood there in the middle of the road, looking off to one side. She called his name again, still unsure if it was really him. As she moved closer, she recognized the white polo shirt he'd been wearing earlier and knew it was him. Oddly, his shirt was covered in dirt, up and down his sleeves and all over the front. Linda stopped running but continued to approach Sam with caution.

Something was wrong.

Linda called his name again, but he was still unresponsive. "Tell me what happened, baby. You're scaring me."

Without speaking, he began walking toward her. He moved with a half-limping, half-sliding motion, dragging his left leg behind him. Linda stopped moving. She could hear his sneaker scrape the dirt road as he inched toward her. His arms were stiff and barely swayed as he moved. And then she heard something else. Something...*inhuman?*

It began as a low growl and then became raspy, like a gurgle. There was also a swishing sound, as if Sam were chewing and swallowing at the same time. Linda tried to ignore the sounds and watched with tear-filled eyes, helpless, as he awkwardly stumbled toward her, until finally she could see him clearly.

It was horrifying.

Sam's shirt wasn't dirty at all; the mud was, in fact, blood. Both sleeves were covered in bloody spatter. The front of his shirt was bloodied as well, and she realized that the chunky masses that stuck to him were pieces of flesh. His face was mangled badly, his upper lip completely gone and his lower jaw hanging down as if it had come unhinged. He had also been hit hard on the side of his head; he was missing a large part of his scalp, and his skull was exposed.

Shocked, Linda drew in a loud breath, and at that, Sam's head jerked, as his mind came back from wherever it had previously gone.

"Sammy?" she called out softly, desperation in her voice.

He took off running, straight at her. Linda screamed and ran back toward the site. She could hear the gurgling and chewing, and the scraping of the ground as Sam chased her. She saw other people now, too, among the trees and in the campsites around her, but nobody was doing anything.

Nobody was helping.

What the fuck are they doing???

She looked back and saw Sam was still running after her. Her previous life as a track and field star served her well; she was able to outrun him to the car. She got in the driver's side, slammed the door shut, and brought her hand to the ignition.

Except there was no key.

Where are the keys?!

Then it all came back to her. She looked through the windshield, past the fire pit at the folding camp chair in front of the tent. A jacket hung off the back of the chair she had sat in just hours ago; the keys were in the pocket of the jacket. She was sure of it. Every hope and prayer of getting away from Sam was now fifteen feet away. She looked out the window and reached for the handle to open the door.

But Sam had reached her.

He knocked out the driver's window; broken glass sprayed onto her face and hands. He reached inside the car and pulled her by the hair and the arm. She kicked and punched as hard as she could as he dragged her out of the car. Sam pulled so hard that he ripped out some of her hair and she fell to the ground. He lunged at her again and she continued kicking wildly, finally striking him in the neck. As he staggered backward, stunned, Linda got up and ran to the other side of the car. She thought about running to the chair and grabbing the keys. She could lead him away from the site and then run back to the car. She had outrun him once; she could do it again. It was her only chance, so she went for it.

She saw Sam on the other side of the car as she ran by the passenger door. He still looked confounded.

This just might work!

She reached the chair and shoved her hand into the jacket pocket. There were no keys! She swore as she tried to remember where they had left the keys. She was sure she had stuffed them into the pocket. And then it came to her: Sam always made sure the keys were in the tent at the end of the night. It hadn't occurred to Linda until now because they had made love before falling asleep. And now she heard Sam panting and growling, along with heavy footsteps running toward her.

Out of options, she remembered Sam's knife; he always kept one in his bag when they went camping. If she jumped inside the tent, she'd have a few seconds to find the knife before Sam came tearing through the door. At least she would be armed, better prepared to fight him off.

The footsteps were coming faster, louder, and

much closer now. Without thinking, she dove into the tent and zipped up the door. She felt around the inside of Sam's travel bag and found the knife. She braced for the attack.

But there was no attack. There was only silence. Silence and the sound of her own terrified breathing. Linda looked above and around, waiting to see the shadow of a figure cast over the tent, but there was nothing.

When it seemed like there would be no immediate attack, Linda looked down quickly, searching each corner of the tent. She saw the keys on the floor next to her bag. Quietly, she picked them up and waited, unsure as to where Sam had gone. She began to think that maybe the other campers she had seen in the woods had finally helped her. Maybe she was saved.

Linda waited in the tent for what felt like an eternity, and when it appeared that nobody was coming to the rescue, she decided to make a run for the car. She unzipped the tent and waited; waited for the attack, once again, but she heard nothing. No footsteps, no growling, no chewing-swallowing sounds. She stepped out into the night and stood still for a moment.

She listened.

There was an eerie stillness. The air felt stagnant

and lifeless. And then, a slight breeze swirled through the trees, the wind seemingly calling her name, imploring her to leave. A few pebbles dug into the ground below her bare feet as she shifted her weight slightly. Satisfied that she was alone, she quickly began walking toward the car.

The attack came from the left. And amazingly, she never saw or heard it coming. The force of the hit knocked her completely off balance and they both fell together, with Linda going back-first into the fire pit. She screamed, arching her back and pinching her shoulders as the hot coals immediately burned through her thin blouse and melted her skin. She tried to get up, to roll, to kick, to push him away, but Sam was on top of her. The weight of his body intensified the pain of the scalding hot cinders.

As the embers quickly burned her hair completely off and seared her scalp, Sam clawed and bit at her flesh, tearing skin and muscle off her body. He was a wild animal. Linda weakly tried to defend herself, but Sam had already bitten off half her hand and part of her arm. She could only pray that death would come quickly.

Amid the smells of flesh and blood and sweat and mucus, Linda now noticed a different smell: the smell of charred skin. She was being eaten *and* burned alive. Her legs cooked and sizzled over the remains of the fire. She looked at her arm, at the place where there used to be a hand, and felt a warm sensation as she watched her own blood travel down her arm to her shoulder. It was the last sensation she would ever know.

Pain faded away as shock settled in. Linda only wished her four other senses had abandoned her as quickly. She could still hear the ripping and tearing of flesh, like a cotton shirt being torn to pieces. She heard the cracking and snapping of bones as he savagely tore her limbs apart. She could smell raw flesh, singed and charred. She could taste her own blood as Sam feasted on her. And worst of all, she watched it all happen before her. The last thing Linda Ashley ever saw was the others. They had finally come to eat as well.

CHAPTER 1

Present Day

"What the hell is that!?" Grace yelled, repulsed.

Over the last twenty miles of highway, she had noticed that many of the trees were coated with a thin, white, threadlike substance.

"I think it's the gypsy moth," her husband said, referring to the giant, web-like masses. "It's like a huge cocoon or something."

Grace tucked her head back, feigning nausea. She wasn't a fan of things foreign to her, especially insects. Instinctively, she knew she'd soon be having nightmares of giant, man-sized moths invading her room and spinning webs around her while she slept.

The ride up Interstate 93 was uneventful, and that was a good thing. It was August and children were out of school, but Charlie and Grace were lucky enough to miss most of the vacation traffic. After all, they weren't headed toward the coast or to an amusement park; they were going camping in the woods. And while the average vacationer might find camping to be less desirable than spending a week in the Caribbean or on a glorious beach somewhere in the Pacific, Charlie and Grace were diehard climbers. No mountain too high, no cliff too sheer.

They were only a couple minutes away from the campground, and Grace had already begun making a mental checklist of things to buy. She had written a few things down on a small pad of paper when a must-have item came to mind. She turned to Charlie.

"Do you think they'll have 'em?" Grace asked. Charlie looked at her out of the corner of his eye. He said nothing and only returned a sideways grin. She dropped the pad and pencil in her lap and tilted her head. "What?" she asked.

He laughed. "I'm sure the camp store will have your roasting sticks," he said, only slightly condescending. "And if they don't," he waved a hand out the window, "there's a whole forest full of them!"

She pinched him under the arm as he continued laughing. Grace had only one ritual she stuck to every time they went camping, and that was to roast marshmallows over the fire at night. However, she wasn't too keen about the prospect of contracting poison ivy or oak or sumac (or any of the "poisons") while searching for sticks in the woods, so she had been ecstatic to learn during their last visit five years ago that the camp store sold pre-shaved and sharpened roasting sticks.

After enduring several harsh seconds of one of Grace's trademark "evil eye" stares, Charlie finally gave in. "I have to stop and get some propane anyway," Charlie said. "So you can get your precious little sticks then." He blinked rapidly and offered a placating smile. Grace continued to stare at him with narrowed eyes for a few extra seconds and then returned to her list.

For all the teasing, Grace knew Charlie was very much in love with her, especially with her childlike impulses. Whether it was roasting marshmallows over an open fire, stopping for ice cream on the way home from dinner, or watching old Tom and Jerry cartoons on Saturday mornings, she had taught him not to take life too seriously and to appreciate the simple things.

Grace was aware that Charlie had dated many women before her—women who seemed to forget that fun sometimes meant acting a little childish. But Grace hadn't forgotten. At thirty-one, she was a child at heart, and she knew Charlie couldn't help but feel like a kid at times, too.

When the sign for the campground came into view, Charlie slowed the Subaru. The four-and-a-half-hour drive from Connecticut was over; the hustle-

and-bustle of big city life behind them. They were now in the woods, in the fresh, mountain air. The smell of pine blowing in the windows was a welcome change from the smog and pollution they had left at home.

As they pulled into camp, they noticed the place hadn't changed in the five years since they'd last been there. The store was immediately on the right-hand side of the camp road. Behind it, there were trash receptacles of all kinds, fenced in to keep out animals. Charlie pulled into an empty spot in front of the store.

"I'll meet you by the propane," Grace said as she exited the car. "I'm going to use the bathroom first."

Charlie was still getting out of the car as Grace walked into the store. He took a look around as he stretched his arms over his head. There were no people around. *Must be on the mountain,* he thought as he bent and flexed his surgically repaired knee. Most people came here to conquer the big mountain. Known for its incredibly rough terrain and unpredictable weather, Mt. George was also the tallest mountain in the northeast, a trait that attracted climbers of all experience levels. For Charlie, it was also "the one that got away."

Many years prior, Charlie and Grace had set a

goal to summit the tallest peak in each of the fifty states. Five years ago, they had attempted to climb this mountain during what turned out to be the worst storm of that year. Because they were unable to predict such weather, Charlie and Grace decided to prepare for the elements and take what they got. Charlie got an overnight stay at the county hospital and Grace got to sleep by his side. A torn ACL and some bruised ribs later, he was off his feet for weeks. It wasn't too long, however—just several months of rehab—before he was back on the trails, good as new. A long ride in the car still caused his knee to stiffen up, but it was nothing some calisthenics couldn't help loosen.

After a few minutes of limbering up, Charlie went into the store. It was built like a small log cabin on the outside, complete with a brick chimney and a swing on the front porch. On the inside, Charlie was greeted by the delightful smell of cedar and pipe tobacco. There were a few racks of clothing: shirts and jackets with "New Hampshire" printed on the front. There were two aisles with everything from food and water to bug repellent and ponchos. Grace was already perusing the snack aisle to his right.

"Did you find your sticks?" he asked. She excitedly held up two roasting sticks above the store fixtures so he could see.

"Awesome. Let's get some propane and get our site."

They brought their items to the counter and were met by an older man, probably in his fifties. He was slightly overweight, but reasonably so for a man of his age. His red flannel shirt, draped with a pair of suspenders, was tucked into brown corduroy pants, just below a stomach that protruded a few inches past his belt. The nametag pinned to the left suspender read "Roy." Roy had a thick, bushy beard that looked less like a beard and more like someone had hung a Christmas wreath on his face. The pipe in his mouth barely moved when he spoke.

"That'll be all?" he asked, a puff of smoke escaping from the middle of the wreath.

"Yes," Charlie said. "And we're here to check in."

Charlie produced his license. Roy accepted it with a hand that showed the wear and tear of both age and a life of manual labor. He moved easily to the opposite end of the counter to look up some information on a computer. After a few taps on the keyboard, he told them they would be at site number seventy-nine.

"You folk's climbers?" he asked as he walked back. His uninterested tone and the fact that he didn't even look up clearly said, *I don't care. This is only small talk.* Charlie decided to try the kill-him-with-kindness method.

"Yes," Charlie said, slightly puffing out his chest. "We're here for the big guy." He pointed over Roy's shoulder toward a picture of the mountain hanging on the wall.

"Of course you are," Roy said, unimpressed.

Grace was immediately put off by the remark, but she attempted not to show it. "Is there something wrong with that?" she asked, forcing a smile.

Roy stopped across from them and rested his hands on the counter. "Now take it easy, lady." His voice was calm. "Everybody who comes here wants to climb the mountain, and that's wonderful. I've done it myself. It's a helluva climb." Grace was afraid she and Charlie were about to get a lesson on climbing. "But I should warn you—there was a death yesterday."

Charlie's jaw slackened. "Oh my God, where?" he asked. "What trail?"

"About five miles up," Roy said. "On Arrowhead. A man just lost it."

Grace stared at him. Arrowhead Trail was certainly one of the more difficult hikes on the mountain, but by no means was it considered deadly. "What do you mean, he 'lost it'?" she asked. "Was he hiking alone?"

"No, ma'am. He was with his wife. She said he started acting all delusional, said he started seeing things."

"How were conditions yesterday?" Grace asked.

"Conditions have been shit all week. Fog, rain, sleet, hail, you name it. Anyway, I guess during one of his *delusional fits*," Roy said, making quotation marks with his fingers, "he was walking backward, opposite the direction of the trail. His foot caught some loose rock and he just went over the cliff. Three-hundred-foot drop until—well, more rock."

"Jesus," Charlie said, wincing. "Were they able to find him?"

"Oh sure," Roy said. "Rescue teams found the body and hauled him out pretty quick. Poor wife was a mess though."

"I can imagine," Grace said, still in shock. But Roy put his hand up as if to stop her from saying any more.

"No, you don't get it. When I say she was a mess, I mean, she was babbling on and on about how her husband had been up the whole night before, talking about 'the people in the woods.'" Charlie and Grace exchanged a curious glance. "When paramedics helped her off the mountain," Roy continued, "she said he was singing the same tune, even as he went over the cliff."

"What exactly was he saying?" Charlie asked.

Roy leaned in a bit closer.

"Something about how the people in the woods were *waiting* for them...for *him*."

Grace felt a cold chill in the small of her back. "*Waiting* for them?" she asked. "What does that mean?"

Roy stepped back from the counter.

"Heck, lady, I don't know what the hell she meant by that. Clearly she had some issues of her own, don't you think?"

After several seconds of uncomfortable silence, Charlie removed his wallet from his back pocket to pay for the site and the supplies. He inhaled and cleared his throat loudly. It was about time to wrap up story hour.

"Well, I guess we ought to go get set up since it'll be dark soon," he said.

"Probably a good idea," Roy agreed. He punched some numbers into the register. "It'll be four dollars, twenty-three cents. You can pay for the site when you leave."

Charlie handed him the cash, and he and Grace left the store. They stopped on the porch, just outside the door. From the corner of his eye, Charlie could tell Grace was a little shaken.

"Well, that's some scary shit, huh?"

It was a reflexive comment, but Grace could tell he was underplaying the whole story. It was Charlie's attempt to not dwell on it, and Grace decided she was fine with that. She didn't want to ponder the horrors of what they'd just heard now that it was getting dark.

"Probably just a couple of inexperienced climbers," she said, more to herself than to Charlie. "Not to mention, I wouldn't doubt that Roy here tells that story to most of the people who come into the store."

Charlie nodded in agreement and forced a smile. Grace smiled back, squinting as the rays of the low-lying sun pierced through the trees and into her eyes.

As they walked back to the car, Charlie couldn't help but notice the thick layer of clouds moving in overhead. It had been clear all day, but then, this was typical New England weather. Growing up, Charlie's father used to say about the New England climate, "If you don't like the weather, wait a minute."

"What's so funny?" Grace asked. Charlie hadn't noticed he'd laughed to himself.

"Oh, nothing. Just remembered something my dad used to say." He looked again at the clouds moving through the sky. "We might be in for a wet night," Charlie said, and they drove off toward site seventy-nine.

26

CHAPTER 2

A cold front moved in shortly after the sun dipped below the cloudy horizon, and Charlie and Grace had traded their T-shirts and shorts for hoodies and sweats. By nightfall, the temperature had fallen below fifty degrees, far from the eighties they had enjoyed during the day.

Camp setup had gone quickly. After all, this wasn't their first rodeo, and it was only the two of them, so the tent, chairs, and rain canopy were up in less than half an hour. After dinner, they sipped a couple beers as they huddled together in front of a small flame; it was all that was left of the fire Charlie had managed to build.

"That's, uh, quite the raging inferno there, don't you think?" she teased. She watched him squint at her through the corners of his eyes. "Someone might call the Fire Marshall if we're not careful."

"You're such an ass," he said. She laughed and snuggled against his shoulder. He chuckled and slowly shook his head.

Charlie, the youngest of three brothers, hadn't been taught many "manly" skills as a young adult. His parents divorced when he was seven years old, and he was raised in large part by his mother. She had taught him kindness, loyalty, and forgiveness—all of which had served him well into adulthood, but he always felt insecure when it came to hands-on tasks like changing the oil in his car, fixing a clogged drain, and, especially, building a fire. He was no handyman, but not for lack of trying—only lack of experience. Every time they went camping, Grace knew not to interfere, but only to "assist" in ways that would make Charlie feel like he had accomplished something on his own.

"It was hot enough to cook your dinner," he said. "And I didn't hear you complaining then."

She laughed and took another sip of her beer. "You know I only tease you because I love you."

Grace met Charlie shortly after college. As a child, she had lived all over the country with her mother and younger sister, never staying in one place for longer than a few years. As a result of the constant moving, she never grew attached to people out of fear she'd only know them a short time, anyway. But then she met Charlie and her habit of detachment was broken.

Grace had finished her beer, but she didn't feel

like sleeping, not just yet. "What do you think of our friend Roy at the store?" she asked.

Charlie finished a sip. "Not sure. Maybe somebody pissed him off and he's just taking it out on others."

Grace was still uncertain. "I'm serious. You've got to admit, he seemed pretty sure of himself. That was a very detailed account."

"Seriously?" Charlie asked. He was still downplaying Roy's story. But whether it was for her benefit or his own, Grace couldn't tell. "I don't buy all that 'people waiting in the woods' crap. He's talking out of his ass. Who knows if that guy really said any of that? Do *you* feel like people are waiting in the woods for us?"

Grace didn't like the question. She felt goose bumps rise on her skin. What if there *were* people in these woods, hiding just out of sight? Spying on them. Stalking them. *Hunting* them? She tried to erase these thoughts from her mind.

"And like you said earlier," Charlie continued, "if it really happened, they could have been inexperienced. Maybe it was their first time camping. You know how some people just don't take to being in the woods."

She shrugged her shoulders. She wasn't fully convinced yet, but Charlie made a good point. People unfamiliar with the outdoors often had trouble blocking out the idea that they were exposed and vulnerable to their surroundings.

"You'll see," Charlie continued. "Tomorrow night, we'll be sleeping at the hut with a bunch of other people, and they'll probably be able to tell us the real story." He paused. "If it's even true."

The plan was to hike to the Silver Lake Hut, which was about a seven-hour trip from camp. The hut earned its name because it sat on the northern shore of its namesake. In the late morning and afternoon, the sun's light reflected off the surrounding granite mountains, which caused the lake's surface to appear silver. There, they would spend the night. The following morning, they would begin their final ascent to the summit, a three-hour hike from the hut. In total, it would be a three-day round-trip.

It was possible to hike to the summit in one day, but most people did it in two out of concern for the weather. The terrain was dangerous enough without having to worry about the ever-changing climate. In fact, a man once wrote a book about his experiences hiking the mountain. He had started at six a.m. with clear, sunny skies. By the time he reached the hut, visibility had been null due to foggy conditions. An hour later, on his way to the summit, thunder and lightning rolled through, and marble-sized hail pelted his fleece coat. Once he reached the summit, there was a whiteout due to a blizzard. On his way back down, he encountered more fog, thunder, and lightning and, once again, sun and blue skies. He vowed never to hike the mountain again, stating, "I'd much rather spend three days in hell, if only I knew the weather was more consistent."

Fatigue was also a concern. Even the most experienced climbers encountered enervation from time to time. If Charlie and Grace weren't prepared with enough food and water, chances are they were going to run into problems. Conversely, too many supplies might weigh them down and cause burnout. Hence, most people took minimal supplies, stopped overnight at the hut to eat and recharge, and then continued to the summit in the morning. That was also the plan the last time they attempted to hike the mountain.

Before going to sleep, Charlie double-checked the backpacks to see that they both had enough water and snacks for the seven-hour climb to the hut. He also checked to make sure they had rain gear and medical supplies.

He packed a small handgun too. Though he didn't admit it to Grace, he was frightened by what Roy had told them. And just in case they encountered

31

any harm, he wanted to be armed.

CHAPTER 3

The man coming down the trail looked like a hiker. He was wearing a blue North Face shirt that showed about a day's worth of sweat and khaki shorts that appeared bloodied, perhaps from the wiping of cracked and weather-torn hands. His dark brown boots were caked with mud. The only part that seemed odd was that he wasn't wearing a backpack and appeared to be carrying no supplies of any kind. He moved with an irregular gait as well, slumped over, with one shoulder lower than the other and feet dragging as he walked.

 He was mumbling something under his breath as he approached Grace. It was then that she realized she was all alone on the trail. She never hiked without a companion. She always went out with Charlie or with a friend. Something wasn't right. The man coming down the trail was now staring at her as he got closer. Grace continued walking, her head lowered; her eyes toward the ground. She felt like turning around and running back down the mountain, or perhaps turning to her right and heading straight into the woods. The only option on her left was a sheer rock-faced cliff. If she ran into the woods, however, she could simply wait until he passed. She would then be able to get back on the trail and keep moving. She looked up again and saw that the man, closer now, was still staring at her. With no further hesitation, she veered to her right, directly into the woods.

She didn't think about where she was going or how far. She only wanted to have some distance between her and the man when she decided to turn around. She swatted branches and leaves away from her face and clumsily stepped over downed trees and stumps, an ounce of panic in her efforts as she walked deeper into the woods. She didn't want to turn around, but this wouldn't be over until she knew he was gone.

When she felt comfortable with how far she'd gone, she stopped and turned around.

The woods were so thick she could barely see the trail. She looked up at the sky, trying to focus on the sound of footsteps. If he, or any other hiker, had been walking down the trail, she would have heard. But there was nothing. She expected to hear the clomping of his boots, but there was no sound. It was as if he had completely disappeared.

Curious, but satisfied she'd lost him, she took a step back toward the trail.

A hand grabbed her arm. Startled, she turned to her left.

It was him. He had followed her into the woods! She tried to run, but his grip held and he pulled her closer to him. Grace screamed as she looked straight into two black, hollow sockets; the man was missing his eyes! All that was left were a few stranded veins inside two dark holes.

As he opened his mouth to speak, worms came tunneling out like hamburger out of a meat grinder. Grace screamed even louder. She swung at him with her free arm and tried to break free from his grasp but he wouldn't let go. He only pulled her closer, digging his soiled fingernails into her skin. The man's face was now only inches from hers. She could smell rotted flesh as he opened his mouth even wider. She felt a few of the worms tickle the side of her neck and shoulder as they gushed from his mouth...

Charlie was shaking her, grabbing both her arms. She was having a nightmare. Grace opened her eyes and saw him kneeling over her.

"What the fuck?!" she yelled, thrashing her arms and legs.

"Take it easy," Charlie said. "You're having a bad dream. You're okay."

Grace, still dazed as sleep surrendered to awakening, started to calm down and allowed herself to let go of the dream. Charlie rubbed her arm as she sat up, clearly shaken. She looked around, analyzed her surroundings. She ran a hand through her hair.

"What was I doing?" she asked.

"You must have had some kind of nightmare," he said. "You were punching and kicking me."

She paused for a second, taking in what Charlie had just told her. "I was trying to get away from the man on the trail." She started to recall the dream. "He followed me into the woods. I—"

"You're all right," he said. "There's nobody following you anywhere. It's just you and me inside the tent." He made a sweeping gesture with his arm.

She rubbed her hands over her face, slightly embarrassed, and took a deep breath. She looked back at Charlie, apologetically. "I'm sorry, that was just insane."

"You looked like you were having quite a dream," he said, exhaling in relief. "But, no worries, I won't ask you to tell me about it." He stood up and moved toward the door. "Anyway, we've got a mountain to climb. Get dressed. Breakfast is ready."

Charlie left the door unzipped as he walked out of the tent. Grace scooted toward the edge of the air mattress. She rubbed her eyes, attempting to get her bearings. She could still feel the man's nails digging into her flesh. He had had a very cold grasp, with skin that felt like wax. She foolishly looked down at her arm, where he had grabbed her. There were no markings. She was finally convinced that the dream was *only* a dream, likely a result of Roy's story lingering in her subconscious. She reached across the floor, grabbed a pair of hiking pants on the top of her duffel bag, and began to get dressed.

The sun rose around 7:30, but its rays could barely compete with the clouds that blanketed the sky. The morning dew was heavy thanks to a thick, low-hanging fog. It appeared the weather wasn't going to cooperate, much like the first time they had attempted to climb the mountain. However, just like they did on their previous attempt, they had come prepared for all conditions. Grace only hoped that this attempt wouldn't end in the emergency room.

Grace and Charlie ate oatmeal and drank orange juice for breakfast, just as they did before every hike. Afterward, they made peanut butter and jelly sandwiches and trail mix for the journey to the hut. The sugar in the jelly was good for quick energy; the protein in the peanut butter and the carbohydrates in the wheat bread would help sustain it.

They left camp just before 8 a.m. and walked back toward the camp store. The trailhead was only fifty yards from the campground entrance, so traveling by car wasn't necessary. Scorpion's Shadow, the first trail on their ascent, was an easy, meandering trek through the woods for the most part, with a gradual elevation gain. They would be under the cover of trees for the next three hours or so. From Scorpion's Shadow, they would take Jagged Rock Trail. A bit more aggressive than Scorpion, Jagged

Rock presented climbers with very rocky, slippery terrain. Also, many exposed roots could easily bruise one's feet if one wasn't careful with one's steps. Many an impatient climber suffered a rolled ankle injury on Jagged Rock.

After Jagged Rock came Silver Lake Trail. Ironically, the trail with the least intimidating name was also one of the most dangerous—very steep with exposed rock. This trail posed a problem for most inexperienced climbers, as endurance was the key to mastering Silver Lake. Of course, if you were able to survive and make it to the hut, you were doing all right.

The last trail was Arrowhead. Arrowhead started at the hut and ran straight to the summit. Arrowhead was like Silver Lake's older brother—it's bigger, badder, more intimidating, excruciatingly exhausting older brother. If Silver Lake was a ten-out-of-ten, then Arrowhead was a thirteen. Just as steep and with even more exposed rock, Arrowhead was more a test of mental gumption that anything else. Endurance was crucial on both the Silver Lake and Arrowhead trails, but endurance alone wasn't enough. Anyone in good health could endure Arrowhead's physical challenges; it was the psychological challenge that ultimately defeated many an aspiring climber. The trail was only four feet wide. On one side, trees, brush and thicket; on the other, a three-hundred-foot drop. If hikers were able to survive the climb, mentally, all they had to do after that was make it back down.

Charlie and Grace were about an hour into Scorpion's Shadow, still battling the fog, when Grace started thinking about her dream again.

"You think that guy knew he was losing his mind before they even got to Arrowhead?" she asked.

"Are we really talking about this again?" Charlie asked, rolling his eyes.

Grace, who was walking ahead of Charlie, stopped and turned around. Because he was walking with his head down, he almost bumped into her.

"Well, what if we run into someone like that?" she asked

"Gee, I don't know. What if?"

She paused and glared at him to prompt a more sufficient response. He only stared at her blankly. She placed her hands on her hips and arched an eyebrow. No reaction. Finally, she took in a deep breath, ready to unleash a verbal rage on him, when he held up his hands in surrender.

"Fine, fine," he began. "If he was losing it, then he wouldn't have *known* he was losing it, hence the phrase 'losing one's mind,'" he said, smiling. "If he *knew* something was up, then clearly, he hadn't lost anything at all."

Grace wasn't impressed. "You know what I mean," she said. "What if someone tries to attack us? Are *you* going to defend us?"

"Don't worry," he reassured her. "I have a plan."

"What plan?" Grace asked dubiously.

He stared at her in silence. Grace folded her arms and waited to hear his plan. He narrowed his eyes and pursed his lips. She could see the wheels of thought turning in his head. She knew this look only too well. He was considering whether or not to divulge something. Something important. Something to which she might otherwise be disagreeable. Then, the light bulb flickered above her head.

"You brought your fucking gun, didn't you?" She glared at him.

He shrugged. "Yeah."

Charlie had bought a gun a few years ago, before they were married. At the time, there had been several break-ins in their neighborhood. Faced with the lack of security, Charlie had become uncomfortable; they didn't own a security system or a dog. So he bought a gun. Grace had implored him to return it, but Charlie insisted on having a weapon in the house. To Charlie, it was a safety precaution. To Grace, it was an unnecessary weapon of violence.

Ultimately, they compromised; the gun would stay locked away in a box and never come out. Then, he proceeded to take it out every weekend to practice shooting targets at a local gun range. It was easy for him to sneak around since Grace had been attending grad school on Saturday mornings. But one Saturday, class was let out early and Grace came home to find him cleaning the gun after a morning of target practice. She moved out for a week. She swore she wouldn't move back in until he got rid of the gun, but after many apologies and much groveling from Charlie, she finally moved back in. There was only one condition: the gun stayed in the box and she kept the key. Charlie agreed, and that was that.

Then, on one glorious Saturday morning, when Grace opted to ride her bike to school, Charlie removed the key from her keychain, drove to the hardware store, and made a copy.

"I can't believe you brought that thing," she said.

He tried to defend his choice. "Just pretend like it's not there. It won't even come out of my bag anyway."

"Then why do you have it with you?!" she insisted.

"Because I feel safer with it!"

Grace threw up her hands and continued hiking

up the trail. Arguing was counterproductive at this point, and it wouldn't lead to any resolution. Not to mention, it would unnecessarily expend a lot of much-needed energy.

Things were quiet for the next hour. They hiked up Scorpion's Shadow, single file. Charlie led the way. He had always been the stronger hiker, but since his injury, he'd begun to realize his limitations. So, rather than struggle to keep up with Grace, he set the pace.

Charlie's mind wandered back to past arguments. He thought about how long the silent treatment would last this time. Sometimes Grace would come around in a couple hours, as if nothing had happened. Those were the quick arguments. Other times, she might be livid for twenty-four hours. This kind of anger usually followed the long, drawn-out arguments. Granted, they hadn't argued long, but the issue of the gun had long been a bone of contention. He wasn't holding out hope for a quick resolution, which was unfortunate since they were on vacation. He was content to walk along in silence for now and allow Grace time to cool off.

Charlie wondered if Grace, hiking just a few steps behind him now, was even thinking about their argument anymore. He wondered if she was simply stressed by the nightmare she'd had. She had told him about it, briefly, after breakfast. She hadn't experienced a fright like that in a very long time. And Charlie knew her dreams didn't often wander into such territory so he'd become concerned at first. Ultimately, however, he was convinced it had been Roy's story that had gotten to her. The issue with the gun, which was already a sore subject, had come at a *very* bad time.

After a few seconds of mulling around in his own thoughts, Charlie realized he could only hear one pair footsteps.

"I'm still mad at you," Grace said, several feet behind him.

He stopped and stood there, ashamed. He didn't turn around right away. He knew better than to try and establish any eye contact with her.

"I was just thinking about my dream again last night," she said.

Her tone told Charlie that what she really meant was, "*Yes*, I'm *still* thinking about it!" However, the fact that the first words out of her mouth didn't include "gun," "inconsiderate," or "asshole" shone a glimmer of light into the end of the doghouse.

He slowly turned around.

"What about it?" he asked.

"I didn't like it," she said matter-of-factly. "I don't dream about those kinds of things."

"Roy probably got you worked up with that story, that's all."

She shook her head. "No, it's more than that. At least, it feels that way to me."

Charlie saw his opening grow a little wider. He took a few tentative steps toward her.

"What do you mean?" he asked.

She took a deep breath and sat down on a giant boulder. "Well, we've been hiking this trail for almost three hours now and we haven't seen any hikers. We didn't even see anyone at the campground. Doesn't that seem strange to you?"

Charlie knew she made a good point.

"And, this goddamn fog hasn't lifted since we got here." she continued.

"Yeah, but you know what the weather's like here," he said. "It's probably sunny with blue skies at the summit."

Grace heaved another breath of frustration. "Okay, fine. It's foggy. That I can deal with. It's just—" She stopped and stared at the ground.

"What is it?" Charlie asked. When she looked up, he noticed genuine fear in her eyes.

"It just feels like there's evil here." she said.

"*Evil?*" Charlie asked. The word hung out there like a dark, malicious presence enveloping them both. "What the hell does that mean?"

44

"I can't explain it," she said, clearly frustrated. "It's in the air, on my skin. I can taste it, you know?"

Charlie was concerned now. Grace had never been one to talk like this in all the years they'd been together. Feelings of "evil" were certainly new to her, and to him. His eyes darted back and forth as he tried to think of something to say, something that would comfort her.

"Never mind," Grace told him. "We should keep moving."

She stood there, impatiently, her eyes again scanning the ground. Charlie knew it was his cue to get moving. The discussion was over, at least for now. Charlie turned and continued up the trail. They walked in silence, both of them pondering exactly what Grace had meant.

CHAPTER 4

The sky was like a giant, gray comforter, but the overcast conditions, while disappointing, hadn't slowed their progress. They persevered through the dense fog and mist. They had been hiking for several hours on Silver Lake Trail, but despite the cloud cover, Grace could still make out the position of the sun. It was low. Her feet were sore from the hike up Jagged Rock, her legs numb from the physically demanding Silver Lake Trail. Each leg felt like a fifty-pound weight; her thighs burned with each uphill step. She would sleep well tonight. *If we ever get to the hut*, she thought.

Grace had taken the lead about halfway up Silver Lake. She had initially refused, but Charlie insisted he could keep up. She looked back at him now. He labored uphill, head down, bearing down on his hiking poles for support. The ring of sweat that once appeared around his collar had now grown into a large, very long "U" that stretched down to his waist. He must have sensed her staring back at him, because he looked up at her and smiled. She smiled back at him. She knew he was in pain, but she admired his determination.

"Only ten more minutes," she said.

"You said that a half hour ago," he said, panting. "And a half hour before that."

She laughed and faced forward again to mind her footing. She had forgiven him hours ago, but now she felt pity as she listened to his feet stumble on loose rock as he slogged up the trail. Charlie was in top shape, certainly cut out for a hike like this, but watching him lumber up the mountain using his poles as crutches, she was certain his knee was bothering him. He hadn't complained about it, but knowing Charlie, he wouldn't say anything about it anyway. And she wasn't going to ask, either.

Grace had first met Charlie ten years ago at a nightclub. A friend of hers had invited her out one night to see the band that was playing. Charlie was the singer. Grace felt an immediate attraction to Charlie, a well-built man of average height. She found his on-stage confidence to be magnetic. She was, therefore, surprised by his reserve and modesty when she first spoke to him, which only added to the mystery that became Charlie.

She had to know more about him, so she

attended more shows and, little by little, Charlie caught on to what was happening. It wasn't long before they began seeing each other more often, outside of the performances. Within a few months, Grace knew everything about Charlie: where he grew up, where he went to school, his favorite color, and his best friend. She was amazed at how quickly she had fallen in love with the man singing on stage.

They were married two years later in a small ceremony in central Connecticut. The marriage was in October; Grace had always dreamed of having wedding photos with the fall foliage in the background. The Red Sox would go on to win the World Series just a few weeks later. Charlie called it, "a good omen."

Grace's eyes fixed on the trail ahead. They were coming to a clearing. She noted a large gap in the landscape. At first, she wasn't sure if it was simply a break in the trees or something else.

Then, she saw what it was. She nearly pinched herself to make sure she wasn't dreaming. She exhaled a long breath of relief.

Ahead of them was the lake.

"We're here!" she yelled. Charlie jerked his head and, with renewed energy, ran the last few steps of the trail, his poles bouncing in the air as he held them out in front of him.

When he reached the top, he stood next to Grace. He was out of breath and had to lean against one of his poles for support, but Grace knew he'd be okay. The view was enough to cure all ailments. It was even better than she had remembered. The sun was low, so the lake no longer retained its silvery appearance; instead, it now appeared black and ominous, almost bottomless. But Grace didn't let this spoil their accomplishment.

Charlie took a deep, rewarding breath. "We made it," he said. He looked over and gave her a wink. "The hard part's over."

Grace laughed. "I wouldn't go that far," she said. "We may only have a three-hour hike tomorrow, but it ain't gonna be easy."

He gave her a carefree smile and blinked his eyes slowly. "That's fine by me."

They sat by the edge of the lake, taking in all the sights and surroundings. The mountain range that seemingly wrapped around the lake was no less impressive than the last time they'd been here. They both recalled how long it had taken them to reach this point five years ago and determined that they'd matched that time. Grace remarked about how Charlie's knee didn't really slow him down after all.

Charlie joked, "I didn't really have a choice at

the end there since I was chasing a Sherpa."

Grace slapped him in the shoulder. Charlie turned and nodded toward a large cabin off to their left. "Let's go see who's at the hut."

They arrived at the hut at about five-thirty in the evening.

They had allowed themselves plenty of time for scheduled breaks. Aside from stopping to argue and talk about Grace's nightmare, they also took time to admire the views, something they often did during long hikes. It helped, if only a little. And Grace certainly needed the distraction when her mind wandered back to the previous day's events. More than anything, she needed people around; she needed to hear the voices of other hikers. She needed to feel that she and Charlie weren't alone.

The hut was actually quite big for a hut. *"Lodge" is probably a more appropriate term,* Grace thought as they walked along the shore of the lake. As they drew near, she studied the outside of the building. The shelter consisted of two long, rectangular sections, most likely dorms, between which was a large, round central gathering area. Wisps of smoke emitted from the chimney in the middle of the center section; a fire was burning.

They reached the entrance at the end of one of the long sections. Beaten and weary, they hobbled up the steps to the hut. From the opposite side of the door they both heard a familiar, welcoming sound coming from inside: people talking. From the sounds of it, lots of people.

Charlie opened the door to a long hallway with rooms on either side. They didn't see any people, but the din of voices was louder now. They were coming from the central area.

Walking further into the hut, they noticed that many of the doors to the rooms had been left open; backpacks, air mattresses, boots and climbing equipment of all kinds filled these areas. As they continued down the hall, the voices became louder still as they neared the large room in the middle of the hut.

They reached the end of the hall and stepped into the common area. There were a couple dozen people moving about the large room. Surprisingly, it looked even bigger on the inside. The room was split, albeit unevenly, so that it was part cafeteria, part lounge. To their left, in the cafeteria section, people sat at picnic tables, eating soup and sandwiches and drinking water and hot chocolate. At the far end of the cafeteria, a set of steel double doors led into a kitchen.

To their right was the lounge area. It was much bigger than the cafeteria and with nicer décor. People sat on sofas and reclining chairs; men were smoking pipes while women shared drinks with one another. The only thing that kept this area from being one large study was the lack of a tall, mahogany bookcase.

At the far end of this space, the hut overlooked Silver Lake. Grace and Charlie walked over to the large bay windows for a better view of the water. Even on a day so overcast and dismal, the scene was still majestic. The calm, blackened water juxtaposed the soaring peaks, and the threatening skies created a sense of foreboding.

"I'd be surprised if it doesn't storm," Charlie said. He turned from the window and started to walk off. Grace lingered a bit, admiring the view from the window. Her arms and shoulders shook as a chill ran through her, and she turned to follow him.

Tired and hungry, they walked across the lounge, toward the picnic tables. Most of the tables were full, except for one occupied by an older couple. They sat quietly at the far end of the table, facing each other. They were having dinner.

Charlie asked if it was all right if they sat at the other end. The old man regarded them both silently, nodded, and continued eating.

Grace slipped off her backpack, which could have weighed a hundred pounds for all she knew, one arm at a time. She let it fall to the floor next to her feet. With a slight groan, she sat down, resting her elbows on the table. She closed her eyes and rubbed her face with her hands. Exhausted, she felt the dirt and dried sweat combine into a sticky mixture between her fingers and her palms. She had never before considered the idea that one could actually smell fatigue, but she did now.

The weight of her body now off her feet, she still felt as if she was walking. Little swells of pressure continued to jab the soles of her feet. Slow and lethargic, she removed one of her boots and began massaging the bottom of her foot.

The old man at the other end of the table watched this ritual as he ate a sandwich. "You two must have come from the base," he said between bites. Charlie and Grace turned toward the man who just spoke. He had thick, gray hair, which had begun to whiten around his ears, and looked to be in his mid-to-late fifties. He was fit for his age, though; his weathered face showed the lines of someone who had kept in shape for many years and never let the softness of aging set in. His cut-off, moisture wicking shirt revealed muscular, toned arms. "We looked just like you when we came up yesterday," he added.

"Ah," Charlie said. It was more of a tired exhalation than an acknowledgement. "So you must have gone to the summit today?" The man nodded.

"How were conditions?"

The man tilted his head back and forth, considering the question. "Visibility could have been better," he said. "I mean, we lost the fog halfway up Arrowhead, so the summit was dry. So, maybe a tenth of a mile? Maybe a bit more?" It was more of a question to himself. "All we could see from the top was that damn fog below us," he added with a chuckle.

The woman across from him nodded in agreement. "Like looking down just after a good snowfall, ya know?" she said.

Charlie and Grace nodded. The woman, who looked to be in her early fifties, was also in great shape. Her shoulder-length hair hadn't begun to gray yet; it was still a healthy blond. Her face hadn't shown the same lines as the man's, perhaps from daily application of lotions and other age-defying facial products. Grace figured the woman could probably pass for early forties, maybe even late thirties. She wore a T-shirt that had a picture of a rolled-up sleeping bag and a campfire, with a caption underneath that said "Bed and Breakfast."

"We're going to go up tomorrow morning, come back to the hut, and then head back down the day after," Charlie said.

"You have rain gear?" the old man asked.

54

"Yeah," Charlie said. "Coats, hats, water-resistant pants. Never know what to expect up here but, I think we'll be okay."

"Well, just take care going up," the old man warned. "Wouldn't want a nice couple like yourselves getting hurt. And keep an eye on the weather."

The man's polite advice was beginning to sound like a lecture. Charlie, a veteran climber himself, was also a bit too proud of his hiking skills and knowledge of weather patterns.

"Yep, yep. I think we'll be all right," Charlie said with a wink. "We've got youth on our side." His arrogance clearly hadn't gone unnoticed, as Grace kicked his foot under the table. He glared back at her. *What?* he mouthed.

Unimpressed with Charlie's hubris, the older man set down his sandwich and turned to him. "Well, young man, I'm glad you have confidence."

Charlie immediately began to regret his previous statement; he sensed that one of life's lessons was about to be bestowed upon him.

"I have *experience* on my side," the old man stated proudly. "And experience tells me that that limp you strolled in on isn't from some little bang against the kitchen cabinet."

Charlie hung his head. The old man clearly saw through him.

55

"And all I'm telling you," the old man continued, "is to be careful."

Charlie nodded, apologetically. But the old man stared at him for a few seconds after he said this. Charlie looked away, his eyes wandering uncomfortably, as he tried to break the old man's stare.

"I think he understands, Bruce," the old woman said. She turned to Charlie, extending her arm and placing her hand on his. "Don't mind Bruce, he's just a know-it-all old coot who doesn't like to be upstaged by a man half his age." She gave Charlie a wink. Bruce scoffed and continued eating.

"It's okay," Grace cut in. "Charlie could use a lesson in humility. Isn't that right, Charlie?" she said, flashing him a condescending smile. Bruce laughed under his breath and continued eating. In an attempt to clear the air, Grace extended her hand to the woman. "I'm Grace, by the way." The woman shook her hand.

"I'm Cheryl. Obviously, this is Bruce," she said, casually nodding toward the old man without breaking eye contact with Grace. "It's a pleasure to meet you both. Are you from New Hampshire?"

"No, we're from Connecticut." Grace said. Again, Bruce scoffed, but this time he tried to disguise it with a cough. Charlie again glowered at

Grace, shaking his head only slightly. She could read his mind. *One more time,* Grace thought, *and Charlie will snap at this man.*

"Are you staying at the campground?" Cheryl asked.

"Oh, uh, yes," Grace said, forgetting about Charlie for the moment. "We got in yesterday. We camped last night, then jumped on at Scorpion's Shadow this morning. Figure we'll summit tomorrow, spend another night at the hut." She paused as she glanced at Charlie. "And then either we'll explore a little more around here and spend one more night at the hut, or we'll head down to the base the day after we summit."

At this point, Bruce rejoined the conversation. "You say you're staying at the campground?" he asked.

"Yes," Grace said.

"So you folks must have bumped into Roy then, yeah?"

Grace and Charlie exchanged a nervous glance. Ever since they had reached the lake, Grace had forgotten about Roy and his story. The peacefulness of being a mile above street level had set her at ease and erased her fear and tension. But now, just the mention of Roy's name brought it all back, flooding her mind with the memory of her dream and the story of the man who had died on the mountain. She became uneasy for the first time since they had entered the hut.

"Yeah," Grace said tentatively. "We had to stop at the store and pick up a few things." She looked back to Charlie, hoping that he would ask about Roy's story, but Bruce continued before either of them had a chance to speak.

"Roy's good people," Bruce continued. "He's been running a tight ship at that campground for years. Keeps the riff-raff out, is good to the people who come there. I've known Roy a long time. Good man." He nodded his head as if to reaffirm his opinion.

Seeing an opportunity to ask about Roy's account of what happened on Arrowhead Trail a couple days ago, Grace prompted Charlie again with wide eyes. Charlie took the hint.

"Yeah, uh, speaking of Roy," Charlie began.

Bruce turned toward him, arching his eyebrow. "Yes?" he asked.

"He told us about what happened up on Arrowhead the other day," Charlie said. "Isn't that awful?"

Bruce furrowed his eyebrows, trying to figure out what Charlie was talking about.

"Something happened on Arrowhead?" he

asked.

Oh boy, Charlie thought. *Wrong person to ask.* He couldn't back up now, though. The cat was just about out of the bag.

"Well," Charlie said, fidgeting, looking to Grace for support. She offered none and pretended to focus on something on the table. Charlie was on his own now. The story would have to come out. He reluctantly continued, "Roy told us about the guy who died. Says he fell off the trail? Fell straight down the cliff?" Charlie paused and waited for some kind of recognition of the account. Bruce simply stared in disbelief. Even Cheryl looked dumbfounded. "You guys didn't hear about that?" Charlie asked.

Bruce put his hand to his head, squinted his eyes. "Well now, let me think for a second," he said. "We got in two days ago, hiked up here yesterday," he was counting on his fingers. "We went to the summit today..." His eyes darted up and down, as he retraced the events of their trip so far. "We didn't hear anything about that." He looked at Cheryl who was also shaking her head. "Roy told you this?"

Bruce seemed genuinely concerned now, and Charlie began to wish he had kept his mouth shut. He attempted to downplay it.

"You know, it was probably just some kids playing a prank on him. You know how that can be, kids and their stories."

Bruce didn't appear to be impressed. "You saying Roy's easily duped by children?" he asked, annoyed by Charlie's comment. "Is that what you're sayin'?"

Charlie began to backpedal. "Not at all," he said, his voice rising in pitch. "He just gave us a really vivid account of an accident that happened up on Arrowhead. We hadn't heard anything about it until we arrived yesterday."

"Well, if Roy said it happened, then it must've happened." Bruce was defensive now. "All I'm saying is we hadn't heard about it." He was about to take another bite of his sandwich when he turned to Charlie again, pointing his finger. "Roy's no liar."

Charlie stared down at the table and nodded. He was content to just drop it.

"It's all right, dear," Cheryl said. "I'm sure the young man isn't calling Roy a liar."

Unable to think of anything else to say, Charlie leaned over and pretended to look for something in his backpack. Grace, too, busied herself with meaningless tasks: checking the zippers on her pack and counting the number of plastic snack baggies, bottles of water. It was after a few minutes of staring at empty food containers that they realized they hadn't had a decent meal all day.

Grace turned to Cheryl.

"Do you know where we can get a couple of those sandwiches?" she asked.

Cheryl must have been ecstatic that someone had changed the subject, because she brightened right up.

"Oh, just ask Terry, dear. She'll get you guys set up," Cheryl replied. "She's basically in charge of the place. Does most of the cooking, maintenance—the only thing she doesn't do is clean up after you. So just pick up after yourselves and she'll be your best friend."

"Yeah, Ter's great," Bruce added. His temper appeared to have subsided, much to Grace's relief. "You guys need anything, you just go see her. In fact, I'm surprised she hasn't been by in a while."

"Thanks for the heads-up," Charlie said. "Maybe we'll go set ourselves up in a room and come back and eat."

"Oh no," Bruce said. "She'll set you up. She has to check you guys in anyway."

"Oh, okay," Charlie said. He turned to Grace. "I guess we'll just hang out here 'til she comes around."

Charlie and Grace, once again back on Bruce's good graces, made small talk with the old couple. They talked about their jobs, where they grew up, where they met, when they married. After a while, Grace found that speaking to Bruce and Cheryl felt like speaking with the parents of a close friend. They had been hiking for thirty years together. They'd hiked out west in the Rockies, up in Alaska in Denali National Park, even got to join an expedition to the summit of Mt. Kilimanjaro. But they loved the northeast. It drew them back year after year. Grace was telling them about her and Charlie's goal of summiting the tallest peak in each of the fifty states when a woman came through the kitchen doors.

"Ah, here's our girl now," Bruce said. He waved her over to their table. Terry was tall for a woman; nearly six feet, and heavyset. Her curly red hair was cut short, but perfectly framed her round face. She wore an apron that said "Kiss me, I'm Irish." Grace assumed that Terry would have old-world charm, but that assumption proved erroneous the moment Terry opened her mouth.

"Bruce, Cheryl!" Terry bellowed, smiling. "How's the food?" She leaned over their end of the table and rested her hands on the corners; the wooden table creaked under her weight. From the opposite end, Charlie noticed that, for a woman, she had hands like a bear.

"It's delicious," Cheryl said. "Actually, Ter, we've been waiting for you. We'd like you to meet our new friends, Grace and Charlie. They're looking for a room."

Still smiling, Terry looked back and forth at Charlie and Grace. "Hey, folks! Welcome to the Silver Lake Hut! I don't recall ever seeing you here before. This your first time?" Her voice had a gravelly quality that Grace suspected was the result of a pack-a-day smoking habit.

"Yes," Charlie said. "We're hoping to get a room for a couple nights and maybe a hot meal if the kitchen is still open?"

Terry let out a deep, raspy laugh. "Well, if the apron's still on, so is the grill!" She laughed again, at herself this time, and Grace and Charlie forced a laugh along with her. "Tell you what," she continued. "Let's go find you both a room and then we'll get you both something to eat. How's that?"

"That sounds great," Grace said. She and Charlie stood up and grabbed their backpacks. Grace turned back to Bruce and Cheryl. "It was nice meeting you both."

"See you two later," Bruce replied.

Charlie and Grace followed Terry out of the cafeteria, through the lounge, and down the hallway opposite the one through which they had arrived.

"Have to put you down here," Terry said over her shoulder. "The main hall is full at the moment."

"No problem," Charlie said.

As they walked down the hall, Grace admired the various pictures that hung on either side. One of the images was of the summit in winter. It was a widely-known fact that the mountain recorded snowfall every month of the year, whether it was a light flurry or a blizzard. In fact, conditions were so treacherous during the winter months that the state closed off that part of the mountain between the hut and the summit from October until March. The only vehicles allowed on that part of the mountain during those months were the snowcats. They patrolled the mountain in the event that any would-be skiers tried to take advantage of the untouched powder.

Grace also stopped to admire a shot of the lake, presumably taken during the fall given the colors of the leaves. She also noticed it was extremely overcast in the picture, much like this day, and wondered how often the hut saw the sun.

As if awoken from a dream, Grace flinched when she heard her name called, rather loudly.

"Grace!" Charlie said, nearly shouting. Terry laughed. "Are you with us, Grace?" Charlie said, laughing at himself. Grace shook her head, eyes wide.

"Wow, sorry," she said. "I was admiring the photography you have along the walls here."

Terry looked around. "Oh yeah, we've got a lot

of talented folks that come up here. Most of them locals," she said, matter-of-factly. "Well, I was just telling Charlie, here we are!" She motioned toward a room on the right side of the hall. "You two will be in room nineteen."

Grace and Charlie walked into the room. There was a window straight ahead that overlooked the lake and, to their right, a full-size bed with only a mattress and sheets. Next to the bed was a nightstand with a small lamp.

"You folks bring pillows?" Terry asked.

"Yep," Charlie replied.

"All righty. Bathroom's at the end of the hall if you need to use it," she said, pointing toward the far end of the hallway. "There's another one in the hallway you came in at the end closest to us. Showers are outside, there's four of 'em. And, with a full house like we have here tonight, as you can imagine, it might be a little bit of a wait before you can get in, but the line moves quickly."

Charlie was amazed that she knew precisely where they'd entered the hut.

"How'd you know we came in at the other end?" he asked.

"Because that door," she said, pointing again toward the end of the hall, "is broken." She let out another scratchy, hoarse laugh. "The door you came in is currently the only way in or out. Well, there's a door in the kitchen of course, but you probably don't want to be running through there now, do ya?" When she said "do ya," her blue eyes became big as silver dollars and she'd pulled her head back so much that her extra chins had now spread her face into the size of a platter. Grace had to stifle a laugh.

"Okay, sounds good." Charlie said, allowing the straps of his backpack to fall off his shoulders and into his hands. Terry stood there and kept nodding. She looked around the room, out the windows, toward the lake. There was an uncomfortable silence as nobody could think of anything to say.

"So, um..." Charlie said, trying to break the lull.

"Right," Terry said, remembering their meals. "You folks get yourselves settled in and give me..." she paused to think. "Ten minutes? That sound good?" Charlie and Grace nodded. "Okay! See ya back at the caf in ten!"

Grace set her backpack on the bed while Charlie took a seat on the mattress. He took a deep breath and ran his fingers through his hair. Grace looked at him while he rested and combed through his pack. She smiled. They'd been through so much just to get back to this mountain, Charlie especially. In that moment she had never been more proud of him for all his hard work: rehabbing his knee, getting into

66

shape, never giving up. There were times when he felt like quitting, when the rehab became so intense and exhausting, he just wanted to settle and live a life devoid of any strenuous physical activity. Those were the times when she picked him up and helped him see his potential, when she helped him to regain his inner physical and mental strength. But she never claimed or accepted credit for helping him get back on his feet. She would assert, "It was in you all the time," and she believed it. All she did was make sure that he never lost faith in himself.

She was pulling a few toiletries from her pack, her mind back in the room once more, when Terry poked her head in the doorway.

"Hey!" she said. Grace flinched so wildly, a small bottle of shampoo flew out of her hand and hit Charlie in the back of the head.

"You folks going to bed early or are ya stickin' around for the campfire tales?" Terry asked.

Charlie rubbed the back of his head. Grace squinted her eyes and tilted her head, not certain what Terry was referring to.

"After the sun goes down—maybe about eight-thirty, nine o'clock—a bunch of us sit around by the fire and share some stories. Sometimes spooky ones!" she said, raising her eyebrows excitedly. She didn't elaborate any further—only nodded, urging them to say yes.

Grace looked at Charlie. "You know, we didn't really have any plans so, yeah, that sounds like fun."

"Fantastic!" Terry beamed. "Okay, you two. I'll have your food ready in a jiff!"

Terry bounded down the hall toward the kitchen. Charlie turned to Grace and raised an eyebrow. Grace laughed.

"Sorry," she said. "Ter needs to knock next time."

CHAPTER 5

Charlie and Grace dined on Terry's specialty: pulled pork sandwiches and lentil soup. Because they had arrived so late, only one other couple and a family of three ate dinner with them in the cafeteria. Most of the other campers had eaten earlier and were now using the bath houses to get cleaned up for the night.

They spoke about the hike while they ate, recalling many of the day's challenges, and compared them to what lay ahead the following morning. Charlie apologized for the gun again. Grace forgave him, if a bit reluctantly. She did not want to see or hear about it for the remainder of the trip.

They showered after dinner and changed into bed clothes. From their room they could hear "oohs" and "ahs" and laughter coming from the common area. Apparently, story time had begun without them.

Grace felt a bit guilty that they hadn't arrived in time for the first story. "I think we're missing it," she said.

Charlie snickered. "I wouldn't say we're 'missing' it. Are we?" He laughed at himself. Grace sighed and threw a pillow at him.

"Stop it." She arched her eyebrows into a pleading stare. "This is like a community for these people. They probably love this kind of stuff." Charlie stared straight back at her for a second before rolling his eyes. Grace gave up. "I don't care what you say. I think it's going to be fun."

Of course Charlie never honestly intended to blow off the evening's event; he only used it as another excuse to mock the child in Grace. Truly, he was more than happy to entertain the idea.

They finished dressing, turned off their light, and headed down the hall toward the lounge area. To their surprise there was actually a large number of people gathered around the fireplace. Most of them sat on pillows on the floor. Grace guessed that this was everyone who was staying at the hut that night. There were old couples, young couples, and families with children. They spotted Bruce and Cheryl seated toward the back of the audience.

Charlie quickly scanned the crowd. "I wonder when Barney the dinosaur is showing up," he whispered.

Grace pressed her lips tight, nearly breaking out in laughter. She pinched Charlie on the inside of his bicep and he pulled away, rubbing his arm. Grace motioned toward Bruce and Cheryl.

"Oh, seriously?" Charlie said with a reluctant sigh.

"Shut up," Grace whispered. "We're sitting next to them. It's not even like we have to talk to them."

They sat on the floor next to the old couple. Politely and quietly, Grace asked Cheryl if they had missed much.

"Not much," Cheryl said, her voice low. "This chap Joe is telling a ghost story."

Joe, a lanky beanpole of a man, sat on a chair as the rest of the people sat on the floor, looking up at him. As he told his story, he moved his hands around in wide, arcing motions, trying to add effect and tension as he spoke. "And when she got to the top of the stairs... *THERE WAS NOBODY THERE!*" he exclaimed. A few small children jumped and screamed.

These are probably the "oohs" and "ahs" I heard, Grace thought.

Charlie, unmoved by Joe's story-telling abilities, turned to Grace. "Is this guy for real?" he asked. He grunted slightly when Grace elbowed him in the ribs and nodded in acquiescence after she shushed him.

She looked around and saw lots of attentive faces: couples sitting arm in arm, children playing

71

quietly on the floor next to their parents. Terry was sitting toward the front. She caught Grace's eyes and smiled, acknowledging her with a slight nod of her head. Grace smiled back and continued to scan the crowd while Joe told his story.

"She entered the room to find the baby, still sleeping in her crib," he continued. "So how did the man know where the baby was?" he asked quietly, scanning the crowd. Several people looked at each other and shook their heads, anticipating the conclusion. *"BECAUSE HE WAS STANDING RIGHT BEHIND THE MOTHER!"* he shouted with dramatic flair. A few people in the audience even jumped. Charlie turned to Grace, yawning, and she shook her head in disapproval.

"HE WAS IN THE BABY'S ROOM THE WHOLE TIME! BWAHAHAHAHA!!!" Joe yelled, concluding his story. He stood up from his chair to much applause. Several children whimpered to their parents, frightened by the story they'd just heard.

"Sorry folks!" Joe said. "Didn't mean to scare the little ones." He walked around the front of the audience and sat down at the far side of the room, to Grace's left. As the applause died down, Terry stood up and walked over to the chair.

"Thank you for sharing your ghost story with us, Joe," she said. A few more people applauded. She took a deep breath and exhaled loudly. "I have a story," she continued, "but, uh, some of you parents might want to put the kids to bed for this one!"

Some moms and dads stood slowly, gathering their things. Several of them shook hands with their neighbors as they shuffled their kids off to bed. Some folks stood up just to stretch their legs. The ones who left thanked Terry and the other storytellers for an enjoyable evening, but there was still a large audience. Some families with older children stayed to listen.

Terry sat down in the chair and looked around the room. "I still see a few young'uns here," she said. "Well, suit yourselves!"

She reached for a glass of water from a table next to the chair. After taking a sip, she set the glass back down and rubbed her hands on her thighs. She leaned forward slowly and rested her hands on her knees.

"This story," she began in a very soft voice, "didn't happen in anyone's home." She took a long, deep breath, allowing the audience a moment to settle in. "It didn't happen in some mental institution, either." She paused to look around, a gesture that commanded everyone's attention. "It didn't happen in a boat or a ship or a plane or a car." She spoke very calmly and deliberately, making eye contact with as many people as she could. Grace found her voice to be very soothing–yet, at the same time, unsettling. "That's because," Terry continued, "there were no cars when this story took place." She paused another moment, attracting several puzzled looks. "That's because, this story took place right here."

Several people shifted uneasily. Grace noticed the attempts of others to get more comfortable. She leaned in closer. *The woman sure can command an audience*, she thought. As Terry looked around, her eyes caught Grace's, but it was too late; Grace was already hooked by Terry's inflection. *She's got them*, Grace thought. And surely Grace was one of "them."

"This story takes place around four hundred years ago, back when the settlers first came to the New World, when the Pilgrims landed at Plymouth Rock. You see, the settlers arrived in what is now Massachusetts, but they soon migrated west, south, and north.

"New Hampshire was founded by John Wheelright, along with a number of other early settlers. It was also one of the original thirteen colonies." This earned a few "good-to-know" looks from people who were impressed with Terry's knowledge of local history. "Folks came north and found the lakes and rivers of New Hampshire full of bass and trout. They were able to hunt deer, bears, and moose for food and kept the animal hides for

74

clothing and warmth. Farming was also a big industry in the colony. So with that, they decided they could live up here.

"Unfortunately, weather, as most of you know, was and still is *very* unpredictable in New Hampshire." Several people nodded in agreement.

"Most of you little ones," she continued, pointing to a few of the remaining children in the audience, "grew up with electric or gas heat. Well, the settlers didn't have such forms of heat because that technology didn't even exist yet!" The kids' eyes went wide with awe.

"Back in those days," she continued, "the only source of heat was fire. Now, Massachusetts was certainly colder in those days than it is today. After all, there were no such things as cars and buses, smog and pollution, buildings and skyscrapers. But it wasn't cold like New Hampshire," she said, shivering as she spoke. "You see, New Hampshire is far more mountainous than Massachusetts and, well, the early settlers weren't familiar with weather conditions in the New World. Many people died very unpleasant deaths due to the harsh, unforgiving winters. Especially in the mountains...especially here" She paused a moment and allowed the implications of what she just said to sink in.

More people shifted nervously on the floor. A

couple with three small children got up to leave.

"Sorry, folks," Terry said. "I warned ya's to put the children to bed!" The father of the family turned back, half-smiled, and continued with his wife and children back to their room.

"Well now," Terry said. "Where was I? Oh, right, the mountains." She drew in a deep breath. "Now, weather in the mountains is quite different from weather at sea level, as many of you probably experienced today." She gestured toward the audience. "I saw many of you arrive in T-shirts and shorts, and now look at you. You're all in sweatshirts and pants." Many people looked around at each other. Some grinned as they noticed that, in fact, they were all in much warmer clothes than those they'd been wearing upon arrival.

"Well, the first settlers weren't aware of exactly *how* much colder it got in the mountains. So when they tried to cross, they were unprepared for the elements and ended up dying in their attempt to cross through the mountains into what is now Vermont."

"When does this story get scary?" a teenager mocked from the audience. Several others giggled along with him. Terry stared at the young man. Her face was stoic.

"The story gets scary when you find out what happened to these people—*after they died*."

The young man's smile quickly faded away. Grace noticed a heightened sense of unease around the room. She nudged Charlie in the arm. He turned toward her and shot her a concerned look. She shook her head, as if to say, "I'm not finding this fun anymore."

Charlie nodded. "We'll go when she's done," he whispered, and returned his attention to Terry. Grace turned to Bruce and Cheryl. Their eyes were glued to big woman as she spoke.

"There's an energy here, friends," Terry said, her voice a bit louder than before; her face completely emotionless. Any hint of friendliness in her tone was completely gone at this point. Her story began to sound less like a story, and more like a warning.

"An energy, in these mountains," she continued, pointing toward the ground below her. "An energy that, when triggered by the right forces," she paused before finishing this most crucial sentence, "*brings the dead back to life.*"

Grace, not one to believe in such fantasies, didn't realize the pace of her breathing had increased so much. She felt winded. Charlie noticed it, too.

Are you okay? he mouthed.

Stunned, Grace looked back to him. She swallowed hard, took a deep breath, and regained her composure. "Yeah," she whispered with a nod, but even she could hear the uncertainty in her own voice.

Charlie nodded back and turned to continue listening.

"But they aren't exactly *living*," Terry said. Her eyes were now less focused on her audience. She stared blankly toward the opposite end of the room. "No, no, these people," she continued, "or more appropriately, these *beings,* are far different from you or me because of the lives *they* lead."

Every person in the audience now hung on her every word.

"They are the *undead*," she said, pausing again to allow the words to sink in.

Nobody on the floor stirred this time. Grace felt as if a pair of hands were holding her down permanently to the floor. There was utter silence because everyone was either too tired to move or too frightened, like her.

Grace looked over at Bruce and Cheryl. Cheryl, wrapped in Bruce's arms, turned toward Grace and gave her a knowing glance. Grace smiled thinly and turned back to Terry.

"They don't remember the lives they led when they were alive," Terry said. "They don't try to go back to work or drive a car or find their loved ones." She stared down at the floor, a trace of sadness on her face. "They don't eat food or sleep or do any of the things normal living humans do. They don't do much of anything." She then looked up and faced her audience. "They do nothing...except crave human flesh."

Grace's stomach began to turn. She saw where this was going and didn't find herself enjoying this as much as she had anticipated. But Terry continued.

"The undead don't just *crave* human flesh," she said. "They *need* it. Human flesh to them is like air and water to the rest of us. They need it to survive in their state of unliving.

"And that's just what happened, right here, four hundred years ago. The settlers died, trying to cross the mountains. But the energy was strong, *very* strong, and they rose again, undead, feasting on the flesh of the living."

Several members of the audience now had looks of disgust on their faces. Even Charlie stared straight ahead, appalled at what he was hearing.

"Those who didn't die right away, the ones who were more fit and able to carry on, died soon after, when the undead caught up to them." Even Terry looked terrified as she recounted the story. "And they didn't just eat them, oh no. The undead *devoured* the living." More looks of disgust. "They ripped and tore the living apart limb from limb, chunk from chunk."

Now there were several groans from the

audience; people turned their heads, horrified at the idea of being eaten alive by another person—another *creature.*

Terry leaned forward again with her hands on her knees as she lowered her head even further toward the audience. "They bit through skin, chewed through bone, gorged on intestines and brains."

A man in the middle of the audience had heard enough.

"All right, Ter, I think that's enough," he said. He stood to leave, but Terry tried to call him back.

"Jake," she said very quietly, raising a hand. "I'm sorry, dear, but it's a story that has to be told."

"But it's not even true!" he protested. Everyone else remained still on the floor, looking up at Jake as he navigated through the audience. "The entertainment value left when you started talking about people being eaten alive. What's wrong with you?" He stormed off, down the hall, and Terry did not try to stop him.

A woman, Barbara, sitting in the front row, asked, "What happened to the," she paused, hesitant to say the word, *"undead,* when there were no more people left to eat?"

Terry slowly turned her attention to the woman asking the question. "I'm glad you asked," she said. "After a while, the living began to thin out, the undead having nearly wiped out the whole lot of them. Those who were not completely devoured suffered the same fate; they became cursed as well, forced to carry on as creatures of the undead.

"And when none of the living remained and no more continued to pass through, the undead just perished."

Not knowing what to think about all this, Grace looked down. But Terry was quick to elaborate.

"But every now and then, the energy generated by these mountains and by the land becomes just right." The last part she said with a half whisper: *"And the dead DO rise again...and again...and again!"*

At this, most of the campers stood from where they sat and wordlessly began making their way to their rooms. Many of them exchanged worried looks. Fathers walked away with their arms around children whose faces were pale and ashen. Grace looked down at her hands; her palms were red from holding on to Charlie's arm so tight. Her neck was tingly, much like the feeling when the hair on the back of one's neck is standing on end. Not knowing whether these people were sickened by the story itself or by the way Terry seemed to have believed every word she said, Grace nudged Charlie's arm. It was time to go.

Charlie nodded and they both stood. From the corner of her eye, Grace noticed Bruce and Cheryl getting up to leave as well. Cheryl's face was white.

"Is this typical for 'story time'?" Grace asked her, keeping her voice low.

Cheryl's eyes filled with shock and terror. "I don't know what the hell this was," she said, and without another word, she and Bruce walked down the main hall toward their room.

By now, Terry was up and making her way toward the kitchen. Grace rubbed her hands nervously, not sure whether they should stay and wait for the crowd to disperse and *then* leave or try to leave now. If they stayed, chances were they'd be alone with Terry; if they left immediately, they ran the risk of meeting her face-to-face on the way to their room. Grace pulled Charlie by the arm and decided now was a good time to go to the room.

As the room started to clear out, Grace and Charlie still found themselves having trouble weaving through the crowd of people. Some were headed toward the main hall, some toward the secondary hall with the broken exit door. Grace continued to push through. She couldn't see very well where they were going but she knew they were headed toward their room. Grace stopped abruptly so as not to get run over by a tall man walking through. After the man passed, Grace stepped forward again.

Terry was there.

If she shrieked, Grace couldn't tell. Her ears filled with the overall din of feet mulling through the hut, voices trailing off in every direction, and of fluid pulsing through her veins. She had been trying to avoid this moment. But here she was, face to face with the woman who had all but cleared the room with her macabre tale. Grace's eyes darted back and forth, looking for a distraction. She didn't want to engage in conversation. Unfortunately, Terry spoke first.

"Hey, you!" she said. "I'm so glad you two came out tonight!"

Grace was amazed at the lightness of her tone. It was as if she'd just participated in a child's recital. This was the same woman who, just minutes ago, had woven a tale of the undead tearing at and feasting on the flesh of the living. Now she put on an air of lightheartedness. Did she even realize that she had just alienated the entire hut? Did she not understand? Grace wondered if something might truly be wrong with this woman. She tried to think of something to say, some kind of exit strategy. Luckily, before she needed to open her mouth, a man wearing a ball cap walked up.

"Hey, Terry," the man said. "That stuff you mentioned about the dead rising again, you know, when the energy is right..." Terry nodded, understanding. "Has it happened before?"

Grace was stunned. Was this guy joking? Did he *really* buy into this? And further, did he *really* want to hear more?? Stuck between the two of them, Grace and Charlie were unfortunately going to find out.

"Oh sure," Terry said plainly. "The last big event happened sometime in the fifties."

Grace slowly turned her head to Terry. "Are you serious?" she asked.

"Why, yes, dear. Of course I'm serious. It happ—"

"No," Grace cut her off. She was disgusted. "I mean, are you serious about continuing this filth? People are really upset by what you said."

"But, dear, it's the truth," Terry said. The calm, nonchalant manner in which she spoke only stoked Grace's rage.

"You honestly believe people are waking from the dead and eating people?"

Before Terry could respond, a voice from behind Grace confirmed Terry's account.

"It's true." Grace recognized the voice before she and Charlie even turned around. It was Joe. "There was a couple that'd come to the campground in the early fifties. People say the man went crazy. Say he got bit by one of them..." he hesitated, "...one of them *undead*."

Grace felt the blood filling her face. What was once fear had now turned into sheer anger. She clenched and unclenched her fists. Her body went rigid. She felt the muscles in her legs tighten and release.

"All right," Grace said, pointing to both Terry and Joe. "Both of you need to stop!" Her hand shook as she reprimanded them. "I am done with the fucking storytelling for tonight! Okay? Enough with this *undead* bullshit!"

Charlie put his hands around Grace's shoulders. "All right, I think this camper is up *way* past her bedtime!" He forced a nervous laugh. Grace whipped her head around and glared at Charlie, but before she could say anything, he was already steering her toward the hallway. "Good night," he said to Terry, Joe, and the man wearing the ball cap. Grace turned back and took one last look at the three of them. All three stared at her with quiet confusion as Charlie guided her down the hallway.

When they got back to their room, Grace's temper was still boiling over.

"Lock the goddamn door," she said as Charlie turned to close the door behind him.

"Okay," Charlie said, holding his hands up submissively. "It's all right, you're just a little wound up, that's all."

Grace paced back and forth in their small room, from the window to the door. She pressed a palm against her forehead, as if fighting the onset of a headache. She tried to control her breathing, but to no avail.

"Wound up?" she asked. "*Wound up?!*"

"Okay, bad choice of words," Charlie said. "Look, we were expecting some children's stories. Obviously these people take their story time a little bit more seriously, that's all. You just have to take it with a grain of salt."

She continued pacing, her hands now at her sides, still balled up in fists. "We're not staying here tomorrow night," she said firmly. "We are getting up early. We're heading to the summit." Charlie was already shaking his head. "And afterward, we're going straight down to the base."

"You know that's impossible," Charlie said. "We don't have the supplies for that kind of hike."

"So then we take whatever we can from here before we leave and then we see if there's a store at the summit. Isn't there a fucking road that goes to the summit?"

Charlie stood silently, his arms folded. He knew he'd have to wait her out, to let the frustration run its course. He also knew Grace hadn't expected an answer to her question, so he ignored it and went about busying himself by packing extra supplies for the following day's hike to the summit.

While Grace turned and stared out the window, uttering things like "Who would *say* that kind of shit? What's their *problem?*" Charlie could only assume this outburst was compounded by the story Roy had told them and the dream from last night. She'd woken up screaming and shaking that morning. And in the years Charlie had known Grace, she wasn't one to be easily rattled, certainly not by a bad dream. But it *had* been an awful story about the man who killed himself. *Terry's story couldn't have helped at all*, he thought.

After a few minutes of silence, broken only by the occasional huff-and-puff, Charlie looked over at Grace. Now he saw resolution in her eyes. Her shoulders loosened and her hands became more relaxed. Quietly and unassumingly, he sat down on the bed. Grace walked over and sat down next to him. He put his arm around her shoulders and she leaned toward him. He breathed a sigh of relief and let his chin fall onto her head as he spoke.

"We won't spend a lot of time at the summit," he said. "We'll just take a few pictures, grab some food, and head back down. That cool?" She inhaled deeply, nodding her head against his shoulder. "All right, let's get some sleep."

He stood up to turn off the light. Grace moved

to the far side of the bed, got under the covers. "Lock that door," she said.

CHAPTER 6

Grace woke up early. There was very little visible light coming through the windows in the room. She turned her head. Charlie was still sleeping. Stifling a yawn, she carefully stretched her legs under the covers, hoping not to wake him. She picked up his watch from the nightstand. The time read 5:53 a.m. Sunrise was in twenty minutes. The events of the previous night flashed quickly in her mind and she started feeling guilty—guilty about the way she had gotten so upset with those people. She never liked being upset with someone, even with someone who had upset her. To Grace, being angry was a waste of energy. She always strove to take the high road and not allow others to get under her skin.

Grace shook off the memory. She rubbed her eyes and slowly removed the covers. She sat up and slid her legs over the side of the bed. The wood floor was cold, and she quickly slipped into a pair of moccasins she'd left next to the bed the night before.

As she stood, she thought about waking Charlie. He could get ready while she used the restroom, perhaps even order some breakfast. In the end, however, she decided to let him rest a bit longer. After the long hike the day before, she knew his knee could use the rest.

She quietly opened the door. The air in the hallway was still, but the light was a bit brighter out here, as the large windows in the common room allowed the morning light to flood into both hallways.

Grace found it strange that she didn't hear a sound. Surely, someone should be in the kitchen by now—likely Terry, if anyone. The hut was near capacity, so there must have been someone awake, getting ready for the day's hike.

She waited.

Thirty seconds passed and it was still quiet. She shrugged it off and walked down the hall toward the bathroom. The silence allowed her to hear the floorboards creak as she walked, but only slightly. When she reached the bathroom door, a different noise replaced the creaking of the floorboards.

Did that come from the kitchen? Perhaps a pot or a pan clanging against steel?

She paused and waited for the sound again.

Only silence.

Must be in my head.

She opened the bathroom door. There were three stalls on the left, two sinks on the right-hand wall. She stepped inside the first stall and sat down.

She stared forward, at the back of the door, and let her mind wander. *I wonder if we'll start a family this year. Charlie always said, 'as soon as I turn thirty, we're having kids.' We're both 31 now.* She had thoughts of building their dream home, vacationing as a family, wondered if they should even have kids, given their active life style.

A sniffle from the third stall brought her back. She flinched and cocked her head to the side.

Was that someone breathing?

What was strange about it though, was that it didn't sound like someone taking a breath. It actually sounded as if someone's breathing had skipped or stuttered; it sounded like a cry.

Grace waited, listened. She quieted her own breathing, hoping to determine whether she had in fact heard what she thought she heard.

Another sniffle.

She wasn't alone in the bathroom. Was someone crying in the far stall?

I'm probably jumping to conclusions.

The sniffling sound was very faint, and didn't necessarily suggest that someone was crying two stalls over.

Perhaps it's someone with allergies.

Then, she heard the slightest sob.

They're definitely crying.

"Hello?" Grace called out. She wasn't even aware she'd spoken out loud until the faintest echo of her own voice reached her eardrums. Rather than pretend she hadn't said anything, she called out again to whoever was in the stall two doors over. "Are you okay?" She waited for a response. The sniffling came to an abrupt stop. Someone was definitely crying in the far stall, and now that person was trying to be as quiet as possible. Grace called out again.

"Do you need help?" she asked. Again, no response. Maybe this person hadn't even heard Grace enter the bathroom. Maybe this person only wanted to be left alone.

Grace waited a bit more, hoping the stranger would make herself (himself?) known. Instead, the person in the other stall remained quiet. Grace thought about and it finally decided that, whatever was going on, it was none of her business.

"Listen, I don't want to be a pain, but if you need anything, I'm in room—"

"Someone hurt my parents," the voice cut her off. It sounded like a little girl. She was scared. Grace heard her begin to cry again.

"What do you mean?" Grace asked. "Who hurt

your parents?"

"A man," the little girl said.

"Which man?" Grace asked. "Where are your parents right now?"

The girl took a sob-filled breath. "My mom and dad are in our room."

Grace asked her next question, even though she wasn't sure she was ready for the answer. "What did the man do?"

There was a long pause before she said, "He bit them."

An icy sensation washed down Grace's neck and across her shoulders. She felt her entire body, right down to her hair and scalp, go cold. If Grace hadn't already been sitting down, she would have been knocked over for certain. She noticed her hands shaking and felt a tingling sensation, as if her nerves were now on fire. Grace realized quickly that she was probably three times the age of this little girl, and the girl was likely far more scared than she was. She composed herself before speaking again.

"Wh-who bit your parents?" Grace asked, trying to disguise the fear in her voice.

"I don't know," the little girl said. "He's a man I didn't recognize."

"Do you know where the man is now?" Grace asked.

"I don't know," she said. Her voice started to waver. "He came into our room and he bit my parents. I crawled under the bed. And then after he left, I came in here and locked the door."

Grace suppressed her fear for the moment and left her stall. She walked around to the far stall and stood at the door.

"Do you want to come with me? We can go outside and find someone to help you."

"I don't want to leave here," the girl said. She started to cry harder now.

"Okay, hun, it's okay. You don't have to go anywhere." Grace tried to think. What could she do to help?

Maybe I should just try to keep her talking.

"How long have you been in here, honey?"

"A long time."

"How long?"

"It was really dark outside. It was dark for a long time. Then I saw light coming into the bathroom from outside. Then you came in."

Grace deduced the little girl must have been in the bathroom for at least a couple hours, maybe longer. She'd managed to remain safe this long, so Grace decided to go wake Charlie, and when they both came back the three of them would all go and find help.

"All right, listen. My name is Grace. I want to help you. I know you're scared, so I'm going to go wake up my husband. His name is Charlie. Then we're going to come back in here and all three of us are going to go find help. Okay?"

The little girl sobbed a few times before saying, "Okay."

"What's your name?" Grace asked.

"Caitlin."

"How old are you, Caitlin?"

"Eleven."

"Okay, Caitlin. You stay right here, stay quiet. Keep the door locked, and I'll be right back."

"Okay."

Grace walked across the bathroom, looking for anything that might work as a weapon. She saw nothing useful. She walked to the door, opened it slowly, and stepped into the hall.

It was just as quiet as before. In fact, the place actually felt deserted. She looked to her right, through the window of the broken door. It was a little bit lighter outside. She could make out trees and several of the surrounding mountains. She turned to her left and looked down the empty hallway.

Nobody.

She hurried back toward the room. Immediately, she felt guilty about leaving Caitlin behind, but she would be fast. Besides, surely nobody *really* had bitten her parents. The idea was absurd.

Grace tried to convince herself that the little girl had only been frightened by Terry's story. She might have had a nightmare. Her parents were probably still asleep in their room.

A loud crash from the kitchen interrupted Grace's thoughts. She stopped walking. The next sound was a dragging of sorts, as if something was being dragged across the floor in the kitchen. Grace waited to see if anyone would emerge from the steel double doors. The dragging seemed to be approaching in stops and starts.

Drag...pause. Drag...pause.

Grace took a tentative step forward.

The doors to the kitchen started to flutter. Grace froze again. This time, she was unable to move. A man nudged open one of the steel doors, then stumbled a bit. He turned and reached down toward the floor. In the dim light, Grace couldn't tell at first what he was pulling out of the kitchen. Then, as the man exited the door completely, she could clearly see what he was dragging. Her body stiffened.

The man pulled stubbornly at a hand. On the other side of the door lay the rest of the person being dragged on the floor. The man jerked and twitched as he tugged hard at the person's hand. Eventually, the man pulled the person out far enough for Grace to see the head and shoulders of another man. The second man lay on the ground. Lifeless.

Grace wanted to help, but she also wanted to be somewhere else. Anywhere but where she stood now. Why was this man dragging the other man across the floor? Was the second man injured? And if he was, why didn't the man seek help from the others?

Grace got a swift, violent answer.

With one sharp tug, the man ripped the arm off the second man. The sound of the arm pulling completely away from the unconscious man's body was like a tree branch breaking in half. Grace felt her stomach lurch, and she wanted to vomit.

The man stumbled backward against the wall and landed hard on the floor. Grace could see his face now. She raised her hands to her mouth to refrain from screaming.

The man's face was covered with blood. He wore a light blue button-down shirt that was bloodstained around the arms, shoulders, and chest. He continued to hold on to the arm that had once belonged to the man on the floor.

Just when Grace thought it couldn't get any worse, the man did the unthinkable: He brought the arm to his mouth and bit into the flesh. Or, rather, he gnashed at it like a wild animal tearing into live prey.

Grace could only stand there and watch while the man devoured the arm. In that moment, her brain became temporarily disconnected from her muscles. Even if she wanted to run at that moment, she couldn't. She no longer had control, mental or physical.

The guy is fucking eating a person's arm!

Grace gaped as the man ripped off shredded pieces of fabric that were once part of a shirt and continue to eat. She wondered how she was going to get to Charlie and Caitlin.

Caitlin.

She's still in the bathroom!

Grace's brain function finally came back to her. She clenched and unclenched her hands just to be sure. There was no exit behind her; the door was broken. She couldn't lead this man back to Caitlin. Her only option was to get to the room. To Charlie.

She took a step forward. The man flinched, as if sensing her next move. He stopped eating what was now a blob of flesh, bone, and tendons. His head turned and he stared at Grace. She stared right back at him and took another step forward. The man growled and dropped the arm in his lap. With no hesitation, Grace broke out into a full sprint toward her room. The man crawled to his feet with amazing speed. He ran at her with his arms outstretched. Grace reached the door before him, but only by a few steps. She threw the door open and, with equal haste, tried to slam it shut, but the man was already there.

"Charlie!" Grace screamed, as she pressed the door on the man's hands. Charlie jumped out of the bed the moment Grace burst into the room. He saw Grace struggling to close the door. A man with bloodied arms was reaching for her, groping and clawing at her. Charlie stared at the thick, dark blood. It was the kind of blood that comes from deep within a person's internal organs. Charlie jumped from the bed and picked up a hiking pole off the floor. He ran to Grace's side and jammed it into the man's hands, trying to force him back from the door.

"I got the door!" he yelled at Grace. "Grab the gun from my bag! It's loaded!"

Grace let go of the door as Charlie leaned against it with his back. She ran to the end of the bed, reached into his bag, and grabbed the pistol.

"Turn the safety off!" Charlie said. "Aim through the opening, and shoot this fucker!"

Grace jumped up and stood on the bed. Her hands shook as she held the gun out in front of her. She could hear Charlie shouting, "*SHOOT, SHOOT,*" but all she could see through tunneled vision was a pair of blooded arms reaching into the room. She aimed and fired twice. The man's arms went limp in the doorway. A second later, he fell backward and disappeared. The weight of Charlie's body slumped against the door as it slammed shut.

Grace stood on the bed. Her heart pounded and her arms and shoulders shook as she held the gun aimed at the door. Charlie stood up and ran to her.

"You're all right," he said softly. "Give me the gun. Give me the gun." Grace let the gun fall into Charlie's hands; her face whitened with panic. Charlie held the gun away from the both of them as he helped her off the bed. He held her as she sat down. "What the fuck just happened?" he said.

Before Grace could answer, the man came crashing through the door, sending splinters of wood in every direction. Grace screamed, her hands shaking in front of her face. Charlie turned and fired three shots into the man's head. He fell backward with the dead weight of a felled tree. Charlie kept the gun aimed at the man, even as blood pooled on the floor.

Without turning around, he pointed toward the far corner of the room. "Get over there," he said. Grace, doubled over as if in pain, walked over to the corner of the room. Charlie stepped over the man's legs and kicked his feet. No reaction. He kept the gun aimed at the man's head and squatted low next to the body.

"Charlie," Grace said, her voice shaking,

imploring him not to get any closer to this man.

"Shh," he said. "It's okay. He's dead."

The peak of the adrenaline rush was over, but Grace's heart still raced savagely inside her chest. She stared down at the body and quickly realized the horror that lay on the floor in the doorway of their bedroom. The man lay dead, his mouth open. She could see bits of flesh and shards of bone and fingernail in the man's teeth. Charlie retched as the combined stench of blood, urine, and decay became unbearable.

Grace stood in the corner, unable to comprehend what had just occurred.

This must be the man who bit Caitlin's parents.

Just then, Terry came hustling into the room.

"Is everybody okay? I heard gunsh—" She took a step back when she saw the body on the floor. Charlie looked up and said nothing. He couldn't yet find any words to describe what had happened.

Terry's jaw dropped and her eyes grew wide. "Oh, my God. Are you folks all right?" she asked. Charlie nodded. Grace, huddled in the corner, shook her head.

"The bathroom," she mumbled and tried to swallow. "In the bathroom..." She pointed down the hall.

"You were in the bathroom?" Terry asked.

Grace shook her head again. "A little girl," she said. "In the bathroom. I, I think this man killed her parents."

"Oh, my God," Terry said.

"He just came busting through our door," Charlie said. "Grace ran in, he was covered in blood. I had to protect us."

Terry nodded. "I'll go get the girl."

"Farthest stall," Grace said.

Terry disappeared from sight. Charlie got up and walked back over to Grace. Her hands, cupped around her shoulders, trembled violently as her brain tried frantically to make sense of it all. Charlie reached out and gently grabbed her hand.

"It's okay," he said. "Everything's fine now."

Grace shook as a horrific scream from the hallway pierced through the silence. Nothing was fine. She shut her eyes and again began shaking her head.

No! No! No!

Charlie turned toward the door. He aimed the gun at the opening and waited. The man was still dead, lying on the floor. The scream had come from down by the bathroom. Charlie wondered if it was Terry. It sure sounded like her...

Another scream. This one was even more alarming than before.

Because along with it came the sounds of

tearing and ripping, gnawing and scraping.

What the fuck IS that? he thought. No longer aware of Grace's convulsive responses to what was going on, Charlie found himself approaching the door, as if gliding in a dreamlike state. He didn't even bother to step around the corpse that lay in the doorway; he stepped through the blood and tissue and wandered out into the hall.

At the far end of the hall, lying in the bathroom doorway, Terry's body was being savagely ripped and torn apart by—a little girl? Charlie turned to Grace, asking her with his eyes if this could possibly be the same little girl she had found in the bathroom. He was unable to form the words with his mouth. He simply shook his head in horror.

Grace, nearly comatose, and with tears flowing, slid down the corner she had been standing in and curled into a ball. She rested her head on her knees and began to rock back and forth. Anything to keep her body from shaking.

In the hallway, Charlie crept along the wall. He wasn't sure what made him decide to approach the two people on the floor. His mind was too busy trying to grasp the idea that a person, no more than ten feet from him, was currently kneeling down over Terry, masticating and clawing at her flesh. After a few steps, he stopped. Frozen. He watched as the little girl took bite after ravenous bite of the big woman's midsection.

The girl attacked with an animalistic ferocity. She wasted no time lacerating Terry's abdomen and pulling out her intestines. Charlie gagged as the little girl gnashed at the long, sausage-like organ. He looked down, attempting to avert his eyes from what he just saw.

"Shoot her!" Terry screamed. "Shoot us both!"

Charlie jerked his head back toward the scene, stunned that Terry was even still alive. She was lying on her back, head tilted to one side, screaming commands at Charlie with her last remaining breaths. But Charlie had lost temporary control of his limbs. He stared at Terry's face. Her left eye was completely gone and the whole left side of her face looked like shredded beef.

"Shoot us!" she screamed again. At this, the little girl stopped gnashing at Terry's organs and looked up at Charlie. With a twitchy, jarring motion, she stood up and charged him.

Adrenaline finally rushed back. Charlie felt restored control over his arms and legs. He raised the gun and fired two shots; both made contact with the little girl square in the forehead. Her feet collapsed underneath her and she stumbled face-first onto the floor. Blood spattered against the wall and against

Charlie's legs. He involuntarily stepped back as her head came to rest at his feet.

"You have to shoot me!" Terry shouted, but Charlie was somewhere else, somewhere far back in the reaches of his mind. He looked down at the little girl, his gun still pointed at her head. She couldn't have been much older than ten years old, he thought as he stared at her lifeless body, twisted and contorted at his feet. What had he done? He just shot a little girl in the head. He looked down at the gun between his hands and asked himself how he'd managed to pull the trigger on a small child.

He looked back at Terry screaming from the floor, grabbing at her insides as she bled out, but her shouts were hollow and distant. *This little girl is dead*, he told himself. But there was nothing he could do now. He needed to see how he could help Terry, if he could at all. He stepped around the body and walked down the hall.

"I'm gonna turn soon if you don't shoot me!" Terry screamed.

"You're what?" Charlie asked, shaking his head.

"I'm gonna turn!" she said again, reaching out to him. "You have to shoot me in the head!"

He knew he was out of bullets, but that wasn't the issue. The issue was that he wasn't about to shoot another human being.

"I'm not gonna shoot you," he said. "You need help."

"You have to!" Terry yelled, blood erupting from her mouth in a geyser. "She's become one of the undead!"

"The *what?*" he asked. He shook his head again. "I'm out of bullets, anyway."

"Well then get something and bash my fucking brains!"

Charlie was appalled. "Don't you understand?! You need medical attention!" Charlie's confusion had slightly morphed into aggravation. Nothing Terry said was making any sense.

"I'm already dead, can't you see?" She reached down to her abdomen and lifted exposed organs that looked like long, bloody sausage. "Look! Look! *See?* I'm gonna be coming after you soon if you don't kill me!"

Charlie fought back the urge to vomit, and tried to understand this rationale. Why did Terry need him to kill her? What the hell did "undead" mean? He also wanted to get back to Grace. God forbid Grace stepped out into the hall now, Charlie wasn't prepared to offer an explanation about the little girl.

"Let me think for a second," Charlie said as he paced back and forth next to her body.

"There's no time to think, you have to fucking

kill me!" she repeated.

"What the fuck is your problem?!"

"Listen," Terry said between gasps. This time, her voice was low, blood gurgling in her throat as she spoke. She reached out to him with the hand that was still somewhat intact. Charlie saw she still had four fingers on this hand. "I'm dead. Okay? The little girl turned. She was an undead. Remember? From last night? The man in your bedroom must have bit her. Now, before I turn into that, you have to kill me. Okay? Just kill me."

She's delusional, Charlie thought.

"Lady," Charlie began, "You need help. There's nobody around here, as far as I can tell. Otherwise, they would have heard your screams by now. So now we just have to figure this out."

"There's nothing to figure out!" she yelled. "Just fucking kill me already!"

Charlie waved his hands down. He paced some more, tried to block her taunts from his mind. He had to find a way to get help up to the hut. And why was nobody else out of their rooms? Where was everybody?

"You fucking pussy," she provoked. "You're lucky you survived two attacks. Wait 'til there's more! There *will* be more!"

"Shut the fuck up, lady" Charlie warned.

"Pussy!"

"Lady, you need to calm down or else-"

"PUSSY! PUSSY!" Terry turned her head to the side and coughed up a mass of blood. She then stared back at Charlie. "You and your little whore are next ya know."

Charlie closed his eyes, tried to clear the anger from his head.

"You're a sick, fucking bitch. You know that?"

"HAHA!" Terry taunted. "You're not going anywhere! You'll never get off this fucking mountain! You and your whore wife are going to die up here, just like me! Because you're a fucking little city, pussy boy!"

Charlie ran to the side of the hall and kicked the wall. The sting in his toe shot through his foot and he stumbled to his right, but managed to stay on his feet.

"HAHAHA! You can't even do that right, you little fuck!"

"LADY! Shut the fuck up and let me think!"

"That's all you pussies do is think!"

"Shut UP!"

"You better go check on your whore! She's probably already being eaten by one of those things! *She's probably going to die the worst fucking death you could ever imagine!!!*"

Charlie screamed, his mettle finally lost. A large

picture frame hung on the wall to his right. He hurried over and pulled it down. Then, with blinding force and a rage he never knew existed within him, he brought the frame down on her forehead. Blow after blow, the frame dug deeper into the front of Terry's head. He screamed uncontrollably as he repeatedly crushed her skull. After a while, Charlie unconsciously tilted the frame so that the next blows came from the large corner. The heavy, triangular edge sliced through her weakened frontal bone, scattering bits of skull and brain matter. He wasn't even looking at her anymore. He was a savage, crushing any last bit of life that remained inside Terry. His eyes were closed tight, but salty tears rolled down his face and over his lips.

Finally, fatigue began to set in as the pain in his stomach, caused by his own guttural screams, began to overtake him.

Exhausted, he let the frame hit Terry's mutilated head one final time. He slouched over and tried to catch his breath. His alertness now returned. He remembered Grace all by herself, crouched in the corner of the room. He swore at himself, dropped the picture frame, and ran back toward the room.

He called out her name as he ran. He needed to hear her voice, to see her. After what had happened with the little girl, he'd never forgive himself if he let something happen to Grace, inadvertently or not.

He reached the door only to find her curled up in the same corner of the room. She sat still. Her head rested on its side in her arms; her eyes looked isolated and disoriented as she stared past him.

Please God, no, he thought. He crouched by her side. Not knowing what to do or say, he simply reached out and held her. He didn't see any injuries. No blood (none that was her own, anyway). She was in a trance.

"Please stay with me, Grace," he said. His voice trembled as he began to sob. "I'll never leave you again." Like a new parent caressing an infant to sleep, he rocked back and forth with Grace in his arms.

As he let his mind drift away from the macabre scene in the room and in the hallway, he suddenly became very aware of the silence around them. The quiet was haunting and calming at the same time. He was aware that a scream or a shout could break the silence at any moment, but he allowed himself to find peace in it, if only for five seconds. Inside, he willed it to be an eternity.

CHAPTER 7

Grace blinked. Daylight filled the room. Disoriented, she looked around and took stock of her surroundings. She recognized the room. They had spent the night here. She looked to her right; Charlie's head rested on her shoulder, and his arms were wrapped around her body. Why were they sitting in the corner of the room on the floor when they had a bed to sleep in?

And then she saw it. In front of her, lying on the floor and bathed in blood, a man was dead.

In an instant, it all came flooding back into her memory. She remembered being chased into the room by a madman covered in human blood. She remembered gunshots in the bedroom. She remembered pulling the trigger herself. She had awoken to the same nightmare from which she thought she had escaped.

And then she remembered the little girl in the bathroom, Caitlin.

111

"Charlie," she said. Her mouth was dry. She tried swallowing before speaking again but it felt like sandpaper scraping and scratching her throat. "Charlie," she said again. This time she nudged him with her right arm and knee. "Where's Caitlin?"

Charlie lifted his head, looked at Grace. His eyes were bloodshot. "Who's Caitlin?" he asked.

"The little girl in the bathroom. I have to go back for her."

As she tried to stand, Charlie stood with her but didn't let her go. "I couldn't save her," he said.

Grace's eyes filled with tears. The pain of defeat crawled back into her body once more. "I promised her," Grace said. "What happened?"

She studied Charlie's eyes as he fought for an answer. She could tell something was wrong, but she couldn't get a clear read from his expression.

"She was already dead, Grace." He nodded to the body on the floor. "He might have gotten to her before you went to the bathroom. She was probably already dying by the time you spoke to her. I found her dead out in the hall. Terry got attacked, too, but I didn't see who it was."

Grace shook her head as she cried. Charlie reached an arm around her and caressed her face with his other hand.

"We have to get out of here," he said.

"We have to leave now."

Grace looked up at him. There was despair in her eyes. "Where are we going to go?"

"We'll go to the summit," he said. "It's close and there will be people up there who can help."

"Shouldn't we call someone?" Grace asked.

"They don't have phones in a place like this," Charlie said.

"There must be someone here with a cell phone."

Charlie looked her straight in the eyes. "Grace, I don't think there's anyone here."

It took a few moments for Grace to realize what Charlie meant. If there had been anyone left at the hut, someone would have heard the gunshots. But nobody had come. They were alone. There was nobody left. Nobody alive.

Charlie must have read the panic on her face. "There's a store at the summit, though! We can see if there's a phone there. From there we can take the access road all the way down to the base. All we need is to find a car."

Grace wasn't sure. She looked around the room, hoping for an alternate solution, but she knew she wouldn't find one.

"It's only three hours to the top," Charlie reasoned. "Maybe only two if we hurry. And I don't

113

know about you, but two hours to the top sounds better than seven hours to the base."

Realizing this was the only sensible plan, Grace nodded in agreement.

They quickly scanned the room, looking only for things they needed. Charlie reached into his backpack and grabbed more bullets. He would have enough to refill the gun two more times. After that, they'd have to find something else to defend themselves.

Grace grabbed a multi-tool from her backpack and slid her feet into her hiking boots. They both stood up, facing each other.

"Bruce and Cheryl!" Grace blurted out, remembering the old couple from the night before.

Charlie shook his head. "There's no time."

"They're staying in the other hallway. They're on our way out!" Grace reasoned.

Charlie sighed.

"You know I'm right!" Grace begged. "They're older, but they're strong. We'll be safer with them, much safer than if we're by ourselves!"

"Okay," Charlie said. "We'll check a few rooms, but if we don't find them, that's it. I'm not checking this whole place." Grace nodded.

Charlie led them out of the room, into the hallway. Grace followed. Immediately upon entering the hall, she glimpsed Caitlin's body lying on the floor, bloodied and maimed. She drew in a sharp breath that caused Charlie to flinch. He spun on his heel and put a finger to his lips. Grace, with her hands covering her mouth and tears spilling through her fingers, shut her eyes and reluctantly nodded. Charlie lowered his hand in a calming gesture and motioned toward the common room.

The lounge area was deserted. Grace couldn't believe that only twelve hours ago, this place had been alive and full of energy. There was surely an energy still, but it was of a different kind. What had once been a warm and inviting hearth was now a cold, darkened tomb. Grace could feel it. She could feel the chill, the tingle in her arms like electric pulses, the ache of stress and tension along her spine. She had to leave this place.

They walked stealthily through the silent lounge so as not to be heard by anyone. Suddenly, Grace stopped. Charlie continued for a few steps, but when he no longer felt her presence, he turned around and offered a questioning look.

Something wasn't right.

"There really is nobody here," Grace whispered.

Charlie found the realization to be unnerving. He only stared back at her. He had no answers.

"How is that possible?" she asked. "Where did they all go?"

Charlie shrugged.

Grace's eyes wandered around the room, down the hallway from which they'd just emerged, over to the large windows that overlooked the lake. Charlie looked around too. There were no signs of life.

But Charlie's eyes were far more focused; he wanted nothing more than to get out of the hut as quickly as possible. "We don't have time to find out," he said. "Let's just go get Bruce and Cheryl and get out of here."

Grace put her curiosity on hold and they continued walking toward the main hall. They checked doors as they walked by. Each time they opened a door, they found an empty room. One after the other, they found beds that had been slept in, windows with the curtains drawn open—backpacks, shoes, and hiking equipment on the floors of most rooms. Where had everybody gone? And why did they leave everything?

Charlie opened another door. The room looked just as the others did. The bed was unmade. Bags, clothes, and other things were tossed around the room. He drew a quick, sharp breath when he recognized an item on the floor: the shirt they'd seen Bruce wearing the day before. He tugged Grace's sleeve.

Grace, who had been half-searching, half-keeping watch, turned to him. Charlie's eyes went straight to Bruce's shirt lying on the floor. Grace saw it and froze. Instinctively, they both looked around for signs of a struggle but found none. No blood. No bodies. No body parts. The room was abandoned. Bruce and Cheryl were either dead, or they'd somehow managed to escape whatever was going on inside the hut.

A loud bang drew their attention back toward the hallway. Grace jerked her head the moment she heard it. She looked back at Charlie. His eyes darted in the direction of the lounge, from where the sound had emanated. Grace opened her mouth to speak but Charlie held up a hand. His eyes slowly went to the ground as he tried to concentrate. He waited for the sound again. Grace took in short, shallow breaths, staying as quiet as possible.

Another loud noise. This time, it was more of a scuff, like the sound of a table leg scraping across the tile floor in the dining area. *Someone must have bumped into a picnic table*, Charlie thought. He stepped around Grace, walking softly back out of the room and into the hallway. Grace began to follow, but Charlie raised his hand and signaled her to stay. She watched from the door to the room.

Charlie raised his gun and aimed in the direction of the lounge. He moved stealthily toward the sound, inching his way along the wall.

He saw movement, flinched, and nearly squeezed the trigger. The gun shook in his hand. Someone had moved just around the corner. Charlie's chest burned as his heart beat faster and faster, each step more tentative than the last. He drew in a breath, and readied his finger on the trigger.

A figure stepped out from around the corner. It was Bruce. He waved his hands submissively. Charlie closed his eyes and exhaled in relief.

Bruce turned slightly and thumbed toward the double doors of the kitchen. "We're in there," he whispered. "I saw you two walk by, but I didn't want to make a noise so I thought I would follow you, let you know where we are."

Catching his breath, Charlie felt relief continue to flood into his body.

"'Tried not to make a noise,' huh?" Charlie asked.

Bruce shrugged, embarrassed.

It was only then that Charlie grew nervous, wondering if Bruce had heard or seen what had happened to Terry or the little girl.

"How long have you been in there?" Charlie asked, sticking his gun in the back of his waistband.

"I don't know," Bruce said. "A few hours, I guess."

Charlie swallowed hard and hung his head a bit before asking, "Did you see what happened earlier?"

"We didn't see," Bruce said. His face was somber. "But we heard."

Charlie nodded. He closed his eyes again as shame filled him.

"It's not your fault, son," Bruce whispered. He reached out a hand and placed it on Charlie's shoulder. "You did what you had to, to protect your wife. I would have done the same thing."

Charlie looked up. Bruce's eyes were honest. For that, Charlie was grateful.

"Now, go get Grace and come into the kitchen," Bruce said. "You'll be safe in there."

"How many of you are there?" Charlie asked.

"Just me and Cheryl," he said, his voice still low.

"Where are the others?" Charlie asked.

Bruce shrugged.

Charlie turned to Grace. She was still standing in the doorway to the room. He waved her over.

"We're going to go to the kitchen," Charlie whispered as she approached, uncertainty apparent in her every step. "Bruce and Cheryl are there, and they're safe. We should go to the kitchen." He was trying to convince himself just as much as her.

Grace looked at him and shook her head. "What about the summit?" she asked.

"It's okay," Charlie said, trying to reassure her. "We'll be safe, right?" he said and turned to Bruce, begging his reply. Bruce nodded. "All right, then. Let's go to the kitchen."

They followed Bruce back through the dining area. Grace couldn't help but feel vulnerable to an attack. The common room was such a large area and the windows were so large, they could easily be seen from outside. But to her relief, they made it through the lounge unnoticed.

They passed through the steel double doors and walked into the empty kitchen. There were fewer windows, so it was much darker than the rest of the hut.

"We were afraid to turn on the lights," Bruce explained as they walked in.

The kitchen had an altogether different atmosphere than the rest of the hut. The air felt sterile and desolate. To their left was a long, wooden counter, on top of which sat knives and other utensils, neatly filed away in blocks and metal canisters. Pots and pans hung from racks installed in the ceiling. Beyond the counter were the grill and a broiler.

They continued walking. To their right there was a large, industrial-size dishwasher. Just beyond it was a long, stainless steel drying rack. A trail of thick, viscous blood painted the floor from the end of the drying rack back to the double doors. Grace had hardly noticed it. She was already becoming desensitized to the sight of so much blood and gore. It occurred to her that numbness to such horror was not a good thing.

"Where is Cheryl?" Grace asked.

"She's in the freezer," Bruce said. "Safest place for us both. We've been bundled up in there a while. I had her wait there while I came out to get you folks."

There was a large walk-in freezer on the other side of the broiler. Bruce was about to open the door when Charlie stopped.

"Wait a minute," he said. "This is the plan? To wait in the freezer?"

Bruce removed his hand from the door, turned to face Charlie.

"Is there a better idea?" he asked.

"Well," Charlie began matter-of-factly, "I told Grace the best move would be to get to the summit, see if we can get some assistance from whoever's running the store up there. From there, we can take the access road to the bottom of the mountain."

Bruce looked at him dubiously.

"And how do you plan to get there, hotshot?"

"We run!" Charlie yelled. Bruce and Grace stared at him with alarm on their faces. "We run," he said again, much more softly. "We run as fast as we can, as long as we can. It's a three-hour climb, but I think we can cut that in half."

Bruce let out a "hmpf," belittling Charlie's idea. "Well, you go right ahead. And while you're running to the top of the mountain, I'll be calling for help."

Grace perked up. "You have a phone?" Bruce nodded. "Then why haven't you called anyone?"

"We were waiting to see if anyone else was here. Any other...*survivors*." The word itself indicated that something massively tragic had occurred.

"Well, shit," Charlie said. "Let's call the park ranger service. But I still say we run to the summit. Grace and I are not staying here. This place is a morgue and we're not sticking around."

Bruce put his hand on Charlie's shoulder. "It's okay," he said. Bruce now appeared reassuring, almost to the point of patronizing. Grace could tell that Charlie was confused at the way Bruce's manner seemed to switch back and forth. She herself began to question Bruce's motives. Just a second ago, he was downright angered by the idea of hiking to the summit. Now he was caring and mindful, much like he had been when he first bumped into them out in the hall. Grace was feeling more and more unsure about the man.

Bruce looked at Grace. "Why don't you go wait in the freezer with Cheryl? Charlie and I will make one more round to see if there's anyone else, and then we'll make the call." He held his hands open, a gesture that said, *Why not?*

Grace looked at Charlie for support. The look on his face was one of cautious optimism.

"Go ahead," Charlie said. "We'll be right back."

Grace walked toward the freezer. Bruce opened the door. And with one, swift motion, he put his hand on her back, shoved her inside, and slammed the door shut, locking it behind her.

Charlie panicked. He drew his gun. "What the fuck is going on?!" he yelled. He could hear Grace pounding from the inside of the door.

"Now just take it easy," Bruce said, quietly, his back pressed against the door. "You don't want to go alarming one of those *things* now, do you?"

Charlie kept the gun aimed at Bruce. He looked up and down the door to see how he might be able to pry it open.

"It's locked," Bruce said. "Ain't nobody getting it open. But I know where the key is. If you shoot me, you'll never find it."

Grace could hear muffled voices on the other

side of the door, but she couldn't make out what they were saying. She pounded on the door a few times.

"What's going on out there?!" she yelled. She heard a scraping noise behind her.

Then a slurping noise. The sounds were coming from the back of the fridge. She turned around. She saw the figure of a woman standing alone among the racks of frozen meats.

"Cheryl?" she called out.

The woman stood in the opposite corner, hunched over.

"Cheryl, is that you? Bruce and Charlie are going to call for help."

As Grace's eyes adjusted to the dim, yellow light in the freezer, she realized it *was* Cheryl. She also noticed that her arms and mouth were covered in blood. *Oh shit,* Grace thought as Cheryl licked at her hands, trying to consume as much of the red, plasma-like fluid as she could. Grace looked down at Cheryl's feet and saw four carcasses torn to shreds. Flesh and bone twisted, broken, and bent into forms unrecognizable to her lay scattered on the floor in front of her.

Panic set in. Grace stayed still. She didn't want to try anything that might set Cheryl off in a rage. She looked around quickly, tried to find something with which to defend herself. She saw a mop handle a few feet to her right. She could get to it quickly and easily. She took a step. Cheryl looked up abruptly. She gnashed her teeth and ran toward Grace. She stumbled as she stepped through the pile of corpses. Grace reached out for the mop handle.

"Why the fuck did you lock them in there?" Charlie fumed. Bruce was silent. His face was full of shame. Within seconds, Charlie realized he still hadn't seen Cheryl. He'd only assumed she was hiding in the freezer based on what Bruce had told him and Grace. He quickly understood what had become of her.

He's hiding HER in the freezer!

"I did what I had to, to protect her," Bruce said, his voice shaking. "You did the same thing." Charlie could hear noise and commotion coming from inside the fridge.

"Cheryl's one of *them?!*" he asked, ignoring Bruce's claim that Charlie had acted in kind.

"She's my wife!" Bruce pleaded. "My Cheryl! I can't let her die!"

Charlie took a step toward Bruce. A fire grew inside of him. He couldn't believe what he was hearing. This was madness. "You're going to open that door, or I'm going to open a hole in your fucking head."

"That's all right," Bruce said, raising his chin,

125

challenging Charlie to shoot him. "At least she'll have been able to live a little longer. I would have given her that much."

Cheryl ran toward Grace. Grace clutched the mop so tightly she could feel splinters digging into her hands. She caught Cheryl in the stomach, which slowed her down, but only for a second. Cheryl stumbled back, her bare, blood-soaked feet skidding across the cold, frozen floor. Grace grabbed the mop at both ends and broke it over her knee. She dropped one half and held on to the end with the sharpest edge.

Cheryl regained her footing and charged forward again. Grace thrust the shiv forward, plunging the sharp end of the stick into Cheryl's side. Cheryl let out a terrible roar as the wooden spear tore into her body, slicing through skin and tissue. Grace squeezed the mop handle even tighter. She twisted and jammed it deeper into Cheryl's flesh. Cheryl roared again. She reached down and tried to pull the skewer from her body, but Grace held on tightly. Blood and pus now oozed out of the wound, down the handle, and onto Grace's hands.

Cheryl lunged toward Grace and attempted to bite her. Grace stepped to her right, letting go of the weapon momentarily. As she did, her foot slipped on the wheel of the mop bucket and she fell to the floor, landing on her wrist. She cried out as pain shot from her hand, up her arm and into her shoulder.

"Get the fuck out of the way, Bruce!" Charlie yelled. He could hear Grace screaming from the other side of the door.

Bruce remained steadfast. "Not until my Cheryl's had enough to eat."

Charlie began to search the kitchen for the key to the freezer. He opened the oven. No key. He shook the pots and pans; several of them clanged as they crashed down to the floor. He paused to look up at Bruce, who was still standing by the door.

"You're not going to find the key," he taunted.

Charlie ran to the dishwasher and slid the door open. There was nothing inside. Sweat rolled from his forehead and burned his eyes as he continued his search. The fight from within the freezer only added to his consternation. He tried to take comfort in the fact that a struggle meant Grace was still alive and still fighting. He had to find the key fast. He cursed at Bruce for hiding it. Assuming Bruce was telling the truth, and they'd been hiding in the kitchen for hours, then the key had to be in the kitchen as well.

Frustrated, Charlie rested against a counter for a moment. His eyes caught on a bloody trail on the ground, likely left behind by one of those monsters.

Charlie wondered if it had been left by the man who had attacked him and Grace in their room. He wondered whose blood it was. Was it from the little girl he'd shot in the hallway?

He shut his eyes and focused. He tried to think like Bruce. *Where would he hide the key?* He couldn't block out the horrible sounds coming from inside the freezer. He also couldn't block out Bruce's taunts.

"Give up yet?" Bruce said.

"*FUCK YOU!*" Charlie yelled, swinging the gun at Bruce.

"It's a near certainty that Cheryl's going to get what she needs—"

"Fuck you, you fuckin—" The noise from inside the fridge came to a sudden halt. Charlie caught his breath. He and Bruce stared at each other in silence. There was a thud, then scraping. They both screamed their wives' names at the same time. Bruce ran to the back door of the kitchen. He pushed it open, crouched down, and lifted the mat on the back steps. He picked up the key.

Grace lay on her back in agony. She held her wrist tight, not sure if it was broken. Her shirt stuck to the floor; the ice-cold swirls of blood smeared on the concrete were like an adhesive. Cheryl, with half a broomstick stuck in her side, lunged at Grace again. Grace kicked at her from the ground, tried to knock her off balance. But Cheryl kept coming. She grabbed and clawed at the air, narrowly missing Grace by only inches. Grace screamed in pain as she mashed her injured hand against Cheryl's face. Cheryl gnashed at Grace's wrists, but Grace was quick with her feet, sending kick after kick into Cheryl's stomach.

In the midst of the struggle, Grace saw a familiar object out of the corner of her eye: the other half of the broken mop handle. But Cheryl continued to attack. Lunge after lunge, she kept coming. Grace did not have the energy to keep up a defense for much longer. She stuffed a fist under Cheryl's chin and she finally got some leverage. As she steadied herself, she pushed Cheryl's face away hard and unleashed a violent kick that caught her in the jaw. As Cheryl stumbled back, Grace reached across her body and picked up the broken stick.

Cheryl lunged again. Her hands thrashed, reaching for Grace. Grace held the stick out and gripped the handle as tight as she could. Cheryl slipped in blood as she advanced and fell forward. As she fell, the pointed end of the broken wooden handle found her eye socket. It squished into her head, passing through the retina and the optic nerve. The force of gravity alone was enough to drive the mop handle straight through her brain, but not through the back of her skull. It just stayed there, extending from her head like the nose of Pinocchio. She fell forward. Grace rolled to move out of the way, but Cheryl's now lifeless body fell across her legs. Grace slid out from underneath her. She used both hands to lift herself up off the floor. Stars shot across her vision again as the pain in her wrist caused her to lose her balance. She reached for the shelving in the fridge to pull herself up.

Bruce ran back to the freezer door, fumbling with key. He froze when he saw the gun pointed at his face.

"Open this fucking door," Charlie demanded. Bruce feebly nodded his head, moved to the door, and unlocked it. Charlie stood behind him, gun aimed and ready. Inside, they saw two figures: one to the right, lying on the floor, one to the left, standing up by the shelving.

"Cheryl?" Bruce whispered.

"Grace!" Charlie called out loudly, causing Bruce to flinch.

"I'm right here," Grace said. She stood by a shelf, holding herself up with her good hand.

Bruce, realizing that the lifeless form on the floor was Cheryl, slowly moved into the freezer toward the person who was once his wife.

"Oh, Cheryl!" he cried. He knelt down on the

floor beside her. He picked her up by her shoulders, cradling her in his arms. His hands trembled over the wooden spear that jutted out of her head. "Cheryl!" he screamed again, as he held her head close to his chest.

Charlie stepped around Bruce and grabbed Grace's hand. He gestured with his head to leave the fridge. Grace stepped away from the shelf that supported her, and followed him out.

Bruce, sensing he was being left behind, looked back at Grace and Charlie.

"Wait a minute!" he called. "Where are you going?"

Charlie pulled Grace completely out of the fridge. Then he turned to Bruce.

"Fuck you, old man," he said. "You wanted to be with your wife. Well," he said curtly, "now you got her."

Charlie turned to walk out of the fridge. Bruce crawled after him, through the blood and gore. Charlie heard the movement and pivoted. He pointed the gun at Bruce's head. Bruce stopped. He sat up on his knees. He put his hands together in a praying position.

"But she's dead!" he pleaded.

Charlie stared at him with soulless eyes. He cared nothing for this man and wanted nothing more than to kill him right now.

"I guess you can make that phone call now," he said.

He slammed the door shut, turning the key that Bruce had left in the door, and locking it as it closed. He leaned against the freezer and listened to the sounds of Bruce beating the inside of the door. He rested his head against the back of his hand, tried to control his breathing. From behind, Grace tugged hard at his shirt. As he turned to face her, a figure caught his eye.

No. *Two* figures.

There were two more of those *things* standing in the double doors of the kitchen. Their mouths dripped red; their hands and lower arms were stained with the same uncongealed fluid.

Charlie shoved Grace hard toward the back door.

"Run!" he shouted.

The two monsters ran at them. Charlie reached for the broiler and pulled open the oven. The first of the undead slammed into the oven door, stumbled backward, and knocked over the one that ran behind him. Charlie thought about shooting them but didn't want to waste bullets if he didn't have to. He turned and ran toward the back door.

Once outside, he quickly scanned the yard for

Grace. He saw her by the bathhouse. She was waving him over.

"Come on!" she urged him.

She disappeared into the shower rooms. Charlie ran in after her. As he reached the bathhouse, he heard the two undead crash through the back door to the hut. He made his way into a shower stall. Grace was there. She was huddled in the corner, motioning with her hand for him to get inside. He thought about looking out to see if the two undead had followed them into the showers.

"Get in!" Grace whispered urgently.

Charlie jumped into the shower stall. Grace leaned forward and locked the door behind him. They both sat down on the floor, facing the door. Inside the stall was a small changing space with a seat and a towel rack. Behind them was the shower itself. They were locked inside a concrete cube, safe for the moment.

Charlie looked over at Grace. Her face was red and drenched with perspiration.

"Do you think we're safe?" she asked.

He didn't honestly believe they were safe, but he nodded anyway.

Grace let her head fall forward; her shoulders drooped. Her eyelids fell shut and she exhaled a long, tired breath. Charlie looked over at her. He was happy they were able to finally rest. He could see she was physically and emotionally drained. What was worse; they didn't have any food or water, and he wasn't about to risk going back into the hut to look for food. They were going to have to find the energy to make it to the summit.

Alive.

CHAPTER 8

They spent an hour sitting on the floor of the shower stall, attempting to reenergize for the eventual climb to the summit. They passed the time playing tic-tac-toe on the tile floor using pebbles that had accumulated with years of foot traffic. They stopped every time they heard the occasional shuffling outside. They'd also heard a couple loud bangs, but they never opened the door once, not even to check if it was a survivor.

They never heard any screams, though. A scream would have indicated that there *were* survivors. However, at this point, they weren't sure if anyone from the hut was even alive. At best, they were long dead. At worst, they had become one of the others—one of the undead.

"We can't stay in here forever," Grace said, breaking the silence.

Charlie knew this to be true but shrugged his shoulders. The adrenaline rush having long since worn off, his knee now ached from the stress of the morning's events. But he wasn't about to let it show.

"We haven't heard anything in the last twenty minutes," Grace reasoned.

Charlie looked up at her. He was amazed by her resilience. He had been so worried about her mental strength back in the hut. Now, she was ready to put it behind her and move on. And, after all, she was right. They couldn't stay in the bathhouse any longer. If they were going to make a run for the summit, it had to be during the day. And they had to do it while they still had an ounce of energy left. The longer they waited, the hungrier they'd become. The pit in Charlie's stomach was growing. Over the last half hour, he'd begun to feel the pangs of hunger kneading his insides. It was only a matter of time before the headaches started and the nausea set in. The burden of having to climb a mile and a half to the summit on an empty stomach would only compound his declining condition.

"Are you okay?" Grace asked.

Immersed in his own thoughts, Charlie realized he hadn't responded to her last comment over a minute ago. He was sure that his face showed his exhaustion, but he tried to mask it anyway.

"I'm good," he said, forcing a smile. He knew she didn't buy it, but he also knew she wouldn't contest him either.

"Then let's go," Grace said, grabbing his hand.

They stood up together. Grace put a hand on her knee, steadying herself as she stood. Charlie's legs and lower back ached as he straightened. It was going to be a long hike.

Grace placed her head against the door and listened. There was nothing. No shuffling, no banging, no discernible movement of any kind. She looked at Charlie and shook her head. His ear was pressed against the door as well. He nodded to her, indicating it was time to move.

Grace opened the door. The rest of the bathhouse appeared undisturbed. There was no sign that any other survivors had passed through. There were several other shower stalls, all open. To Grace, the absence of blood and gore was a welcome sight, but it didn't guarantee safety.

They stepped out of the stall, walked through the main area of the bathhouse, and glanced outside through the main opening. There was no sign of life. Grace wondered if Bruce was still pounding on the inside of the fridge. *Chances are,* she thought, *the undead probably got to him, too.*

From the opening of the bathhouse, they could see the back of the hut. The door to the kitchen hung loosely by a single, bent hinge. For Grace, it was a dark reminder of the horror from which they'd managed to escape and of the reason they had to get the hell out of there. Above them, the overcast skies had carried over from the previous day, and the dark clouds that hung over the mountains offered little encouragement. Grace knew the chances of a storm were good, but they couldn't wait. They had to make an attempt at the summit now.

Without a word, Charlie pointed past her, indicating an opening in the trees. Grace followed the direction of his finger and saw a sign: "Arrowhead Trail." She looked around, checked both ends of the hut, and stepped out onto the ground.

It was alarming at first, being that exposed, but they walked quickly toward Arrowhead. They didn't turn to speak or even look at each other. It was as if they were trained soldiers in a war, sneaking up on the enemy.

There was no wind, no breeze of any kind. And while this might have seemed tranquil and serene at any other time, the air now felt still and lifeless, mimicking the atmosphere in the hut. It was all very surreal to Grace, who couldn't quite comprehend what had happened, what was *still happening*. Had they really just survived nearly being murdered only hours ago? From people who were once alive, now dead, yet somehow—*undead?* It didn't make sense. She cleared her mind of it and focused on hiking, on putting one foot in front of the other. It wouldn't be long before she would be fighting fatigue, so she had to get herself mentally fit in order to deal with the inevitable physical strain.

They walked along the rear of the hut while staying close to the building. They moved down the forest-facing side of the main hall. As they approached the entrance, Charlie reached out and tugged at Grace's shirt. She turned to say something, but Charlie put a finger to his mouth. Then, using two fingers, he pointed toward his eyes and then around the corner. Grace understood.

Charlie stepped around her as she stood with her back pressed against the building. He looked around the corner, checked the front of the hut, and looked out toward the lake. It was clear. Not a person in sight. He turned back to Grace and waved her on.

Grace took off for the trailhead. She was light on her feet and careful not to step on a twig or anything that might snap or create noise. Charlie immediately shot out after her. Within the first few steps, he felt a pinch in his knee and fell forward; nearly hitting the ground, but he willed himself to stay up and continued running.

Neither Charlie nor Grace turned to see if

anyone had witnessed them running across the grounds. To their good fortune, they made it to the forest, where they would be able to stay hidden under the cover of trees for a short while. After that, they would be exposed for the majority of the hike.

Grace and Charlie had been so preoccupied by thoughts of protecting themselves from the undead, they'd completely forgotten about the natural dangers they'd yet to confront. The exposure they'd soon have to deal with would certainly present its own set of problems; without the cover of trees, the wind and weather could weaken them, making them even more vulnerable to attack.

About ten minutes into the hike, as they hurried through the woods, they came to a downed tree in the middle of the trail. Charlie was lead climber, and he stopped to take a seat.

"We're going to have to find water," he whispered, panting lightly.

Grace rested her hands on her hips and looked around.

"Maybe we'll find a stream or something," she said. "Otherwise, we'll just have to break every ten minutes or so."

The two of them looked around for any sign of water nearby. Charlie looked through the trees, out into the distance. He strained to listen for moving water—a stream, anything. He felt Grace's hand rest on his knee. She cursed under her breath and fell fast to the ground. He jerked his head around to see why she'd fallen.

"Get down!" she whispered. She tugged at his pant leg. Charlie slid off the tree and flattened himself on the ground next to her.

"What is it?" he asked.

"There's someone at our three o'clock," she said.

Charlie rolled himself over on his stomach, propped himself up in a plank position, and looked over Grace's shoulder. It was a man walking in the woods. About fifty yards away.

"Does he look like one of *them*?" she asked.

Charlie narrowed his eyes to try and focus. The man appeared to have a normal gait. He also seemed to be alert, nervously scanning his surroundings.

"I think he might be okay," Charlie said.

"What do we do?" Grace asked.

"I think we should call him over." Charlie put his hand to his cheek, about to yell to the man. Grace quickly pulled his hand down.

"What are you doing?!" she hissed.

"I'm going to yell to the guy."

"Are you sure that's a good idea?"

"Well, if it isn't, we have a gun," he said. Grace

frowned. She wasn't impressed. Good thing for Charlie, he wasn't trying to be funny.

"Okay," Charlie said. "How about I wave? If he waves back, we're good to go. If he charges, I shoot him."

Grace stared off. Charlie waited as she considered the idea. They'd be stronger with three people; Charlie knew deep down that Grace's biggest fear was that this guy might turn out to be another Bruce. Worst case scenario, he *was* another Bruce. But he was alone, and the odds would be in their favor. *Worst*, worst case scenario, he was one of the monsters himself, and Charlie would shoot him. Reluctantly, Grace nodded in agreement.

Charlie got up on his knees, in position so that he could see over the tree trunk. This person would surely notice any movement he made. He waited until the man looked in their direction. *Now!* he thought.

Charlie waved both hands several times. Then he waited. The man stopped moving. He stayed perfectly still, staring in their direction. *Oh shit*, Charlie thought. *This may have been a very bad idea.*

"What's he doing?" Grace asked, her voice barely a whisper now. Charlie shook his head slowly. He held out a hand, indicating to wait.

The man was still staring in their direction. He made no movement. Then, slowly, he raised his hands, and waved exactly as Charlie had.

"Thank God," Charlie said. He let out a long breath. "He's waving back." Charlie waved again, then waited. The man responded in kind, quickly this time.

"Anything?" Grace asked.

"I think he's one of us," Charlie told her. "I'm getting up."

He stood up so that the man could see him. This time, he waved him over to their location. The man slowly began walking toward them. He was carrying something—something big and long, like a tree branch. But it was too straight to be a branch.

"He's holding something," Charlie told Grace. "He might have a weapon."

"Shit," she said. Her heartbeat quickened.

"It's okay," Charlie said. "We still have the gun. I'll be able to shoot him before he can try anything." He reached behind his back slowly. He pulled the gun out of his belt and held it low and out of sight.

The man was now twenty yards away. He was tall and thin, and Charlie thought he recognized him. Charlie could also clearly see now that the object the man was carrying was a very long machete. Charlie swallowed hard as the man closed the distance between them. He tightened his grip on the gun.

The man was now ten yards away. Charlie held

the gun out to his side so the man could see it.

The man stopped moving. They stared at each other for a few seconds. Neither spoke. He looked so familiar, and yet, Charlie still couldn't determine where he'd seen him before, if he had at all. Then, the man slowly raised the machete and placed it into a sheath on his side.

Charlie breathed another deep sigh of relief. He returned the gun to his belt. The man continued walking toward him. Charlie saw that he had blood on his shirt and pants and wondered how many of the undead this man had run into. He wondered what the man thought of his own appearance; he was covered with blood spatter from both Terry and the little girl.

The man reached out his hand. Charlie extended his own, and they shook. Grace stepped out from where she'd been hiding. Charlie introduced them, keeping his voice low. The man introduced himself as Joe. Grace immediately recognized him.

"You were there last night," she said. "During story time." Joe nodded.

Charlie remembered him now. Joe had gone before Terry during story hour. He had told some tale about an intruder and a mother being home alone with her baby. It was only hours ago, but it felt like weeks.

"How long you been out here?" Charlie asked.

Joe rubbed his forehead. The dark crescent moons under his eyes were a clear indication that he'd been awake most of the morning and likely much of the night. He looked down at his watch.

"Been out here since about four-thirty," Joe said. "Woke up around four, heard someone screaming—" He stopped and squeezed his eyes shut for a moment. He was clearly haunted by what had happened to him. "I always bring a machete with me when I go out into the woods." Tears began forming in his eyes as he clenched his fists tightly. "I walked into the room where I'd heard the screaming. This poor woman," he turned his head, appalled by the memory. "There was blood everywhere." His breathing became quick between sobs. "She was being eaten by this man. He was sick. He was so sick." His voice grew louder, and he looked down at the large weapon now sheathed at his side. "I always bring a machete with me when I go out into the woods. So I just brought it down on him." He brought his hand across his body, swinging a blade that was no longer in his hand. He began to cry harder. Grace gently grabbed his arm and motioned for him to sit down. Joe buried his face in his hands as he cried.

Charlie looked around, afraid that Joe's cries may have been heard, but there was nobody in sight.

"Uh, we should probably keep moving," Charlie said. Grace looked up and shot him a blank stare. She didn't need to say anything; Charlie knew they would be sitting for a few minutes.

Grace waited patiently and with much sympathy while the big man sat and cried. After all they'd been through, she and Charlie still had their wits. But here, right in front of her, sat this broken shell of a man. He sobbed like a child. Grace watched as hours of grief rolled down his face and into his hands. She and Charlie had been through hell, for sure. *This man must have* seen *hell,* she thought.

The sobs became slower and Joe's breaths became longer and more controlled. Grace saw an opportunity and patted him on the shoulder, letting him know it was time to get moving.

"Did you see any other...survivors?" she asked.

Joe wiped his eyes and rubbed his hands on his pants, drying away the tears. "There was an old man," he said. "He wanted to stay in the kitchen with his wife." Charlie and Grace exchanged a nervous glance. "He wanted me to stay with them, but I wasn't staying in that hole any longer than I had to."

Charlie and Grace remained silent.

"I saw a couple more of those *things* though," he added.

The blood drained from Grace's face.

146

"Where?" she asked.

"When I came out of the hut, there were a few down by the lake," he said. "There was also a couple in the woods."

For Charlie, his plan to rush to the summit felt futile now. He had tried to make himself believe that he and Grace wouldn't have to worry about the undead once they escaped the hut. He'd hoped they would make it to the top without running into any more of those...*maniacs*. Deep down, though, he knew the possibility was real. And now Joe's account had all but confirmed it was a certainty.

"What exactly *are* they?" Grace asked. "What happened to them? Are they infected or something?"

Joe looked at her with mock disappointment. "You weren't listening last night?"

Grace stared back at him, confused.

Joe stood up and straightened. "It's like Terry said last night: There's an *energy* here. It cannot be explained. I'm sure you've heard hundreds of theories about why planes get lost in the Bermuda Triangle, or how those statues ended up on Easter Island, or how Stonehenge was built." His eyes went to the sky for a moment; then he looked around the forest. Suddenly, his eyes filled with fear. "There's just something about this place." The fear made his voice shake. He finally looked back down and met Grace's eyes.

"The dead come *back*."

She broke his gaze and looked elsewhere. She tried to concentrate on something else, but the words sent a chill up her spine.

The dead come back.

The realization that it was true was almost too much for her to bear. She tried to shut down inside, to turn herself off. She didn't want to listen anymore, but Joe continued.

"And when they kill you," he said, "it's like, *you're* infected, and you become what they are."

"And what exactly is that?" Charlie asked.

Joe turned slowly toward him. "You rise again." He took a step closer to Charlie and stopped. His stare pierced into Charlie's eyes as if he was looking into his soul. "You become the undead."

Charlie held Joe's stare but said nothing. Grace tried to find something in Joe's expression, a tell, anything that might give away that Joe was full of shit. But there was nothing. Joe was as real as they came. He wasn't covered in blood, traveling the woods with a machete, looking for suckers. He was surviving. And, in Grace's estimation, he was doing a damn good job. It was only then that Grace fully understood: They'd have to keep Joe with them as long as possible.

Joe backed off and sat down again. "The only

way to kill them for real," he pointed toward his temple, "is to destroy the brain." He pointed to Charlie. "You've got a gun, you shoot 'em in the head."

"Wait, wait," Charlie began. "How do you know all this? How do you know for sure that they're dead?"

"You ever see a living person behave like this?" Joe asked.

Charlie hesitated. "No, but—"

"And have you killed one yet?"

"Yeah, but—"

"And did you get them in the head or the body?"

Charlie thought about it. He'd shot the first attacker, the one in their room, in the head. Grace had shot him several times. She'd probably gotten him in the chest or the stomach, or maybe an arm. But he didn't go down until *after* Charlie had put two bullets in his head. He'd also shot the little girl in the head, which was purely by luck, but she went down immediately. And he'd killed Terry by destroying her skull with a heavy frame. In other words, he'd killed all three by damaging the head and, in effect, destroying the brain.

Joe started nodding. He could see the understanding register on Charlie's face.

"You got them all in the head, didn't you?"

Charlie nodded.

"Well, good for you. Now you know how to kill them," Joe said.

Charlie remained silent. The understanding that he hadn't killed a little girl but, in fact, something else, something *evil*, helped ease his mind a little. He wasn't a killer, and the fact that these things were not living souls allayed the burden on his conscience. But there was still something missing.

"You talk about this like you've done this before," Charlie said. "How?"

Joe drew a deep breath, composed himself.

"Because it *happened* before."

Grace and Charlie stared at him, their eyes asking him to continue.

"Most folks from New Hampshire don't even know about it," he said. "Only the locals do. You'll never hear 'em talk about it 'cause it's a part of the state's history that people wish never happened. But, it *did* happen. And we choose not to forget because it's made us what we are today."

"Made you what?" Grace asked.

"Prepared," Joe said. "It's a secret, passed on from generation to generation. Usually the firstborn is the only one to know. Knowledge of the past prepares us for future incidents. Like last night. Like

150

right now."

Grace let the gravity of Joe's words sink in. This was not some isolated incident. This had happened before. She wondered how many times it had happened. She wondered how people managed to find a way to survive—*if* they survived. She also realized that this wouldn't be the last time it would happen.

She decided then that it was time to start moving out. "I think we should continue to the summit," she said. She looked at Joe. "You're welcome to come with us. We're going to see if we can get some supplies at the store and then maybe catch a ride down the access road."

Joe's face was grim. "That's if you find anyone alive up there."

"Well, it's either that, or we can hang out in the woods until those things find us. How long did you say you've been out here? They probably see a lot better in the daylight, huh?"

Joe narrowed his eyes. Grace watched him as he tried to think of another reason not to go to the summit, but he knew it was the only idea that made sense.

"Fair enough," he said. "Let's go."

Charlie caught Grace's eyes while Joe wasn't looking and arched his eyebrows.

Are you sure about this?

Grace nodded quickly and she took lead. Charlie fell in behind her; Joe grabbed the rear.

They set off again and headed up the trail. As they hiked in silence, Grace couldn't stop thinking about the history of this place, about everything Joe had told them. She wondered what kind of an effort it might require to completely eliminate these things, these—she could barely form the word in her mind—*undead.*

She hoped they wouldn't have to find out.

CHAPTER 9

The trail had emerged from the woods, and they'd been hiking along the ridge for an hour. Wind swirled around and crashed against them, gusting at speeds of over ninety miles per hour. Grace's face was numb and cracked, the salt from her tears having dried out the reddened skin under her eyes.

She was also starving and dehydrated. The only thing that filled the emptiness in her stomach was the pain like a dull knife stabbing at her insides. Every few minutes, she'd stopped to dry heave. The pounding in her head, accompanied by a ringing in her ears, was no doubt compounded by the wind's relentless assault and almost debilitating. She'd had migraines in the past. Not many, but enough to be familiar with the pain. The pressure she felt now was like a vise, squeezing the sides of her head, tightening just a little more with every labored step. She wanted nothing more than to give up, to just leap over the edge and fall into an unending state of blissful

153

unconsciousness. She wanted to sleep, or to eat, or both. But she knew these were not realistic options. She willed herself to continue. As much as she wanted to stop, she wanted more to escape from what hunted them. She wanted to escape the monsters— or the *undead,* as they were called. They'd almost gotten her and Charlie that morning at the hut, but they'd bested them then and they could do it again. Of course, they were much weaker now, but she had faith that, together, they would carry each other through. They had Joe with them now, too, and he knew a thing or two about fighting these things. But the pain, the pain was unbearable.

Fortunately, Charlie was the one who gave in first. He put up a hand, signaling Joe and Grace to stop. He bent over and rested his hands on his knees, his back and shoulders heaving up and down as he gasped for air. Grace worried about his bad knee, but she wasn't about to bring it up now. She didn't fully trust Joe just yet and she didn't want him to know about Charlie's injury.

Charlie turned to the both of them.

"We've been on this trail for an hour and a half now," he said. He nearly fell over as a hard gust blew from across the ridge and onto the trail. He steadied himself against a large boulder. "I think we should take a break."

Before Joe could protest, Grace spoke up. "I agree," she said. "We should head off the trail. The trees will protect us from the wind. And I could use a rest, too."

"We might be able to find some berries or some leaves to eat," Joe said. Grace was relieved Joe wasn't about to argue about stopping. Selfishly, she was happy that he was just as worn out as she and Charlie were.

"Good," Charlie said. "Let's go."

Charlie walked a bit up the trail until he found a small opening in the thicket. He was about to step in when Joe waved him off. Joe pulled his machete out of the sheath.

"Let me go first," he said. Charlie gestured with his hand, letting him go.

Joe started chopping through branches and twigs. In no time, he'd made an opening big enough to walk through. He stepped into the woods first, and Grace and Charlie followed close behind.

The woods were incredibly thick. Grace had to squint as she walked so as not to catch a branch or thorn in the eye. She shielded her head with her arms, but it still wasn't much of a defense; branches and sticks poked at exposed areas of skin and scratched at her face. And when her stomach muscles twisted and contracted, she gripped her midsection with both

155

hands, grimacing as she pressed onward.

They hadn't walked far when Grace suddenly became very aware of how much noise they were making as they ventured into the woods. She stopped walking and listened to the sound of leaves rustling and sticks breaking as Charlie and Joe continued. The sharp *thwack* of the machete as it tore through the brush made her nervous. Surely, anyone on the trail wouldn't be able to hear the noise above the howl of the wind, but they couldn't be certain that the undead would stick to the trails.

Not wanting to yell, Grace clapped her hands twice to get their attention. Joe and Charlie stopped and turned.

"We're being very loud," she whispered. Joe and Charlie walked back to her, making every attempt to step around sticks and dry leaves.

"What do you want to do?" Charlie asked.

She looked back and assessed the distance they had put between themselves and the trail.

"I think this is fine," she said. "We're far enough away from the trail that we can rest, but close enough if we need to get back on in a hurry."

"I'm going to look around for something to eat, then," Joe said.

Grace opened her mouth, ready to issue a warning, but Joe cut her off.

"I'll be quiet, don't worry," he said. Reluctantly, Grace acquiesced.

Joe walked off; his footsteps much softer as he plotted his advance into the woods. Charlie sat on the forest floor, holding his knee and grimacing as he went down. It was the first time he'd shown any pain since they had begun their hike from base camp. Grace wondered how long he'd been hiding it. She'd expected him to hide it from Joe, even from her, but the fact that he wasn't even attempting to disguise it concerned her.

She knelt down next to him. "How do you feel?"

He looked up at her, his face the picture of agony.

"Never better," he said half-jokingly. Grace didn't laugh. She only offered a look of concern.

"You don't have to be a hero for me," she said. "You need to rest."

"We don't have time to rest," he said.

"Yes we do," Grace insisted. "We're fine as long as we make it to the summit before nightfall. We have plenty of time."

A loud, lengthy groan emitted from Grace's stomach. She shut her eyes tight and tried to ignore the pain. The contractions seemed to work their way from the bottom of her ribcage all the way to her pelvis. She put a hand on her stomach and massaged.

Charlie looked at her incredulously. "Yeah, plenty of time," he said sarcastically.

Grace looked at him. She wasn't going to argue. She knew they had to get to the summit and find something to eat. Aside from the ache in her stomach, she felt herself becoming physically weaker. Each fiber of muscle in her legs burned from fatigue and lack of nourishment. She felt a twinge in her shoulders with each breath she took; her lungs attempted to expand more and more in order to take in more air. Her headache was also wreaked havoc on her vision; with each throb of pain, the woods appeared to open and close in front of her. Tunnel vision was a bad sign. That, along with the nausea, induced a fear of fainting. She looked down at the ground and considered which leaves on the forest floor she might be able to eat. She thought about Joe and where he had wandered off to. He was already gone from sight.

"What do you think of him?" she asked.

Charlie considered the question for a moment. "I think he's okay," he said. "He made it out long before we did and still managed to stay alive."

Grace nodded. She had to admit to herself that Joe seemed okay. And if Charlie gave his approval, then she didn't really have much reason to doubt Joe.

After all, it was good to have three solid people together. The fact that Joe was armed also gave her a little peace of mind.

They both jumped when they heard the scream. Grace shot up from her squatting position and Charlie jumped to his feet. The fatigue she felt through her body quickly washed away as the adrenaline surged through her once again.

Another scream. It came from deeper within the woods. It sounded like a man's scream. It had to be Joe.

Grace and Charlie took off toward the screams. They ran through the woods with no regard for protecting themselves from the branches and scrub that whipped at their faces. Grace saw a figure up ahead. A man. He was attacking something, or *someone*, on the ground. She saw the man's arm raise and lower, quickly and violently. It was Joe. He was swinging the machete.

Grace called his name. Startled, Joe turned around. He froze with the machete held high, ready to swing. His face was spotted with blood spatter, his arms more like they had been bathed in it. Grace and Charlie stopped running and continued slowly. A mangled figure lay on the ground. From the long hair and slight curve of a breast, Grace assumed it was a woman.

159

A *woman*. Eventually, Grace would have to reconcile the difference between living and dead—and *undead*.

She looked at Joe but didn't notice any obvious wounds. "Are you...okay?" she asked.

Joe's chest heaved as he fought to catch his breath. "She came out of nowhere," he said, then paused to inhale. "Fuckin' dead bitch! She almost got me." He whipped his head left and right, quickly scanning both shoulders. He pulled at his shirt and looked for any indication that she had bitten him. "I was looking for something to eat. Then this bitch grabs me. Tries gnawing at my back. So I spun around and just started hacking."

From the corner of her eye, Grace could see that the woman had several deep head wounds. Joe had been merciless in his assault. Her face didn't much resemble a face at all. It looked like a stew of blood, bone, and cartilage. Joe hadn't simply killed this woman; he had exacted revenge on her.

"Are you sure she didn't bite you?" Charlie asked.

Joe turned, pulling up the back of his shirt so they could see.

"I don't think so," he said.

Grace and Charlie checked his back. There were no wounds.

"You're fine," Grace said. "But that was loud. We should get moving."

As she said this, they noticed movement to her right. Two men and a woman were running through the woods, straight toward them. Grace took a few tentative steps backward. She reached back for Charlie's hand. Charlie yelled out to the people, attempting to elicit some kind of response. There was nothing, nothing that resembled any kind of recognition. They just kept running. Their movements were fast and uncontrolled. The wide eyes and open, quivering mouths on otherwise expressionless faces told Joe, Grace, and Charlie all they needed to know: They were flesh-eating beasts that were coming to rip them apart and eat the pieces.

Joe cursed. "Let's go!" he yelled.

"No," Charlie said.

Tired of running, he pulled the gun from his waistband. Grace took a few more steps backward, moving behind him. Joe also stepped back. Charlie took a deep breath and aimed the gun. He waited until they were a little closer. Then, when they were about fifteen feet away, Charlie, patiently and coolly fired three shots.

Three were all he needed.

The retorts echoed loudly through the woods. He hit each one of them in the head and they fell just as fast as they had run. Their bodies lay still on the ground; dark, thick blood oozed from the wounds.

Joe stepped next to Charlie. He stared down at the bodies.

"Nice shot," Joe said. "You know how to use that thing."

Charlie only nodded slowly, his breathing slow and controlled.

"You know," Joe continued, "any other day, I'd say that was loud enough to wake the dead."

Charlie continued to stare coldly at the three bodies that lay before him. "The dead aren't sleeping today," he said.

Joe snickered. He caught Grace staring off into the woods; her face drained of color.

"What is it?" Joe asked.

"We have to go," she said flatly.

Joe turned in the direction of her gaze. "Oh, shit."

At least a dozen undead ran through the woods. They headed straight toward them.

"Run!" Grace yelled.

The three of them took off. Grace jumped over stumps, small bushes, and dead trees. She looked back and saw that Charlie and Joe were close behind. The undead were still farther off, but they were gaining fast. They tore through the brush like it wasn't there. Even when they tripped or stumbled, they never slowed down. In fact, it seemed to Grace that the more they stumbled, the *faster* they came. *How is that possible?* she thought. The three of them would never lose them in the woods. The only place they had a chance of escaping them was on the trail.

"Head back to the cliff!" Grace shouted.

The three of them turned toward the trail. Grace could barely see as she got smacked in the face by branches and leaves. She could hear the sound of the stampede over her, Charlie's, and Joe's footsteps. The sound was getting louder, closer. The undead could have been tearing down the woods, for all she knew. It was an awful sound, one that only fed the terror growing inside her.

She could feel the air turning colder; they had almost reached the trail. The high winds made the air feel even colder. Ahead, she saw the edge of the woods and began to slow down. She looked behind her. Charlie and Joe were close. The swarm of the undead had closed in on them considerably. Another ten seconds and the undead would reach them. *We're not going to make it,* she thought.

Grace exited the woods first, crashing through the trees and stumbling onto the trail. The winds knocked her backward, nearly to the ground. Charlie and Joe exited a second later. Grace could see that the throng of undead was close. They'd be on the trail very soon.

Grace turned and ran, leading the way up the trail. Trees and brush were no longer a hindrance out here. However, the steep grade and exposed, loose rock presented a brand new set of obstacles. Climbing the ridge was going to be slow. She could only hope that the undead would struggle on the trail as well.

She looked behind her. Charlie and Joe were right on her heels. A little farther back, the horde had finally reached the trail. The mob of undead crashed into each other as they spilled out from the woods. Several of them made hard impact and fell over the cliff. There seemed to be only half as many as before.

Grace turned and focused on her climbing. The trail was so steep she had to crawl on her hands and knees. One hand over the other, she fought through the pain, hunger, and dehydration. She didn't bother to make sure she had good footing; she only concentrated on speed.

She looked behind her again. The undead were moving just as quickly as they had moved through the woods. Somehow, the rocky terrain was not an issue for them, as they moved like arachnids across tree bark.

Grace slipped as she grabbed hold of a loose rock. She fell backward a few feet. Several rocks fell past her and crashed into Charlie's shoulder. He fell hard against the trail. The uneven rock clawed into his chest and arms. Joe was able to keep his footing and gave Charlie a hard shove forward.

"Keep moving!" Joe shouted. Grace hesitated, slowing her ascent. Despite Joe's commands, she wasn't going to abandon Charlie.

Charlie looked up and waved her forward. "Go!" he yelled.

Grace looked up at the trail in front of her and continued climbing. The horde of undead grew louder and louder as they inched closer. Grace could hear the rock shifting and grinding under their feet as they plowed forward. She tried to concentrate on her footholds and handholds amid the grunting and snorting coming from behind them. She quickly analyzed every rock on which she placed her hands. She stretched her neck to see if the end of the trail was in sight, but all she could see was more rock.

Suddenly, the thought of being overtaken and eaten by the undead became a reality. She tried to imagine what it would feel like to have her skin and flesh torn apart. Would her skin separate like paper? Would her bones break and come apart like the wishbone of a turkey? She imagined being ravaged right there, her entrails scattered across the trail.

These thoughts disappeared when she heard a

short cry from behind. It was Charlie.

He had stopped climbing and was resting on his elbows. He'd succumbed to the pain in his bad knee.

"Come on, we have to keep moving!" Joe shouted.

"He has a bad knee!" Grace yelled.

Charlie pulled himself up on his hands and attempted to kick off with his other leg. He found a foothold and pressed forward, but when he tried to push off with his bad leg, he let out an anguished scream and collapsed to the ground.

"Charlie!" Grace shouted in despair.

He lifted his head slowly and stared up at her. She saw a painful surrender in his eyes and knew he was done. She knew *he* knew he was done.

Panicked, she moved back down the trail to help him. She grabbed him by the shoulder and tried unsuccessfully to drag him forward.

"Just go, Grace," he said. His voice was soft and tired. He rested his head against the trail, and looked out over the cliff.

Ignoring his request, she grabbed his arm under his shoulder, attempting to pull him up the trail. It was like trying to move a dead body.

"Push!" she yelled.

Joe grabbed under his other arm and tried to carry him forward. Charlie tried to push again, but exhaustion and his weakened knee wouldn't allow him to move.

"Just go," he said again. The resignation in his voice made Grace realize for the first time that, if in fact she did get off the mountain alive, she might be doing so alone. She tried to fight back the lump in her throat.

"It's okay," Charlie said, "I'm just slowing you down."

She stared back at him. Tears now filled her eyes. She heard Joe curse behind them. She looked past Charlie; the undead had finally caught up to them.

"Motherfucker!" Joe shouted. He whipped his body around, unsheathing his machete. He sat on the trail, his back toward Grace and Charlie. He hacked and swung at the undead, making devastating contact with the long blade every time. Blood sprayed in every direction. Hands, fingers, and other body parts shot away from the undead.

Grace saw the bulge in the back of Charlie's shirt and reached for the gun; there were still bullets left. She pulled the pistol out from under his shirt.

"There are only four rounds left—you'll have to reload!" Charlie yelled as Grace scooted down the trail to assist Joe.

He reached into the side pocket of his cargo

shorts and pulled out a handful of bullets. He took the gun from Grace and replaced the empty chambers.

"Shoot at the heads!" he shouted as he handed the gun back to her.

Grace's hands shook as she raised the gun. She took aim at the closest of the undead, a young man who appeared to be his early twenties. His eyes were bloodshot. Blood and pus oozed from his snarling mouth. She fired the gun. The round caught the man in the shoulder and stunned him, but only for a moment. Joe looked to his right, startled by the gunshot.

"The head! The head!" he shouted.

Grace took aim again and fired. This time, the bullet entered the young man's head through his left cheek, and the back of his head exploded with brain matter, hair, and bone fragments. He fell to the side, off the narrow trail and over the cliff.

She shot again at another, this time striking a middle-aged woman in her temple. The woman had been crawling across the trail and lunging toward Joe. She immediately fell limp as the bullet ripped through her skull and destroyed her brain. Her body slipped and tumbled down the rock-laden trail.

Grace looked back at Joe. He was fighting off three more of them; they were attacking him from his left. Grace crawled along the rock, around Charlie, and tried to get in better position to take a shot. From where she was, Joe sat directly between her and the undead. Given her lack of experience with a firearm, she didn't want to risk shooting him.

She stared down at the trail, navigating over loose rock, when she heard Joe let out a painful cry. She looked over at him; one of the undead, a young woman, was biting his leg.

"No!" she screamed.

She raised the gun and fired erratically. She struck two of the undead, knocking them off balance. Joe was able to take advantage while they were stunned; he drove the machete into one's skull and sliced the head off another. Grace continued firing until the gun emptied. She'd managed to hit the third one, the young woman who had bitten Joe's leg, in the head. The woman fell into a lifeless heap.

And just like that, it was over.

Grace sat there frozen on the trail. She stared, as if in a trance, at the bite on Joe's leg. Joe, too, sat there, unable to move as he tried to process what had just happened. *Nobody was supposed to get hurt*, Grace told herself. *This wasn't supposed to happen.* And yet, Joe's wound was deep; blood pulsed out in a thick, deep crimson stream down his shin and over his sneaker.

"Here," Grace said, "let me wrap it." She pulled at the bottom of her shirt, attempting to rip off a piece.

"Don't bother," Joe said in a very sullen tone. He laid the machete across his lap, brought in both his knees, and rested his elbows. He sat there, motionless, with his arms crossed. Grace could only watch as Joe stared off into the distance.

"What happened?" Charlie asked. "We're okay, right?"

Grace turned to Charlie. It hadn't occurred to her until then that, lying on the ground, face-down, he never even saw the woman bite Joe's leg. She closed her eyes and slowly shook her head. "I think Joe's hurt."

Charlie looked from Grace to Joe. "He's hurt?" he asked. Fear crept into his voice. He tried weakly to push himself up, attempting to plant his knee, but he couldn't turn over. Grace took his hand and helped him sit up. Charlie could now see the carnage left by Joe's and Grace's efforts. He also saw the wound on Joe's leg. He turned to Grace and opened his mouth to speak. She shook her head again. *Give him a moment*, Grace thought.

The three of them sat in silence. Fear raced through Grace's head. *What's going to happen to Joe? How are we going to get to the summit? Should we just go back down? I hope Joe's okay. We need him. Is Charlie going to be able to continue?*

After staring at the ground for several minutes, Grace broke the silence. "I think we should head to the summit," she said, "and see if we can get your leg—"

Joe stood abruptly and Grace stopped talking. He turned to face them, and Grace noticed that his eyes were wet; tear streaks meandered through the dirt, blood, and grime on his face. He held the machete in his right hand, the blade dripping with the blood of the undead.

"Why, is there a doctor at the summit?" Joe asked, his voice full of sarcasm. Grace averted her eyes from Joe's, ashamed at her frail attempt to motivate him. "I might not even have ten minutes!"

"I'm sorry," Grace said. And she genuinely was—sorry that he was wounded, sorry that she still didn't quite understand the consequences of this, but mostly sorry for the relief she felt that neither she nor Charlie had sustained any wounds from the undead. Certainly, she never wanted to see Joe injured, but inside, she felt guilty, guilty that she was happy it wasn't Charlie standing freshly wounded before her.

"I've got *no* chance now!" Joe shouted. His face turned red. He turned toward the trail and swung the machete, chopping at a small tree repeatedly.

171

Charlie slowly managed to get to his feet, favoring his good leg. He pulled Grace toward him and stepped back, giving Joe room to vent. Grace held Charlie tight as she watched Joe release his frustration. He cursed and yelled as he hacked at leaves and branches, savagely chopping the trunk until it broke in half. When the top of the tree fell over, Joe turned around. He looked out over the cliff and screamed out, the echo carrying long after he'd stopped.

And then he stood there, motionless except for the heaving in and out of his chest as he tried to control his breathing. Grace and Charlie stood away from him, farther up the trail, huddled together. Grace thought about what was going to happen next. She remembered what Joe had said earlier about being bitten by one of those things. She wondered if in fact this meant that Joe was going to "turn," whatever that meant.

Joe continued to stare off over the cliff. He was slowly calming down; his breathing had returned to normal. He now seemed pensive as he looked off into the distance. Grace tried to imagine what he was thinking.

"You know," he said, a tear forming in the corner of his eye, "I could have turned and walked the other way back there by the hut." He must have been referring to when he met them in the woods earlier in the morning. Grace wondered if he regretted his decision to join them. He turned his head, and looked directly at Grace.

"But if I did, you guys wouldn't know how to handle these things, right?" The slightest hint of a smile began to form on his lips.

"We wouldn't have made it this far without you," Grace said humbly. "Charlie's leg...he may not be able to make it very far." Her voice wavered as tears began to fill her eyes. She looked down at the gun and held it out by her side. "And I don't even know how to use this thing. I don't—"

"It's okay," Joe cut her off softly. "You don't have to."

Grace just nodded. Joe's eyes welled up again.

"You guys will be just fine," he said, wiping away a tear as he spoke. "You just stay on the trail, okay? No more venturing off into the woods." Grace nodded. She was sobbing much harder now.

She finally understood.

"What's going on?" Charlie asked. He looked over at Grace. Tears streamed down her cheeks and over her lips. He looked at Joe. "You're not coming to the summit?" Joe looked away without responding. "Where are you going?"

He turned to Charlie. "You've got a strong

173

woman here," he said. Charlie narrowed his eyes and tilted his head, confused.

Joe looked back to Grace. "You think you can do better with this?" he asked, holding up the machete.

Grace hardly responded. She simply reached out her hand. Joe wiped the machete along the leg of his shorts, removing as much of the blood as he could. Grace turned her head away and squeezed her eyes closed, tried to hold back the river of tears that fought against her eyelids.

"Why are you giving us the machete?" Charlie asked. "If you're not coming to the summit, you're still going to need protection on the way back down."

Grace looked at Charlie. He turned to her, a quizzical look on his face. Grace only half-smiled as she reached out and held his hand. Charlie turned back to Joe.

"Are you going back?" he asked.

Joe didn't respond. He finished wiping the blade and sheathed the machete. He walked up the trail, removed the weapon from his waist, and handed it to Grace. She accepted it reluctantly. He then rested his bloodied hands on his hips and stared at the weapon in Grace's hands.

"My father told me this might happen one day," Joe said. He stepped back to the edge of the trail. He looked out into the distance, seemingly admiring the view.

"He told me what to do if I should ever be injured by one of them," Joe said. "He made me promise. He told me, 'Joey, you do what I tell you, or else you ain't helping anybody.'"

Charlie was visibly confused now. He stepped toward Joe.

"What the hell are you talking about?" he said. "What are you doing?"

Joe closed his eyes and took a long, deep breath. He exhaled slowly and held his arms out like wings. His fingers splayed out and he let his head tilt back and forth with the swirling wind. He looked like every image of Jesus hanging from the cross.

He opened his eyes again and stared at Charlie.

"I'm saving your lives," he said.

It happened so quickly. Joe stepped forward. Charlie lunged, a reflexive reaction to Joe leaping over the edge. But Joe's body fell fast into the abyss. Grace wanted to close her eyes, but she couldn't stop herself from watching as Joe approached the bottom of the ravine. His body tumbled in the air as he descended faster and faster, closing in on the hard, granite bottom.

Seconds after he stepped off the cliff, Joe made contact with a large, smooth boulder below—

headfirst, just as he'd hoped. His body exploded against the rock like a bug on a windshield. Even from this altitude, they could still hear the bones shatter against the solid ground. Grace finally turned away upon impact and buried her face in her hands. Charlie, still shocked, held her close as he stared at the blood cascading down the rock. Having heard the sound of Joe's body hitting ground from up high, Grace was certain that others would have heard it too.

"Come on," Charlie said absently. Grace was sobbing hard. Her tears had begun to mix with the sweat that had soaked through his shirt sleeve. "We have to go."

Grace wasn't sure where Charlie had found the energy to move (Adrenaline? Fear?), but somehow he'd stood up and was now helping her to move on. Grace was sure his knee ached like hell, as he continued on with a severe limp, but she was mentally broken, and willing to let Charlie play the man this time.

And though they had spent just a short time with him, Joe had served as their protector when they needed him most.

As they made their way up the loose rock and pebble, a thought crossed Grace's mind: W*ho would be their protector now?*

CHAPTER 10

The sun was still missing, stowed behind a cloud-filled sky, and it was hard to determine the time of day. To Grace, it felt like it was past noon. Neither she nor Charlie had a watch, but she was certain they'd been climbing for at least an hour since Joe had leaped off the trail to his death.

The temperature had also dropped another ten degrees. The forecast had predicted low 40s, but combined with the wind chill, Grace knew it was much colder. They certainly weren't dressed for this part of the climb, either—Charlie in his cargo shorts and T-shirt, Grace in her track shorts and tank top. They had expected to make the three-hour climb from the hut to the summit in half the time. What they hadn't anticipated was running into Joe. They also didn't expect to see so many of the undead this high up in altitude.

The journey to the summit had left them drained of nearly all their energy. They still hadn't

177

eaten a thing since the night before. Grace's insides churned and bubbled, twisted and gurgled. The retching she'd experienced for much of the day had abated, but now dehydration was a factor. They hadn't found any water during the trip up the mountain. Neither of them was salivating. Grace's throat was sore and dry, and her muscles were beginning to tighten. Charlie had simply decided to not talk, assuming he would save energy and retain fluids that way.

Grace's headache was also still very much in charge of her movements. She tried to time her steps in between throbs. Sometimes she would lose her footing and have to reach quickly for another rock to step on. And when she lost her rhythm, she'd double over, folding up onto the ground as she strained against the disabling hurt that surged through her.

She began to pray.

She prayed that her family would never have to know what happened to her. She didn't want them to have to bear the burden of knowing what she and Charlie had gone through. She prayed that they'd both make it home safe, that they would have children who would never know what happened here, now or at any other time in history.

And then, in her mind, she spoke directly to God. She asked Him why he would allow such a thing to happen. She asked God why He would allow these people to be resurrected from the dead to serve no other purpose than hunting and devouring the living.

She cursed Him. She called Him a coward for not having the courage to save her and Charlie from this evil.

She called Him a bully, because bullies preyed on the weak, injured, and less fortunate. And, by definition, she and Charlie were weak and injured. They were certainly less than fortunate, as they weren't equipped to fight off the undead. They had Charlie's gun and Joe's machete, but two weapons, one of which would soon run out of bullets, would be no match for the numbers of undead she dreaded they might find once they reached the summit.

Then she challenged God. She challenged Him to provide a sign that everything would work out in their favor. She demanded that He make an offering of good faith, anything that might give them reason to believe this would all be over soon, and they would leave this place unharmed.

Grace had become so consumed by her anger and defiance toward God that she hadn't noticed her pace had quickened considerably. She also hadn't noticed that Charlie was now laughing.

What the hell is he laughing about? What the hell is so fucking funny?

179

She continued to climb uphill on her hands and knees with her head down, driven now only by her anger.

"Look up, Grace," Charlie said. His voice was cracking, but there was a slight resolve in his tone. Grace stopped climbing and stubbornly looked up. Her back muscles, stiff and dehydrated, fought against her. But what she saw brought a wave of relief, a warm sensation that crashed over her, from her head down her back and through her legs.

They had reached the summit.

For a moment, she wondered if it was a mirage. She closed her eyes for ten seconds, took several deep breaths, and opened her eyes again. And smiled. Tears of relief filled her eyes. She saw Charlie and noticed a tear fall down his cheek. They'd made it. Alive.

There was a long wrap-around boardwalk with a large building in its center: the summit shops. Along the boardwalk at intervals were several lookouts that offered views of the landscape. Immediately in front of Grace and Charlie was a small parking lot. Those who were unable to climb the mountain could drive up the access road. The road ran from the parking lot, around the opposite side of the summit, and down to the base of the mountain.

But Grace noticed something else, something that quickly turned her joy into trepidation.

The summit was deserted.

There were no other climbers, no other hikers that they could see. The summits of oft-hiked mountains like this one typically generated a lot of daily traffic, however; on this day, there was none.

Grace felt another hunger pang slice through her stomach. They had to find some food and water.

"Let's get inside," she said, throwing Charlie's arm over her shoulders and helping him to the building.

They entered through a glass door into what appeared to be a small outdoor recreation boutique. The lights were off, as if the store was closed. There were no employees. On the far left wall, backpacks and Camelbaks hung from various fixtures. There was a small selection of hiking shoes and ropes. On the floor in front of them, three small hiking tents were set up for display along with two sleeping mattresses. Ice climbing equipment hung from the other wall to their right. Ahead of them, past the tents, was the check-out counter.

Grace walked toward the back of the store. She had hoped there would be some kind of cafeteria inside, but she was willing to settle for any type of sustenance the store might provide. When she reached the glass counter, she looked around, hoping to find a display of Snickers bars, peanuts, anything.

181

There was nothing. The feeling of despair once again crept up her back. She felt the stress and disappointment spread over her shoulders and through her neck like a pair of strong hands pushing her down. Her palms and forehead began to sweat. Her stomach twisted around like a damp washcloth being wrung out. They were in desperate need of food—or at the very least, water.

She closed her eyes and tried to keep from panicking. She would be of no use to herself or Charlie if she was unable to keep it together now. After all, she'd come too far to give up.

She rested her hands on the glass counter and took several deep breaths. When she opened her eyes, she saw something through the glass cabinet. Just past the counter, behind the register on the floor, was an unopened box of energy bars. Excitement and relief filled her chest. She turned to Charlie. He was standing over by the ice climbing equipment, wielding an ice axe.

"Charlie!" she whispered loudly. She could barely contain her excitement. Charlie whipped his head around in her direction. She waved him over to the counter. "I found food!" she whispered again. Charlie dropped the ice axe and raced across the store.

Grace walked quickly around the glass counter,

toward the register. She knelt down on the floor and opened the box. There were at least a dozen bars. She grabbed a handful and stood up. She spread them on the counter in front of them both.

She and Charlie each grabbed one and fiendishly opened the wrappers. They stared at each other as they inhaled their first bars. Grace even used her fingers to collect the crumbs left in the wrapper. She picked up another one, tore open the foil, and bit into it. This time she savored the taste, the feeling of food in her mouth. It might as well have been prime rib—all she was missing was a glass of pinot noir. Charlie was enjoying his second bar, too.

They continued to stare at each other, watching each other chew every bite. Grace smiled and pushed the chewed-up bar through her teeth, her eyes wide and crazy. Charlie nearly spit out his bar when he laughed. *Now we just need something to drink,* Grace thought.

She ducked down below the counter, next to the glass cabinet. She saw a bottle of Poland Spring sitting inside. She tried to slide the glass door open, but the cabinet was locked.

"Think we can smash this open without anyone knowing?" she asked.

Charlie tapped a fingernail on the counter.

"Is that a yes or a no?" Grace asked.

Charlie tapped again.

Grace stood up abruptly. "What?" she asked.

The grin on Charlie's face was gone. His mouth was still full, but he'd stopped chewing. He stared at Grace for a second before his eyes darted left and then came back to hers. Grace looked to her right.

"What the fuck do you think *you're* doing?"

The woman held a rifle aimed at Grace's head. Grace stood still. She averted her eyes so as not to stare directly into the barrel. *Oh my God, this is how it's going to end,* she thought. Her eyes moved over to Charlie. She searched his face for any clue as to how they were going to get out of there. But Charlie didn't have any answers. He simply stood there, motionless.

It had been about fifteen seconds before Grace realized she hadn't taken a breath. "We came from the hut," she blurted out, her voice low. "We haven't eaten since last night. We're starving and thirsty." She continued to stare at Charlie, waiting for the woman to respond. "Please don't kill us," she said.

"You two have any *followers* on your way up here?" the woman asked. Grace turned her head slightly, her eyebrows scrunched. She and Charlie exchanged a look of bemusement. Grace shook her head and shrugged, not sure what to say.

"Zombies!" the woman said, her voice louder now. "Did any of them follow you up here?"

"I don't...think so," Grace said confused. "I thought they were 'undead?'"

"What do you think a zombie is?" the woman asked.

"We ran into a few of them," Charlie cut in, "but we managed to kill them all."

"You killed them? *All* of them?" the woman asked dubiously. "And just how'd you manage that?"

"I have a gun," Charlie said.

"Congratulations," the woman said. "Drop it on the ground. Slowly." Charlie reached behind his back and carefully removed the gun. "Nothing fancy or your girl gets two in the head," the woman said. Charlie dropped the gun on the floor and pushed it toward the woman using his foot. "And I assume you used a machete?" the woman asked Grace. Grace shook her head. "Uh-huh. And do you mind explaining that?"

"Well, we had a third," Charlie said. He struggled to find the words to explain what had happened to Joe. "But...he didn't make it."

"Wonderful," the woman said. "And is he out there running around now, trying to find something that looks like us to eat?" she asked.

"No," Grace said, defensively. Her fear started to turn into anger over the woman's incessant and superfluous line of questioning. "He jumped off a cliff and smashed his body into the bottom of the ravine."

"Smart man," the woman said. "Maybe smarter if he had taken you both with him."

Grace had had enough, her patience worn thin. If this woman was going to kill them, she would have done it by now.

She turned to face her. "Are you planning on shooting us? Because clearly we're not two of those things. And your little power trip is getting old. We're hungry, we're thirsty and we're tired. And we've been fighting those fucking monsters all morning with nothing but pure adrenaline."

The woman narrowed her eyes. Grace could feel her stare, as if she was looking through her soul. Grace tried to hide her nerves, but she could feel her heart pounding against her ribs.

The woman lowered the rifle, and a smile began to crease one side of her mouth.

"All right, get in here. I've got drinks and food in the office."

She turned and walked back into the small room behind the register. Grace and Charlie stood still for a moment. When the woman no longer felt their presence, she stopped and turned around.

"You coming?"

Grace shot Charlie a look of concern. He

nodded slowly. *I hope you're right,* Grace thought.

CHAPTER 11

The woman introduced herself as Rose. Rose was very fit for her age, which Grace estimated to be early to mid-forties. She had arrived at the summit earlier in the week and was staying for two weeks total. She explained that summit employees often worked weekly or biweekly shifts.

She was also single and didn't own a car so, on this occasion, as with many others, she had hitched a ride on the shuttle that went back and forth from the base to the summit twice daily.

When she worked at the store, she sometimes camped outside during the overnights. This time, however, she had stayed in the little room in the back of the store. The room was equipped with a small tube TV, sink, cot, and even a mini-fridge containing cold drinks. There was a microwave for heating up soups or other cold dishes that Rose would get from the cafeteria, which was, to Grace's pleasant surprise, also located in the same complex. Grace and Charlie had simply picked the wrong entrance.

Rose sat on a cot, next to the microwave. She was heating up some food for the three of them. Grace and Charlie sat on two overturned milk crates. They had asked if Rose had a cell phone. She didn't.

"Seriously?" Grace asked. "What don't you have a phone?"

"Didn't say I don't have a phone," Rose said. "I said I don't have a *cell* phone. I have a landline at home."

"I didn't know people still used those," Charlie mocked her.

"I guess I'm just old school then," Rose said.

"There must be a radio then," Grace said.

Rose nodded over toward the TV. A CB radio sat on top of the set. "Already called down to the base on it."

"And?"

"Nobody down there, apparently."

"How is that possible?" Grace asked.

Rose locked eyes with her. "The dead don't answer phones or radios."

The idea that those who would have otherwise come to their rescue might themselves have succumbed to the undead was a harsh bit of reality Grace hadn't yet considered. Even if she and Charlie were to make it to the base, there was still a chance that they'd never walk away alive.

"Well, obviously someone drove up here," she said. "Who owns the cars out in the parking lot?"

"Kitchen folk," Rose said.

"And where are they?"

Rose stared at her with a cold expression that made Grace wish she hadn't asked the question.

"Believe me," Rose said, "you don't want to find them—and you don't want them to find *us.*"

"So they...*turned?*" Charlie asked.

"You got it," Rose said. The microwave beeped and she removed a Hot Pocket. She placed it on a napkin and handed it to Grace. "They tried something stupid and got themselves killed. Now they're probably out there running around looking for something to eat. Hell, they may even be in the kitchen still."

Grace couldn't believe Rose's candor—the way she talked about the undead, about the whole situation as if it wasn't a big deal. Simply an everyday occurrence. Grace looked at Charlie. They both shook their heads, shocked by Rose's attitude.

"So," Grace started, "do you plan on leaving any time, or are you just going to sit on your ass forever?"

Rose stopped passing food around and stared at Grace. Grace saw a look of death in her eyes and swallowed her fear down hard.

"You listen to me now," Rose said. "I've got everything I need here—food, water, shelter. I was perfectly safe before you two showed up. The only way I can get off this mountain is on foot." She looked back and forth at both of them. "And from the looks of it, it seems I'm not the only one who isn't likely to hike off this mountain."

Grace realized her own arrogance. How pompous to think that she and Charlie would just walk down this mountain with no problems. Rose made a good point. Had she and Charlie been stocked with food and water back at the hut, it was possible they would never have left.

Regardless of their current situation, however, Grace knew they had to get off the mountain. They had filled up on Hot Pockets and trail mix and washed it all down with cold spring water. They were fueled, renewed, and energized, and it was time to move on. But as concerned as Grace and Charlie were about one another, Grace felt she needed to convince Rose it was time for her to move on, too.

"Look," Grace said, "you have a gun. We have a gun and a machete. We have a much better chance of getting out of here alive if we all stay together."

Rose stared at her, unconvinced.

"Honey," Rose said, "this gun isn't even loaded.

She handed Grace the rifle. Grace held the rifle, stared blankly back and forth between it and Rose. She felt deflated.

"Are you kidding me?" she asked.

Rose closed her eyes and nodded. "Wish I was, believe me."

Grace set the rifle down and leaned it against the wall. She stood up and pressed her hands against her head, as if to stifle the onset of a headache. She paced back and forth a few seconds. Then she stopped and rested a hand on Charlie's shoulder.

"We're getting out of here," she said. Charlie stood up slowly, supporting his bad knee with one hand on the floor. He followed Grace, who was walking quickly to the door.

"Suit yourselves," Rose said. "But I wouldn't recommend it."

Grace stopped, turned, and faced Rose.

"I don't know how you can be so content with doing nothing, but eventually you're going to wish you weren't sitting alone in this hole." She waved her hand around the room.

"You're welcome for the food and water," Rose said.

"Whatever," Grace said. She turned and walked out of the room. When Charlie exited, she slammed the door shut.

It wasn't even a full second later until she wished she hadn't done that. Grace immediately recognized the familiar stench of rotting flesh and blood. Her back toward the store, she turned slightly toward Charlie. His eyes were wide and his breathing had picked up considerably.

"How many?" Grace whispered. Charlie tapped the leg of his shorts five times. *Shit,* she thought.

"They see us?" she asked. Charlie nodded his head slowly. Grace tried to think quickly. Charlie still had the gun, but it only had four bullets left. Grace wore the machete at her side. They would have to fight their way out. It was the only way.

"How close?" Grace asked.

"Register," Charlie said. The cash register was only a few feet away. *He'll have to kill that one first,* Grace thought. Still facing the door, she quietly let go of the door handle and slid her fingers over the handle of the machete. She looked at Charlie from the corner of her eye.

"Don't miss," she told him.

"I won't."

With the speed of an assassin, Grace spun on her heels, pulling the heavy blade out of its sheath. The undead were already running at them. Charlie pulled the gun from his waist and fired a shot into the forehead of the one by the register. It had already climbed over the counter by the time Charlie got the shot off. But it was a direct hit, and the zombie went down lifeless behind the counter.

Three bullets left.

Grace moved around the side of the counter and swung the machete at an oncoming zombie, slicing his outstretched hands off. She tripped over a box of carabiners and fell to the floor. The handless man fell on top of her and flung his arms at her. Blood and bits of flesh spattered across her face. The zombie gnashed his rotted teeth as he tried to bite her. Grace held onto the machete at both ends and tried to push him away from her.

"Push him up so I can get a shot!" Charlie yelled.

The zombie was relentless in his attack. He snapped his jaws repeatedly, and more bloody drool dribbled onto Grace's face. Blood spilled from the stumps at the end of his arms. Summoning all her strength, Grace pushed the blade as hard as she could until her arms were completely outstretched. Charlie took the shot. The bullet ripped through the side of the zombie's skull, knocking it backward momentarily. It then fell toward Grace. She shoved the limp body to the floor.

Two bullets left.

She pulled her shirt up to wipe her eyes. As she

blinked, she saw another zombie running at her. He was only a few feet from where she stood. From seemingly out of nowhere, the zombie caught a crampon in the face, which knocked it off balance and into a display of canteens. Grace looked back to her right; Rose had emerged from the back room. She jumped on top of the zombie, delivering blow after blow to its head using the crampon. The metal footwear device had spikes two inches long. Blood and brain matter sprayed in every direction as Rose drove the spikes into the zombie's head again and again.

Another zombie ran at Charlie at full speed. He fired the gun and missed. Grace ran and intercepted the monster, knocking it to the ground. She landed on the zombie's back. With no hesitation, she hacked at its head again and again. She'd carved out a hole the size of a fist in the back of its head before she realized its arms and legs were no longer moving.

One bullet left.

Grace heard a terrible scream from behind her. She turned and saw Rose being attacked by the fifth zombie. It had bitten into her shoulder.

"Shoot it! Shoot it!" Rose screamed.

Charlie ran to her. He stood over the zombie and fired his last shot into the back of its head. The zombie immediately went limp. Charlie pulled its lifeless body off of Rose. As she lay there, blood sprayed from the wounds on her shoulder and neck.

"I didn't see him," Rose said. Her voice trembled. "I got the other one, but I didn't see him."

"Shh, it's okay now," Charlie said, throwing an ominous glance at Grace. Grace knew it would never be okay for Rose, whose head bobbed up and down as she went into shock.

"Rose," Charlie said, his voice soft but firm. "You're going to turn. So we're going to have to ki—"

A loud crash from inside the store turned their heads.

"That's more of them," Rose said, her voice just above a whisper. "They're coming in from the stock room."

Charlie looked around, as if weighing their options.

"Just go!" Rose said. "I'll take care of them." Charlie looked at Grace. He seemed as unsure as she was.

"Go!" Rose insisted. "I promise! I'll take care of them." With no bullets left and no idea how many more were coming, Grace knew they had to go.

"I'll take care of myself after!" Rose said.

"Let's go," Grace said. "She'll at least slow them down and then she'll kill herself before she turns."

Rose nodded emphatically. Grace could tell Charlie had little confidence that it would work, and that Rose would easily succumb to the zombies, but Grace was right about one thing: Rose would likely slow them down.

"Okay," Charlie said. He turned to Grace. "Grab the machete." He got up and ran to the display of ice axes and grabbed two.

"Help me up," Rose said.

Grace held her left arm. Charlie tucked the ice axes into his belt and held her right arm. They stood her up by the counter.

"They'll have to come through me before they get to the door," Rose said.

"All right, let's go," Charlie said. He ran to the door, and Grace started to follow. She stopped and looked back at Rose. She stared deep into her eyes. She couldn't bring the words to her lips, but Rose acknowledged.

"It's okay," Rose said. "Besides, it looks like you were right all along." That same half-smile creased her bloodied, painful lips.

Another loud crash in the stock room.

"Grace, come on!" Charlie said. He was standing by the front door. Grace looked back at Rose one last time. She nodded, mouthed the words, "thank you," and ran to the door.

CHAPTER 12

Once outside, Grace and Charlie ran along the perimeter of the building. They could hear Rose's screams shortly after they exited the store. Grace tried to block out the sound as they searched for an entrance to the cafeteria. If the kitchen employees owned any of the cars that were parked outside, surely they'd find a set of keys.

Grace wondered what had compelled Rose to help them after their less-than-pleasant first meeting. She hadn't expected that kind of selflessness out of Rose, and now she felt guilty for allowing her to become food for the undead.

For the *zombies.*

Grace had enough trouble forming the word in her mind. Images of teeth ripping into Rose's skin flashed in her head. She tried to push them away. She could no longer hear Rose's screams; either they were far enough away, or Rose was dead. The wound on her shoulder—the fountain of blood that bubbled out onto the floor—was probably more than a wound at this point. Rose was probably missing an arm by now. Or a leg. Or...

"I think this is it," Charlie said. The words pulled Grace out of her own mind and reset her focus on what they were there to do.

They had reached another door. Charlie cupped his hand to the glass to look inside.

"I can see tables, chairs," he said. "This is definitely it." He reached for the door handle.

"Wait a minute," Grace said. She put a hand on his arm. Fear and hesitation were starting to cloud her judgment. Charlie must have seen it in her face.

"Grace, we gotta get out of here," he urged.

"But what if..." She couldn't finish. All she could think about were the five zombies that had just found them in the store. They hadn't waited around to see how many more had come. They'd simply left.

And Rose had been the sacrifice. Her eyes drifted off. She stared past Charlie, off into the distance at nothing in particular.

"Grace!" Charlie grabbed her by the shoulders. He was shaking her, trying to bring her back from wherever her thoughts had taken her. "We're getting down from the mountain, right?" he coaxed her.

Grace's eyes met his again. She nodded.

"Okay," he said. "Then we're just going to take

a look around for some keys. If we don't find any, then we'll just have to go on foot. Right?"

She nodded again.

Charlie pulled the door open. The cafeteria was much brighter inside than the store had been. The lights were off in here as well, but the majority of the walls were glass—huge windows that overlooked the summit and the surrounding landscape.

The cafeteria was enormous, comparable in size to that of a ski lodge, with many rows of tables and chairs. There was a staircase on the left side that led upstairs to a second floor.

There was no stench of the undead here. Instead, the air was scentless, yet thick and heavy. There was no spirit in the air, no feeling of hope or belief that they were going to come out of this with their lives. There was only the feeling that something, or someone, was about to leap out at them at any moment.

Grace held Charlie's hand as they tiptoed through the tables, toward the back of the cafeteria where the food ordering area was. Beyond this was the kitchen, completely visible to the rest of the patrons—if there had been any.

Charlie stepped to the counter and raised himself up on his elbows. He looked through the order window.

"We should go check the kitchen," he said. "If anybody left their keys, they'd be in there."

Grace was hesitant at first, as she recalled the last time she'd been in a kitchen. But she agreed. They were both armed, and as ready as they could be for anything that came out at them. They walked toward the end of the ordering area and through a revolving door, into the kitchen.

The place was a mess. Appliances, large and small, were left plugged in, sitting on top of dirty counters. Used pots and pans lay on the stove and washing area. A chef's knife lay next to a bowl containing a mixture of egg whites, peppers and mushrooms; no doubt an omelet-to-be left behind in the panic. Grace was certain it had been urgently abandoned in favor of safety. Any self-respecting head chef would never leave his or her kitchen in such disarray.

Charlie found a chef's coat hanging on the corner of one of the counters. He inspected the pockets but found no keys. Grace searched around the old-school punch-clock. There were cups with loose change, cigarettes, paper clips, and matches. But there weren't any keys.

At the far end of the kitchen, opposite the revolving door, there was a small coatroom.

"In there," Charlie said urgently.

They both rushed into the small room. A half-dozen coats hung from hooks nailed into the wall. Grace and Charlie searched through every pocket, frantically trying to find a set of car keys. To their dismay, they found none.

"You've got to be kidding me," Charlie said.

At that moment, Grace heard a familiar sound. It was something she hadn't heard since they'd arrived at the campground two days ago. She heard music. They both stared at each other.

"Where is that coming from?" she whispered. Charlie looked around. Eventually his eyes went to the ceiling. The music was coming from upstairs.

"Should we check it out?" Grace asked, keeping her voice low.

Charlie's expression seemed unsure. Grace watched as he silently weighed the decision in his head.

"Someone might know we're here," he said. "Maybe they heard us come in. Maybe they need our help and this is a signal."

Grace wasn't sure why Charlie felt the need to rationalize his decision. Ultimately, if she didn't want to go upstairs, she wasn't going upstairs. But, on the off chance there *was* a set of keys upstairs, she was willing to take the risk.

"Let's go," she said.

They tiptoed back through the kitchen, careful not to disturb any of the appliances or utensils around them. The music that blared above them grew louder. Grace thought she recognized the melody: a haunting rhythm strummed on an acoustic guitar.

They passed through the revolving door, back out into the empty cafeteria. The music was even louder out here. Grace recognized the song now. Someone was playing Johnny Cash's cover of Nine Inch Nails's "Hurt" over the cafeteria sound system. She stopped and turned to face Charlie. She shook her head, silently imploring Charlie not to go upstairs. *This is a bad idea*, she thought. She suddenly had no interest in finding out who or what was upstairs.

Charlie simply nodded, determinedly. He walked past her and she grabbed his hand, following close behind. Every uncertain step she took now felt one closer to her last. It was all too surreal to Grace as Cash's voice filled the lower part of the cafeteria.

Charlie headed toward the staircase. Grace floated behind him. She didn't seem to have control over her legs and feet anymore. She didn't care. Consumed by the voice of Cash all around her, in her head, she was now being drawn upstairs as if by gravitational pull.

She ascended the stairs. The eerie melody was inside her now. It reverberated through her arms and legs. She no longer felt the steps beneath her. She was moving on an escalator; her head and upper torso simply along for the ride.

Grace took another step.

And another.

Cash's voice was booming now as she and Charlie were halfway up the stairs. Ahead of her, Charlie seemed fifty yards away; tunnel vision had crept into her head and poisoned her vision. She put her head down again and watched as her feet made each step, robotic and uncontrolled.

She looked up again at Charlie, who now stood at the top of the stairs. He looked out over the room. His eyes had glossed over; his face showed no emotion. Grace made the last few steps and looked out across the room. Her body went numb. She couldn't blink. She simply hadn't been prepared for what they found.

Bodies and body parts lay on the floor, scattered and tossed all over. Detached torsos and appendages lay intermingled in a sick game of Twister. Blood— some dried, some still wet and dripping—had sprayed over most of the upstairs windows. Someone, likely in their final stages of life, had managed to write a message in the bloody windows: "HELP US!"

The scene on the second floor was absolutely gruesome. Grace was frozen. All she could do was turn her head from left to right and back again, scanning the carnage.

Grace estimated that there were about a hundred people, all dead, upstairs. Some bodies were still intact; most were not. Some clutched onto their own parts even after they had been savagely ripped off; a final act of defiance.

A mother and father lay dead, their two young sons next to them. The parents had died trying to protect them, but it just wasn't enough. One of the sons was missing his entire lower half. The father lay with his head on the boy's stomach, his arms stretching over his head. He had been reaching for the boy, likely an attempt to hold onto him and keep him from being further defiled by the monsters.

Another man lay with his arms wrapped around one of his own legs, which had been ripped off and partially devoured. What he held onto now more closely resembled a decaying piece of raw meat with a bone protruding from the bottom into a sneaker. The undead, apparently uninterested in his foot, had chosen to take his lower leg muscle and part of his thigh before moving on.

Most disturbing was the man's expression. His eyes were open. And huge. His mouth remained open as well, as if his last breaths had been spent screaming out in pain, a fruitless attempt to draw help. Grace nearly ran out of air before she finally remembered to take another breath.

Charlie found his legs again and began walking into the room, keeping to the perimeter. Grace followed. She imagined how many of the undead it took to kill these people. Certainly, it was more than they'd already seen.

Cash continued to sing from a jukebox in the opposite corner of the room as they navigated around the dead, being mindful not to step on or over the bodies. This was a murder scene now. And while it wasn't likely that police would be there any time soon, it was no excuse to be any less careful.

There was a man slumped over on a stool in the back of the room. He was wearing a white chef's coat. He looked peaceful, resting on the counter; his head cradled in his arms. He looked as if he had been placing an order when the attack happened. It also looked like he had been left unharmed, as he didn't appear to be covered in any blood.

The music finally stopped. It was silent again. Charlie walked over to the man slumped over the counter. He poked him in the shoulder. The man didn't budge. Charlie looked at Grace, who shook her head. *We shouldn't be here*, she mouthed. Charlie shrugged. He turned back toward the man. He reached out with his hand again, slowly.

The man shuddered, letting out a loud, wet cough. Charlie and Grace jumped. The man sitting on the stool lifted his head. He hacked and wheezed, blood spraying from his mouth in a red mist. When the coughing fit was over, he rested the side of his head down on the counter, his eyes wide and staring at Charlie and Grace.

It was then that Grace noticed the man *had* been attacked; the front of his neck had been chewed into what looked like raw hamburger. Charlie held out his arm, a warning to Grace not to come any closer. But it didn't matter. Grace's feet were stuck to the floor. She was amazed and horrified by the amount of blood that had run down the front of his coat. She was further surprised that he was still alive.

His mouth began to move; his lips attempted to form words.

"Is he trying to talk?" Grace asked. To their astonishment, the man was speaking. He spoke very low, lower than a whisper. They couldn't hear what he was saying. Charlie slowly moved closer to the man.

"P-p-" he stumbled. He obviously didn't have the energy to speak. He probably lacked the muscles in his throat too, Grace thought.

Charlie moved in even closer, placing his ear directly in front of the man's mouth.

"Pock-et," the man whispered, exhaling slowly

as he spoke. He was clearly weakened and, quite obviously, close to death. Charlie backed away. He looked at Grace.

"I think he's telling us to take something from his pocket," he said. Grace stared back at him. She wasn't sure they needed to be taking *anything* from this man's pocket, regardless of its importance.

"Pocket," the man whispered again, this time with a little more strength. He gurgled as he tried to speak; blood bubbled out of the neck wound.

The both of them stood there, motionless. After exchanging stunned looks, Grace, admittedly, was curious now as to the object the man wanted so badly for them to have.

"Well," she said to Charlie. "Check his pockets!"

Charlie gripped the ice axe, ready to strike down if need be. He moved toward the man, reached out for his coat, and felt both shirt pockets. Nothing. Cautiously, Charlie moved down and felt both the man's pants pockets. There was something in the man's left pocket.

"Here," Charlie said, handing her the ice axe. He slowly opened the man's pocket with his left hand and reached in with his right. There was a jingle as he felt the object. He turned to Grace. A thin smile touched his lips. Grace looked down at the man's pants. Charlie pulled out a set of keys.

Holy shit, we're getting out of here! Grace thought.

There were a few different keys on the key ring: one resembled a house key, another that of a locker key. However, there was no mistaking the key with the "Chevy" logo on it.

"Did you see a Chevy outside?" Charlie asked. Grace closed her eyes. She tried to take a mental inventory of everything she had seen outside. There was a Toyota, a Ford pickup.

"Yes!" she said, opening her eyes again. "I think there was a small Chevy out there!" She felt a burst of energy course through her. There may not have been a rescue mission forthcoming, but there sure as hell was a car out there that could lead them to safety.

She celebrated silently, inside her head, and her smile stretched from ear to ear. Charlie smiled too. He reached out for the ice axe; Grace handed it back and he stored it in his belt. Relief washed over his face momentarily as he looked past her, toward the windows. He appeared to be savoring the moment. Grace just stared at him, thankful that they still had each other, thankful that they were nearly out of this mess. She knew it might be a few more minutes until they found the car, and that they might have to fight off more of the undead, but the imminent danger did nothing to weaken her renewed confidence. They now had purpose. They were *supposed* to get these keys and they were *supposed* to take this man's car to safety. It was the whole reason they had come to the summit. It was destiny.

But Charlie continued to stare past her. His smile slowly faded away; his face wore a dour expression. Grace became worried about his sudden change in demeanor. Did he forget something? Was there *not* a Chevy outside? She grabbed his hand.

"What is it?" she asked.

Charlie put a finger to his mouth.

Be quiet.

He swallowed hard.

"I just saw movement over by the windows," he whispered.

Grace started to turn.

"*Don't* turn," Charlie said, keeping his voice low. "Let's just quietly leave the way we came."

Grace turned toward the staircase. She tiptoed around the corpses, careful not to disturb the bodies. From the corner of her eye, she too noticed movement by the window.

Fuck!

She quickened her pace but immediately felt Charlie tug at the back of her shirt, slowing her down. She started to take deep, controlled breaths and continued walking slowly toward the staircase.

She wanted to look, to investigate, as she rounded the top of the stairs, but she forced herself to keep her eyes ahead of her. When they were halfway down, she stopped. She turned to Charlie.

"What if it's another survivor?" she whispered.

"What if it's not?"

"That's ridiculous," she said. "That man just helped us. He gave us his car keys. There could be others."

Charlie looked Grace in the eyes. "There is a room full of dead people who may not be dead for very long!" he whispered.

As Grace attempted to stare him down, there was a noise above them. It sounded like a chair knocking against a table.

Then there was a moan—an inhuman sound that quickly turned into a growl.

"Shit!" Charlie said. "Go! Now!"

Grace turned and quickly found the bottom of the stairs. She rounded the corner and ran for the door as Charlie came down the stairs behind her. When she reached the exit, she quickly scanned outside for any of the undead. There were none. She turned back to Charlie.

Her stomach dropped.

Charlie was fighting off one of the zombies. It was Rose. She had burst through the kitchen door and attacked him from behind. She clung to his back, tried to bury her teeth in his skin. Grace screamed. Charlie reached over his shoulder and grabbed Rose's head and tried to free himself, but she held on. Grace broke into a sprint. It felt like Charlie was a mile away. She couldn't seem to run fast enough. As she closed the distance between her and Charlie, she pulled the machete from her side.

But it was too late. Rose sunk her teeth through shirt and flesh and pulled away a large chunk of muscle; Charlie fell to his knees in pain. Tears filled Grace's eyes as she hauled back the machete and swung hard at Rose's head.

She buried the machete a few inches into Rose's skull. Blood gushed out on either side of the blade, splattering on Grace's face and arms. Charlie fell forward to the floor. Grace pulled the machete from Rose's wound, raised the blade, and swung again. And again. And again. Even when Rose's body dropped to the floor, Grace fell to her knees and continued swinging.

She continued to attack until nearly the top half of Rose's head was gone. Blood and bone had mixed with the brain in a viscous stew of grey, red, and white.

Grace looked down at Rose when she was finished. She still had Charlie's flesh in her mouth.

Grace forced open Rose's mouth, separating the lower jaw, and pulled out Charlie's flesh. She scoured the inside of Rose's mouth with her bare hand. She was so intent on cleaning out every last bit of Charlie, she'd forgotten he lay on the floor, injured.

"Grace," he said, his voice weakened.

Grace stopped. She let go of what was left of Rose and went to Charlie. Tears welled up again as she saw the blood squirt from his wound in short, pulsating bursts. She covered the wound with her hand.

"It's okay," she said. "We just have to find a few towels. I'll fix you up." She looked around hurriedly.

"Grace." He tried to get her attention, but she continued scanning the room.

"*GRACE*," he said again, a bit louder. This time, he caught her attention.

She looked back at him slowly, unwilling to accept the inevitable. She stared at him, took his head in her hands. He was already turning pale, his face the color of clay. Her face, covered in Rose's blood, now streaked with tears. *He's already gone...*

"Oh, Charlie..."

"I'm losing a lot of blood, Grace," Charlie said. His body started to shake. He was going into shock.

Grace cried even harder. This wasn't what was

213

supposed to happen. They were both supposed to get in the Chevy and drive down the mountain to safety. They still could. She wiped her face with the front of her shirt.

"No," she said. She slipped an arm under his back and tried to sit him up. "I'm going to help you to the car, I'm going to drive us down the mountain, and we're going to get you help."

"Grace, it's not going to wor—"

"Yes, it is!" she said. She struggled to get him into an upright position. "Help me! Sit up!"

"Grace, baby," he pleaded. "I don't have much time left. You need to accept that. You know what happens now."

Grace let her head hang as she cried. She felt the strength leave her arms as Charlie's weakened body slid back down to the floor. He rested on his side and stared into her eyes.

"You're going to have to kill me."

Grace stopped crying. The horror flashed across her eyes and she shook her head.

"No."

"Grace, you have to—"

"No!" she said vehemently.

She stood up. She paced around the cafeteria, grabbed whatever napkins she could find from every table. When she'd found as much as she could carry, she went back to Charlie. She began applying the napkins to his shoulder, one at a time. Then two at a time, then more...

"It won't stop bleeding!" she cried. She continued to press napkins to the open wound. She watched as the napkins turned a deep crimson and removed them. The blood was coming at such a rapid flow that it covered a large section of the floor now.

"I know," Charlie said. "And it's not going to stop. I'm going to bleed out, Grace."

Charlie now lay flat on his back. His breathing was shorter. The color had completely drained from his face, along with much of the blood from his body. His lips had turned bluish, his face a pasty grayish-white. Grace could only stare at him, helpless, as the life left his eyes. With the only strength he had left, he reached for her hand.

"You... have to... do it, Grace," he said. "You have to... kill me."

She shook her head.

"Please, Grace." He slid the ice axe across the blood-covered floor.

"Just... put it in my head... into the brain. That... ought to do it."

She picked up the axe. She held it to her chest.

"And then... you have to save yourself, Grace," he said, staring into her eyes as her empty gaze

215

wandered around the room.

"I won't do it," she said softly.

"Do it," he said. "For me."

"I can't."

"I don't... want to come back... as that," he said, pointing to Rose.

Grace shut her eyes tight, forcing out more tears. She shook her head.

"You still... have a chance," he said. He wheezed now, and blood trickled out of his mouth. "You're not hurt... you can make it... I know you can. But you have to... promise me you'll get out of here, Grace."

She stared at him, motionless, through tear-filled eyes.

"Promise me, Grace," he said again.

She exhaled the last bit of resistance from her body and weakly nodded her head.

"Okay," Charlie said. "Now you have to kill me."

She shook her head again.

"Please, Grace. Do it fast. Because, soon, it won't be me lying here."

She gripped the ice axe with both hands.

"You can do it," Charlie said. "You'll survive, Grace."

Grace raised the ice axe over her head.

Charlie's final words came out as breath. "I'll always love you, baby."

Grace closed her eyes and wailed as she brought the axe down fast. She felt the metal spike break through his skull. Without thinking or any hesitation, she raised the axe and brought it down again. This time, she felt it sink farther into his head. She raised the axe once more and brought it down with every ounce of strength she had left. She held on to the axe for a few seconds, shaking uncontrollably, before she finally let go.

Grace covered her face with her hands as she cried. She immediately felt the cold, unforgiving arms of guilt wrap around her. She felt a sickness in her stomach, a pit of anguish that temporarily debilitated her. The anguish quickly turned to nausea, and she swung her head to the side and vomited on the floor. The acids burned in her stomach, all the way up her throat. But she *wanted* to feel the pain. Even when she was finished, she forced herself to vomit more. She wanted to suffer, to feel her insides coming out. More than anything, she wished there was still one bullet left in the gun. She'd have ended it right now if she could.

But then, that would have been too easy—a simple way of getting rid of the pain. No, she had to feel the pain, she *needed* to feel it.

In her periphery she saw Rose's body lying still, her head completely destroyed. As much as she didn't want to look to her left, she didn't want to leave Charlie there with the ice axe buried in his skull. She closed her eyes tight, reached out her left hand until she felt the handle, and grasped it tight. She then reached across her body with her right hand and with a hard tug, the axe came free with a sound like slicing an over-ripened tomato.

There was a noise upstairs. Grace's eyes went to the floor above her. She gripped the axe tightly.

Another noise.

People were getting up. There was movement now. Confused movement. The dead were rising— walking into chairs and trash cans, bumping into other people. They were a band without a leader, a symphony without a conductor.

Grace thought about staying where she was. She could simply wait and die at the hands of the undead. She imagined them grabbing at her, biting into her flesh, severing her limbs with their teeth; it would be more pain than she'd ever known. But in her mind, she deserved it, for if Charlie had come down the stairs first, he most likely would have made it out alive. Grace was the faster of the two. She could have easily gotten away from Rose; Charlie would have already been at the door.

But Grace had gone down the stairs first. She had reached the door first. It was only when she turned around that she had seen Rose's teeth sunken into Charlie's shoulder. She had momentarily forgotten about Charlie in her attempt to check the parking lot for any zombies. Charlie's death was all her fault. She deserved to die the same way he did. She deserved to endure the same pain. She deserved—

Bullshit.

She knew Charlie wouldn't have wanted that. His death would have been in vain if she didn't at least try to escape from these creatures. She had to survive. For him. Because he loved her and she loved him.

Grace now heard movement at the top of the stairs. Erratic footsteps began descending. One step, then two steps at a time. Then another set of footsteps that seemed to skip a step and fall down the stairs. She pulled the second ice axe from Charlie's belt and held both in her left hand. She quickly grabbed the machete and shoved it in the sheath. Wiping away tears, she picked herself up off the floor.

There was a loud grunt at the bottom of the stairs. Grace looked up. The same man who only minutes ago had given them a set of car keys now stood ten feet away from her. His eyes were soulless.

Blood and mucous slowly dripped from his mouth; the wound in his neck oozed pus and blood.

Not today, Grace thought to herself.

She turned and ran to the door. Manic, pounding footsteps followed quickly behind her. Those footsteps were soon joined by several others—more of the undead were coming down the stairs.

Grace burst through the door into the daylight and ran left toward the other side of the building. She looked behind her; the undead swarm poured out of the cafeteria. They chased her with rabid tenacity, but Grace was able to keep a safe distance. She would need the separation; she still had to find the car.

On the other side of the building, she found several cars parked in a small lot. She pulled the keys from her pocket and desperately began pressing the remote locking device. To her left, she saw the taillights of a Chevy Cobalt blinking.

Grace ran to the driver's side of the car and yanked the door handle. The horde of undead bound around the corner of the building and pursued at a frantic pace. The sound of running feet, grunts, and groans announced the approach of the crowd. It was deafening. Grace tossed the axes onto the passenger side as she jumped into the driver's seat. She jammed the key into the ignition as she slammed the door shut. The Chevy revved to life. Grace looked down at the shifter and put the car in reverse.

Hands smacked at the windows before Grace could even step on the gas. The undead had surrounded the car. They crawled onto the hood and trunk. They banged at the driver's window using their own heads and limbs, smearing blood, hair, and pieces of skin. A man on the hood of the car pounded both his fists against the windshield. To Grace's horror, the windshield glass began to crack.

She slammed the accelerator to the floor. The car lurched backward, knocking down several of the undead. The man, who had been pounding on the windshield, flew off the hood of the car. His head exploding into a bone-and-flesh goulash as he hit the asphalt. Grace bounced around inside the car as the wheels rolled over several bodies.

When she finally felt the wheels make contact with solid ground again, she put the car in drive. Through the spider-webbed windshield, she watched as the horde continued their frenzied pursuit. Grace pounded the accelerator again. This time, she was going forward. She could barely see the road through the sea of undead. The front end of the Chevy rammed into them, one after another. The hood wrinkled and buckled as the car repeatedly struck the oncoming zombies.

Several bodies crashed into the windshield,

spreading the cracks even further across the glass. The windshield started to bow and cave in. Grace wondered how much longer it would stay in place before the glass finally shattered and the whole thing caved in on top of her.

As she plowed through what felt like a seemingly endless number of them, Grace finally saw the access road. Without taking her foot off the gas pedal, she sped around the building, toward the exit. In the rearview mirror, she saw what remained of the horde running after her. She pressed the accelerator harder. Ahead, the access road began sloping downhill; she was finally getting off the summit! It would only be about fifteen minutes before she reached the bottom.

With the crowd behind her, Grace checked inside the car for some kind of communication device. She opened the glove compartment; only papers and insurance documents fell out. She lifted the center console. There was a cell phone inside. In her excitement, she almost didn't feel the wheels of the car slip off the edge of the road.

Grace dropped the phone. With both hands, she jerked the wheel hard to the right. Both driver's-side wheels had hopped the road and were riding in the ditch alongside the asphalt as the car sped down the mountain. She desperately held on to the steering wheel as the narrow access road bent to the right. She willed the car to stay out of the trees as the passenger side skipped and stuttered on the road. Ahead of her, the road straightened out. She eased out of the turn and slowly straightened the wheel, steering the car back onto the road.

She reduced her speed and looked down for the cell phone; it had fallen into the cup holder in the center of the vehicle. She reached down with her right hand and flipped it open. It still held a charge. Grace hastily dialed 911 and put the phone to her ear. An operator answered.

"9-1-1, what's your emer—"

"*HELP!*" Grace screamed. "I'm hiking in the mountains, by Campground Tamakwa, and I'm being chased!"

"Chased by whom, ma'am?" the operator asked.

Grace narrowly missed going off the road again as she picked up speed.

"I don't know! They're fucking... *dead people!* I don't know what they are!"

"Okay, ma'am, I'm going to need you to slow down. Where are you?"

"You don't understand!" Grace shouted. "They're fucking *DEAD!*"

She pinned the phone to her ear using her shoulder; she gripped the wheel with both hands as the turns became tighter and sharper.

"Ma'am, who's dead? Are you okay"

"There are a ton of them!" Grace said. "I'm on the mountain! I need help!"

As she screamed, the movement of her jaw knocked the phone loose; it fell between her seat and the center console.

"Fuck!" she cursed. She looked down and could see the phone wedged inside the gap. She reached down and inched the phone up with her fingertips, back into her hand. She pressed the phone to her ear.

"Hello!" she shouted.

***

The Chevy made impact with the boulder before Grace was able to hear a response. She had driven straight through a hairpin turn, and the car collided with the large rock without warning. The windshield shattered upon impact.

The driver's-side airbag deployed, but it shoved Grace's head into the roof of the car. She felt a warm sensation on her neck. She couldn't tell if it was blood or paralysis setting in. To her left, she saw the driver's-side door had completely ripped off the car.

To her right, tree branches had entered the car through the passenger window, through the backseat, and into the trunk.

Grace sat there, motionless. Her head throbbed. She tried to lift her right arm and felt a bolt of pain shoot from her hand to her head. Stars rained down in front of her eyes. Suddenly, the steering wheel was twenty feet away. Her circle of vision narrowed. Then, a shroud of darkness lowered over her eyes as she went unconscious.

CHAPTER 13

Grace woke up in a large, familiar room. It was dark, but there were tall windows that allowed in the moonlight. She lay on a couch with her hands resting on her chest. She let her head roll to the side. The room was a lounge of sorts. There were a couple more sofas and some chairs. Grace seemed to recognize it but she didn't know why.

She thought about the moonlight for a moment. She hadn't remembered seeing the moon recently. For some reason, she remembered it being very cloudy the last time she was awake.

Shaking off this notion, she tried to sit up. A crippling spasm smacked the front of her head, as if she'd slammed it into an invisible wall. She squeezed her eyes shut and lay back down, wincing as she pressed the palm of her hand against her forehead. She took several deep breaths and waited for the pain to subside.

When the pain finally lessened, she raised

herself up again slowly and rested on her elbows. She turned her head to look out the enormous windows. She saw the moon in the sky. And, to her surprise, she saw it on the ground as well. Unable to focus, Grace closed her eyes again and massaged her eyelids. She opened them and looked again. Closed them and looked again. The moon did in fact appear to be both in the sky and on the ground.

Grace squinted at the moon on the ground. It was flickering. *The moon doesn't flicker* she thought. *Only stars flicker.* Then she saw tiny waves passing through the moon, kind of like a reflection. The moon was reflecting off a body of water.

Grace shifted uneasily. She turned back toward the room and examined her surroundings more carefully. The tables, the sofas, the chairs—it all came back to her. Grace knew exactly where she was. She was in the common room inside the hut. The moon was reflecting off Silver Lake.

Realizing where she was, she tried to sit up straight. The pain still consumed a large part of her head, but she managed to sit upright on the couch. She tried to remember how she'd gotten there. She remembered climbing to the summit with Charlie. She remembered fighting off what felt like an endless number of the undead. She remembered escaping in a car and hitting a tree.

That was it. She vividly remembered hitting the boulder. She must have blacked out. But where was Charlie? *Why would he bring us back here?* She scanned the area. Perhaps he was resting in one of the rooms? *He wouldn't leave me here to sleep alone.*

Finally, visions of the events on the summit came flooding in as the dam within her memory broke open. Grief and guilt filled her once again, even more now than when she was with Charlie in the summit cafeteria. The pit in her stomach, once left by hunger, now filled with nausea. Her stomach turned even more as she remembered what Charlie had asked her to do, and the terrible act she had carried out. Her heart ached so much, she wanted to rip it out of her chest and throw it on the floor, just to watch it die as she had watched Charlie die—as she was now dying inside.

She had never endured so much pain in her life. She never wanted to feel like this again. She never wanted to feel anything again. She thought of leaving, of climbing back up Arrowhead and leaping off the same cliff from which Joe had leapt to his death. She'd never feel a thing, which is precisely what she wanted—not to *feel*. It would be a quick death. And in the end, she'd be with Charlie again.

Why hadn't she thought of this before? Why hadn't she simply waited on the first floor of the cafeteria? The undead likely would have taken her then. There were plenty of ways she could have taken her life as well. Or maybe that was why she had crashed the car? No, she knew the crash had been an accident. She hadn't intended to crash the car. Then why?

"Ah, you're awake."

Grace screamed as the voice startled her. She had been staring at the floor, trying to make sense of everything; she hadn't even noticed someone had entered the room. She drew back, cowering on the corner of the sofa. The figure of a man came nearer. He stopped next to an armchair, about fifteen feet away to her right.

"It's all right," he said. "You're okay." He continued to approach her. "I thought I warned you and your hubby about this place?"

Grace recognized the gruff voice and the enormous beard as the man walked closer. He still wore his red flannel shirt.

"Roy?" she asked. "Roy, from the camp store?"

"The one and only," Roy said matter-of-factly. He took a seat in a chair next to the sofa. Grace settled down onto the seat cushion, and her heart began to beat normally again.

"What the hell are you doing here?" she asked. Roy chuckled loudly.

"Lady, do you really ask that question of everyone who pulls you from a car wreck?"

She immediately regretted the question upon the realization that she was facing her rescuer.

"I'm sorry," she said.

Roy waved off the apology. "No worries."

Not knowing what to say or ask, Grace remained silent. She watched Roy's hand as he tapped his fingers on the arm of the chair. She noticed as he glanced around, nervously thinking of something to say.

"So," he said, breaking the silence. "Where's that man of yours anyway?"

Grace hesitated before answering.

"He's dead."

Roy's shoulders stooped and his voice took a somber tone. "I'm very sorry to hear that, truly I am."

Grace nodded.

"Did *they* kill him?" Roy asked, likely referring to the undead. Grace nodded again. Roy let out a long exhale. He looked off to his right before asking his next question, not wanting to make eye contact with Grace.

"And is he now," he paused, "one of them?"

Grace shook her head.

"So his head was, uh—"

"Yes, his head is fucking destroyed." She was

already tired of Roy's passive attempt at finding out about Charlie. "I know because I killed him."

Grace stared at him, unblinking, after she said this, and waited for a response. There was none. Roy only stared back in awe.

"You've got some scars, don't you," Roy said.

Grace lifted her hands, stared at her palms. "Yeah, I suppose I do."

"I'm not just talking about the physical kind," Roy said. "Although, those are there too."

Grace dropped her hands. She nodded weakly and began to cry.

"He's gone," she whispered. "I can't believe he's gone." She stood still, in front of Roy, who also didn't move, and let the grief come out finally. Safe for the moment, she allowed the full realization of Charlie's death overcome her. Her chest burned as the emotion filled her inside. As she rubbed at her eyes, she noticed Roy, standing completely still, his arms folded. He wasn't being impatient, though, of that she was sure. He was simply allowing her to mourn.

After a few minutes of silence, Roy spoke.

"When I found you in the car," he said. "I couldn't help but notice the axes in the front seat."

Grace again remembered when she'd last used one of them.

"It's okay, you know. I'm sure you were just doing what you had to do."

Grace's eyes welled up again.

"These people," Roy began, "I mean… these *things*—they're not like us, you know. Not anymore."

Grace's eyes went to the floor. She was not ready to have this conversation. Luckily, Roy seemed to notice and he quickly changed the subject.

"You must be starving," Roy said.

Grace nodded. Roy stood up.

"Come on," he said. "There's food in the kitchen."

The word "kitchen" set off a silent alarm in Grace's head. Cheryl was still in the kitchen. In fact, *both* Bruce and Cheryl were still in the kitchen. Grace tensed and shook her head. Roy saw that the terror in her face had returned.

"What's wrong?" he asked.

Grace gestured toward the kitchen. "There are people in there," she said, her voice very low.

Roy lowered his head. "What do you mean?" he asked. "There's nobody in there."

Grace slowly rose from the sofa. She started to approach Roy but walked past him. She looked down the hallway, toward the room in which she and Charlie had spent the previous night. The bodies that had once lain on the floor in the hallway were gone.

"I moved them," Roy said, as if reading her mind.

She continued walking toward the kitchen. Roy watched her curiously, tried to guess what she was up to. She placed her palms against the steel double doors, but the memory of the incident from that morning prevented her from entering. She turned around.

"What about the people in the freezer?" she asked.

Roy shrugged his shoulders. "I haven't been in the freezer," he said.

Grace pointed toward the kitchen doors. "There was a man and a woman this morning," she said. "She turned into one of those things. The man tried to trick us into helping her, so we locked them both inside."

Roy now stepped closer to Grace.

"Lady, I haven't been in the freezer. I brought you back here, moved those bodies out, and washed up. Nearly got myself killed in the process."

Grace's pulse quickened. She wanted to be anywhere else at that moment.

"What do you mean, 'nearly got yourself killed?'"

Roy hesitated. He'd said too much. But it was too late. It was time to talk. "One of those things saw

233

me when I carried the little girl outside."

Grace remembered Caitlin, the image of the bullet hole in her head still fresh in her mind.

"Did it attack you?" she asked.

"It tried to," he said. "I had already lain out Terry and one other. Then I dragged out the little one." He stared off as he recalled the terrifying ordeal. "I'm not as quick as I once was," he said, tapping his hand on his leg. "Bastard nearly caught me as I was closing the door."

Grace could see he was shaken up. She was surprised. She didn't figure Roy to be the kind of man who was easily rattled. Then again, not many people could say they'd been face-to-face with the living dead.

She put a hand on Roy's shoulder and met his eyes. She suddenly became filled with compassion. "But it didn't, and that's the important thing."

Roy took several deep breaths, nodded his head. Grace rubbed his arm and looked around.

"We have to leave," she said.

"Wait, wait. *What?*" he asked.

Grace's adrenaline was pumping again. Her head was a bit clearer than when she'd gotten up. "We have to get out of here. We have to get off this mountain."

She started to walk away, but Roy grabbed the

sleeve of her shirt.

"Didn't you hear a word I said?" he asked.

"Yeah, every word."

"There's nobody here," he said. "We're safe here."

"We are *not* safe," Grace said, struggling out of his grip. "This place is a fucking tomb. I'm leaving, and if you're not coming with me, then that's fine."

She marched back to the sofa to get the axes and machete. They were gone. She looked behind the sofa. They weren't there, either. She paced around the room, her eyes darting back and forth.

"Where the fuck are my things?" she asked.

"Now just you wait there a minute, miss," he said, gesturing with both hands." You need to take it down a notch. You have no idea what's waiting for you out there.

She stopped and turned toward him.

"I know *exactly* what's outside," she said. "Which is why I'm not staying here."

Roy dropped his hands by his sides and scoffed. He half-grinned.

"Well then, Dr. Confidence, don't let me stop you," he said. "You go right ahead. You know where the door is." He gestured toward the main hallway.

Grace thought she saw something in the way he smirked. She paused, considering Roy's words for only a moment before starting toward the hallway.

"I'm outta here."

"Good, I'm sure you'll be fine," Roy said sarcastically. "Although...you may want to take a look out one of them windows. Might be best to *strategize* your route."

He was fucking with her. She knew it. She just needed to get out of the hut and get down the mountain. She entered the main hallway at a slight jog. She was still unarmed. *Fuck!* She would check the rooms to see if anything had been left behind, anything that could be used as a weapon.

She searched the first room on her left. There was a backpack on the floor. She found a buck knife in one of the pockets. Not bad, but not good enough. She needed something bigger. Something she could swing, like a bat...or a hatchet.

She looked through several more rooms. Each time she crossed the hallway, she noticed Roy in her periphery. He hadn't moved. He was still standing in the same spot in the common room, arms folded, staring down the hall.

What's his deal?

She ignored him and continued searching. She walked into a room that looked familiar: Bruce and Cheryl's room. Grace shuddered as she thought again about the incident in the kitchen. Cheryl had been

such a sweetheart, such a kind lady. But those eyes—
the ferocity. She wasn't Cheryl anymore by then,
though—of that much Grace was convinced. Cheryl
had been incredibly sweet to her and Charlie the night
before. In the kitchen, however, Cheryl was *not*
Cheryl. She was something else. Grace shook the
memory from her head and focused.

She tossed items around the room as she looked
for a weapon. She crouched to the floor and checked
under the bed. There was a day pack. Grace pulled
the pack out from under the bed. The initials "GR"
were stitched on the front. It was Bruce's pack. She
loosened the drawstring at the top. A jolt, equal parts
excitement and relief, shot through her: There was a
small revolver inside.

She dumped the contents of the pack onto the
bed. A headlamp fell out, along with some tissue, a
protein bar, and a box of bullets. *Now we're talking,* she
thought. She'd never loaded a gun before, but she
suspected she'd seen enough cop movies to figure it
out.

As she rose from the bed, fumbling with the
box of bullets in her hands, Roy's last words played in
her head again.

You may want to take a look out one of them windows.

She turned toward the window. The glare from
the light in the room prevented her from clearly

seeing outside; she could only see her own reflection. She turned and reached for the light switch. She flipped it down and turned back toward the window.

The empty revolver fell out of her hand and landed on the floor. Her feet were frozen. She wanted to turn and run. Walk. Fall to the ground. Jump. Any kind of movement that let her know she still had control over her extremities. She began to sway, which apparently was enough. Natural reflex caused her right leg to move out in front of her. She swayed again. Her left leg moved. Then her right again. She was walking. Toward the window. She stopped when she was a foot away from the glass and stared.

There were hundreds of them. Maybe even thousands. Men, women, and children paced the grounds outside the hut. They staggered back and forth, moving in lines, following each other in a confused but seemingly choreographed formation. Grace looked deeper into the mob. The never-ending rows of undead ebbed and flowed like waves, a sea of the dead. Several of them scraped against the side of the building, their decaying fingernails snapping off as they pawed at the window over and over.

Grace slowly backed away from the window. She couldn't tell if they were able to see her; their grayish eyes wandered aimlessly and erratically. Occasionally one would slap at the window. They must have known people were inside the hut. Perhaps they just weren't smart enough to find a way in. Perhaps they were simply waiting. There was nobody left at the summit. Presumably, there was nobody left at the campground either.

And that was it, Grace had deduced. The dead were waiting for the last two people alive on the mountain to come outside and meet their fate.

Grace turned and walked out of the room, hugging the wall as she came back into the hallway. Her eyes glossed over as the reality of the situation pummeled her psyche. She crawled along the side of the hallway and stumbled along the wall, using her other hand for support.

Roy stood at the other end. He remained silent. No further sarcasm would be necessary. He needed no satisfaction; the look on her face was enough. Grace understood now—kind of. The immediate shock and despair would linger for a while, but she understood for the most part. There was nowhere to go. Nobody was coming to save them. They were trapped.

As she walked into the common room, Roy offered his hand.

"Come, sit down," he said.

Her face expressionless, Grace instinctively reached out and gave him her hand. He led her to a table, pulled out a chair, and helped her sit down.

"Feel like eating now?" he asked. Grace's head twitched. She looked up at Roy as if she didn't know who he was. She nodded slowly. He turned and headed for the kitchen. Grace then stared ahead, her eyes unblinking, her jaw still slightly open. She felt paralyzed—by fear, doubt, uncertainty, despair. She couldn't concentrate on a single feeling. The reality was too overwhelming.

Sitting at the table, staring out into the large room, she still saw them. Moving in waves. Waiting for their prey... Somewhere, buried deep within her brain, was the knowledge that these creatures were still outside and unable to get to her, but it would be a while before that knowledge surfaced and materialized into any kind of consolation.

CLANG!

Grace's mind returned as the noise from the kitchen roused her from her temporary catatonia. Roy had banged into the steel kitchen doors as he came through. He carried a plate with a sandwich and a glass of water. He set both down on the table and took a seat opposite her.

"That's fresh deli meat," he said. "I just sliced it now."

Grace's eyes grew wide with horror.

"Not to worry," he said. "The freezer is locked.

This came from one of the coolers. Only shelving fits inside."

Grace let out a relieved sigh. She grabbed the sandwich with both hands and bit into it. Ham, turkey, and Swiss cheese filled her mouth. It was the best food she'd ever tasted. She chewed slowly, savoring every bite of it. She'd needed this all day; the food was finally allowing her to think clearly and rationally.

"Sorry for being an asshole," Roy said.

Grace looked up at him and put a hand to her mouth. "Me too," she said between bites. They sat in silence for a few minutes as Grace enjoyed her meal. When she was finished, she sipped her water, slowly enjoying every drop of that as well. She placed her glass down on the table and looked up at Roy.

"So," she said, "now what?"

Roy shrugged and arched his eyebrows. "Now, we wait."

"Wait for what?"

"Exactly," he said, nodding his head.

Grace's eyes narrowed. "I don't understand. *Are* we waiting for something?" She studied Roy as he shifted uneasily in his chair. Clearly, he had something to tell her. He just wasn't sure how to deliver the news. Finally, after some deliberation, he spoke.

"We may be stuck here awhile."

"What's awhile?" she asked. "For how long?"

"Could be a week, could be longer."

"Are you kidding??? Can't we call someone?"

"Nobody to call," he said plainly.

"What do you mean? I was talking to the police when I crashed the car!"

"Police ain't coming. Doubt they'd believe you anyway."

"Why don't we pick up the phone and find out?" she challenged.

"Phone's out," he said.

Grace let out an exasperated breath. "Why is the phone out?" she asked.

"Protocol."

"*WHAT?!*"

"Protocol," he repeated.

She couldn't believe what she was hearing. "Whose fucking protocol?"

Now it was Roy's turn to express his aggravation. He closed his eyes and leaned forward. He rested his elbows on the table.

"I'm trying to keep my patience with you," he said softly, tapping his fingers on the table. He stared at her but he wasn't quite *looking* at her. His mind was working, strategizing. "Let's try something different," he said. He leaned back into the chair and folded his arms. "What exactly do you know about what's going on here?"

Grace was insulted by the question. She knew exactly what was going on here. At least, she thought she did. Didn't she? She tried to disguise the uncertainty in her voice.

"Sure. There's a bunch of dead people running around the mountain, trying to kill us. That about sum it up?"

Roy laughed at her ignorance. "Lady, you have no idea."

She shook her head, disgusted by his condescension. "You think I'm stu—"

"What did you see outside?" he cut her off. She stared at him in disbelief. Were they really having this conversation?

"I saw a bunch of fucking dead people walking around, who shouldn't be walking around, trying to get in!" she said. "There. Happy?"

Roy shook his head slowly. "No. You didn't see that at all," he said. His voice was even softer than before. He leaned back in, toward the table, as if he was about to tell her a huge secret. "You saw a virus."

Now she was confused. Terry and Joe and Rose had all confirmed that these were the walking dead, brought back from their centuries-old graves by an energy within the mountains. Roy was full of shit. This wasn't a sickness; this was no kind of disease.

243

These people were fucking *dead*.

"Bullshit," she said.

"It's true," Roy said, unwavering. "It's a virus, for sure. And just like any virus, it can't be killed. Just has to run its course."

"What the hell are you talking about?" she asked. "I killed a bunch of these things already."

"Symptoms," he claimed.

Grace threw her hands up. "Are you kidding me with this?"

Roy slammed his fist down in the table. Grace jumped. She was sure she heard a crack, perhaps the table buckling under the pressure of his giant hand.

"Now listen, goddammit!" he yelled. "You killed a *symptom*, understand?" She shook her head nervously. "I've been here for nearly sixty years, miss," he continued. "I was here the last time this happened, back in 1959. You heard that story, I bet?" She nodded. "I was just a little guy back then, of course." His tone began to ease up. "My father ran the camp store in those days. My mom wasn't around; she left us both shortly after I was born. So, I spent a lot of days at this campground." He looked around the hut. "Place wasn't this big back then."

Grace cleared her throat. "Wait... You were *here* when it last happened?"

Roy showed a look of surprise.

"Oh, I've got your attention now, do I?" He paused and waited for her to retort. She stayed quiet. "Good," he said. "Yes, I was *here* when it last happened." He pointed down toward the ground. "My daddy and I rounded up as many survivors as we could and we took shelter in the hut." He turned and pointed toward the back hallway. "Back then, it was just the kitchen and that hallway. The cafeteria, common room, and front hallway were all added years later."

"How long did you have to stay here?" she asked.

Roy looked up as he tried to remember. "I think it was nearly two weeks," he said. "And there weren't many of us. Only five, including my daddy and me."

"How did you know when it was safe to leave?" Grace asked.

"We didn't," he said. "We'd run out of food about three days earlier. But it had been a while since we'd seen any of 'em, so we figured we either die of starvation or take our chances getting off the mountain." He rose from the table and paced around the common room. He stretched his red, flannel-sleeved arms behind his head as he recalled more of the incident. "We grabbed whatever we could use as weapons. We stayed together as a group. Stuck to the trails. God forbid we went off-roadin' and ran into any of those things."

He sat down again on a sofa. His tired eyes gazed downward as he ran his hand slowly over the cushion, remembering the time of the last "outbreak." Grace waited for him to continue. He remained silent for a while, and Grace began to wonder if that was all there was to the story.

"So you guys made it off the mountain and...that's it?"

"Pretty much," he said.

"What about the other survivors? Weren't you afraid they'd tell someone about what happened?"

He chuckled at the thought; his head bounced when he laughed. "I doubt anyone would have believed 'em." He turned and looked at Grace. "Would you?"

She thought about it. It actually made sense. After all, who in their right mind would have believed that the dead were coming back to life and killing people? She needed more answers though. There *had* to be more to it all.

She stood up and walked over to the sofa. Roy sat with his chin resting in his hand, looking off. Grace sat down on a coffee table across from him.

"You called it a virus," she said. He nodded slowly. "Why do you think it's a virus?"

He steered his gaze toward hers.

"Because a virus never dies," he said. "A virus will run its course and then be done with you. Except, instead of going away, it stays with you. Lies dormant."

"Okay," she said. But the confusion in her eyes was enough for Roy to know that she didn't quite follow.

"This," Roy said, pointing toward the window, "all of this will go away, eventually. But it'll never be gone for good. It'll always come back again and again." He leaned forward and looked her straight in the eyes. "You might kill one zombie. Hell, you might kill a hundred. But you'll never kill the disease."

Grace looked into his eyes. He was very convincing. He believed every word he said. It was hard not to trust a man who'd been through it once before.

"So how come some of you refer to some as the 'undead' and some as 'zombies?' Aren't they the same thing?"

Roy brought his hands to his chest and interlaced his fingers in a praying position. "Is a vampire not undead?" he asked.

Grace again stared back at him, confused. "Vampires?"

Roy relaxed his hands and rested them on his legs. "Never mind. Think of it this way: Those people out there..." He pointed again toward the windows. "...and they are in fact *people*. They were just like you and me at one time: living, breathing, regular heartbeats. Except when they passed on from this life, their souls were released from their living bodies. Problem is, their living bodies *expired* here." He raised his arms and made a sweeping motion with his hands. "But the energy that exists in these mountains awoke their bodies after their souls had left. That energy reanimated them, made them what they are now. Not alive, mind you, but not quite dead either. They're something in between. We refer to them as undead. Zombie is just a slang term. For some folks, the term zombie helps them reconcile the idea within themselves. People need to attach labels to things, especially things that aren't easily interpreted. Kinda like the universe. Nobody really *knows* how we got here or how it all started. So, most folks put their faith in God. Or *a* god. Most folks don't like not knowing or not having an answer. Placing their faith in God gives them an answer. It's comforting. Same thing with the undead. 'Undead' is too abstract for some. So a lot of folks adopted the term 'zombie.' Whichever term you use, once you accept what this is, then you move on to the coping phase."

"What the hell is the coping phase?" Grace asked.

"Exactly what it sounds like," Roy said. "It's when you've moved past acceptance and learn what you need to do to cope with this, to manage it."

Grace processed everything that Roy had told her. She wasn't about to delve into her issues with faith—that would have been too much to handle. She needed to learn more about the undead, though. She needed to know why and how this secret had been kept for so long.

"Where does the energy come from?" she asked. "Why is it only here?"

"Oh, there are plenty of theories. The most popular one is that the energy is the result of an old Native American curse."

"And nobody knows how to lift the curse."

Roy nodded. "Of course, when the early settlers first arrived, they knew nothing about native customs or traditions. When the first recorded outbreak occurred, they didn't know what they were dealing with. They just killed as many as they could and ran as far away as possible when they could no longer fight them off."

"How come so few know about this?"

Roy looked at her skeptically. "Seriously?" he asked. "I know I'm not the first person to tell you about this." He waited, but she held firm. "Hell," he said, giving up. "It's a secret. This will *never* get out.

We don't *want* it to get out."

"Who's 'we?'" she cut him off.

"*We* is *US!*" he said, raising his voice. "*We* is ME! *We* is the locals, the people who live and work here! Do you realize what would happen to this place, to the entire state of New Hampshire, if this secret ever got out?! How much money the state would lose? Nobody would visit anymore. State parks would empty. Forget about camping, hiking, fishing— nobody would risk it."

"But what about the bodies?" Grace asked. "What about the people who are killed by the undead? Once the outbreak is over and people come back, won't they find bodies?"

Roy's eyes narrowed, almost sinister. "Assuming you're talking about the ones that don't turn?" Grace nodded. "Well, that's easy," Roy continued. "*The dead don't leave crumbs.*"

Grace felt her gag reflex kick in at the mere words. Visions of the undead feeding on humans— on their flesh, tissue, cartilage, bone, tendons, muscle—were enough to turn anyone's stomach. At that moment, she wondered if any had stayed behind to finish Charlie after she'd left him. It hadn't crossed her mind until now.

She quickly chased the thought away with another question. "What about the undead? What happens to their bodies?"

Roy was slow to answer. He simply stared at Grace quietly.

"You don't...know?" Grace asked.

"That's the million dollar question," Roy said. "Nobody knows. Some think they go back into the ground. Some say they eat each other. Of course, that wouldn't explain how they're able to come back time after time."

Grace looked deep into Roy's eyes. He was holding something back.

"You believe something else," she said. "What is it?"

Roy slowly turned his head and looked out the window. "Doesn't matter what I believe."

"It matters to me."

He turned his head back toward her, but his eyes fell to the floor.

"Tell me," Grace said.

He let out a sigh. "Dead bodies are still bodies, right?"

Grace nodded.

"Well, they're out to consume us for some reason. So, maybe when there's nothing left to consume, they just...perish."

"But they're already dead," Grace said.

"Really?" Roy said sarcastically, but he quickly

changed his tone. "Sorry. I mean, when the soul leaves the body, the body dies. Right? Well, whatever energy is here is only strong enough to reanimate the body, not the soul."

Grace nodded as she listened.

"But," Roy continued, "that energy is only strong enough to *resurrect* the body. It can't *sustain* it. So, they must sustain themselves by eating the flesh of the living. And when there's no more life around, they simply die off. Disappear. Who knows."

Grace took it all in. She didn't know when the idea of the dead rising up from the ground and walking around had gone from pure fiction to stark reality. But this was something that was going to live with her until the end of her days. The dead *can* come back to life. Fact.

But there was still something missing. Roy still hadn't explained what happened to the bodies.

"You still didn't answer my question," Grace said.

Roy turned his head to the side.

"What about the bodies?" she asked. "What about the bones?"

"I can't tell you that," he said.

"Why not? You've told me everything else."

Roy sat forward quickly on the sofa. "Because there are some things that need to remain secret!" he yelled. His hand clutched the arm of the sofa so tightly that Grace thought his fingers might rip through the upholstery. His eyes were red. Grace thought she might have seen a tear forming, but Roy turned away before she could tell for sure.

But she understood. As much as she could, she understood him. Roy had a secret to keep. A secret buried for centuries, known only by the locals who handed it down from firstborn to firstborn. And she'd broken through to him. She wasn't sure how, but she had gotten Roy to tell her things he never should have. However, there was something Roy wouldn't tell her; something he *couldn't* tell her. That part, he would take to his grave.

"So, what?" Grace began. "You're, like, a 'protector' to this place or something?"

The words spilled out of Roy's mouth coldly: "This place is special."

Grace was immediately disgusted by that assessment. "This place is *evil*," she said. "Not special."

"Call it what you want," he said, "but there's something here. The only difference is, the rest of the world will never know about it."

His conviction was unwavering. Grace had no response this time. At this moment, she knew there were only two people on the mountain who knew what was going on. She would eventually have to decide whether or not she would ever tell anyone this story. Just as Roy had made the same choice.

Grace stood from the coffee table. She walked over to the giant bay window. She still couldn't believe how many zombies there were. Surely there couldn't have been this many back in the fifties. Could there have been? She considered Roy's story again and mentally prepared for the lengthy stay. It would be a test of will, of whether or not she could outlast the undead.

She would have to.

She turned back to Roy. He was still sitting quietly on the sofa. His shoulders stooped forward and his eyes looked weary; he had the appearance of someone who'd just been defeated by his worst enemy. Grace wondered if he would once again find the resolve to make it through. He'd gone through it years ago, as a child. And with the help of his father, and others, he'd survived. But the ordeal had clearly taken its toll on him. Even as an adult, it must have been an impossible burden to bear, this *secret*. Grace could only imagine what it had done to him mentally and emotionally over the years.

But she would need him. She could no longer be his enemy in this. She needed an ally and there was only one person available. And just as his father had helped him survive the previous incident, Grace was going to need him to help her if it became unbearable.

"So we wait," she said. It was an agreement. It was also a statement in which Grace had tried to infer, "I'm on your side."

"We wait," Roy said.

CHAPTER 14

They had pulled two mattresses out of the rooms and set up beds in the common room. The last place either of them wanted to be was alone in one of the rooms just in case any of the undead found a way to break in. They had locked the doors to all the rooms and the kitchen. They were prepared for the long haul, however long that might be. Grace's assumption was, it was probably going to be longer than she'd hoped.

When Grace woke up the following morning, she was surprised to find that she'd slept straight through the night. Then again, with everything that was on her mind, the physical and emotional exhaustion had likely been enough to keep her from waking.

The common room filled with weak, overcast light from outside. She still didn't want to believe what was happening. It was all surreal, a dream from which she had seemingly just woken. Except it was not a dream—the situation couldn't have been more real.

Roy was already awake. He stood by the big windows, as if keeping a vigil. He was the image of a statue: arms folded, legs firmly planted, eyes staring straight ahead. Grace pulled the sheets away and stood up. The movement caught Roy's eye.

"How do you feel?" Roy asked. Grace stared at him incredulously. "I know, bad question."

Grace raised a hand and waved it off. She walked over to the window and stood next to Roy. It appeared that the sea of the dead had grown exponentially. She was sure there were more of them. Last night, it was as though there were hundreds. Now, there were thousands.

"I thought they're supposed to start dying or something?" Grace said.

"Only looks like there's more because it's daytime," Roy replied.

"I just can't believe how many there are," she said, rubbing her eyes, half because she was still waking up and half because she simply couldn't believe what she was seeing.

"I made eggs in a basket," Roy said changing subject. "There are some leftovers in the kitchen."

Grace was still reluctant to go into the kitchen, but she couldn't continue to rely on Roy to fetch her meals for her. After all, neither of them knew how long they'd have to stay there, and she didn't figure him to be some kind of manservant. There were no zombies in the hut, of that she was sure. There were plenty to fear outside, but nothing to be afraid of inside their sanctuary.

She walked across the large room, through the cafeteria, and into the kitchen. She pushed the heavy steel doors open and stepped inside. The air was just as cold and as still as the last time she'd been in there. She rested a hand on a metal counter, ran her fingers along the spotless surface. The chill from the steel triggered a horrible memory of Cheryl coming after her in the freezer. She stepped over to the range. A frying pan containing the fried eggs on toast sat on a cold burner. She served herself breakfast on a clean plate left on the stove and walked back out into the common area.

Roy still stared out the window.

"Thank you," she called across the room. Roy turned and nodded. Grace walked as she ate, across the room, back toward the big window where Roy stood. She brought a piece of toast to her mouth and gazed out the window.

They were hideous. She'd seen plenty of them over the last twenty-four hours—fighting, killing, surviving, trying to stay alive. Now that her focus had shifted, she was able to get a good look at them. They all had the same grayish skin, loose and swollen. Some looked like they'd been dead a very long time, most likely members of the last outbreak. They wore torn, outdated clothing. Their eye sockets had sunk in so deeply that a golf ball could probably sit inside without falling out. Their skin was beyond deteriorated, decay having eaten away much of the top layer, revealing dark red and blackened muscle. Much of the muscle fiber itself, maggot-ridden and moldy, had also torn and hung loosely from their bodies.

Then there were the others. *The "new batch,"* Grace thought. Their skin was equally gray and swollen, but it was easy to tell that they were "newer" than some of the other zombies. Modern clothing, hair that looked like hair and not straw, teeth that still retained a lighter shade of yellow versus the brown of the older ones. Their wounds still looked somewhat fresh, too.

Grace looked down at her half-eaten breakfast and realized that her appetite had been spoiled. She set the plate down on an end table and looked around for something to occupy her time.

"Hey," Roy said. "I found a book when I was checking the bathrooms. I'm not much of a reader, but it might help to pass the time."

"Sure," she said.

"I left it over by the fireplace."

Grace walked over to the fireplace. The book sat up on the mantel. The word "Diary" was written in pink letters on the front.

"It's not a book," Grace said. "It's someone's diary."

"Hmm. Well, I'm sure they won't mind if you read it."

Grace quickly flipped through the first few pages. There wasn't much written; maybe ten pages had been filled with text. She flipped open to the middle of the book and dog-eared one of the pages, and then she walked over to an end table and pulled open the drawer. There were coasters, a few magazines, and a rolled-up newspaper. Inside the newspaper she found a small pencil. *A crossword puzzle addict* she thought. She sat comfortably in a chair and flipped the book back open to the page she'd marked. Grace thought for a few minutes about what she might say. Then, she began to write.

CHAPTER 15

Day One Lockdown

Roy found a diary this morning. I didn't read any of it. It's probably bad karma to invade someone's personal thoughts. However, it's barely been written in, so from this page on it's my journal. I'm not really sure what to say.

It's me and Roy, the camp store owner. He's a good guy. He's a little old, definitely twice my age, but I'd still want him on my side in a fight. We're hiding out in the hut until it's safe to leave. The old hut. Back where it all began.

Roy was here in this very hut the last time there was an "outbreak." He says they stayed a couple weeks before it was safe to go, but that's only because they'd rather have been eaten than starve to death. That's a really shitty decision to have to make. I hope it doesn't come down to that. I trust him, though. I just hope he trusts me. I'm not quite sure I'd trust me. I'll just take it one day at a time for as long as I have to. That's about all for today. I'm not sure what else to write right now.

In the evening of "Day One," Grace prepared dinner for herself and Roy: sandwiches and chips.

"How domesticated of you," Roy joked. Grace laughed slightly. It was the first time she'd done so since she first came to the hut with Charlie.

"You know, there are some meats and stuff in the freezer," he continued. "I don't mind going in and taking something out."

Grace curled her lip, her thoughts immediately drifting toward the evil that might still be lurking behind the freezer door.

"Maybe tomorrow," she said. "I'd rather check it out in the daytime."

"Okay. That'll work."

They ate slowly in silence. To Grace, every bite was better than the last; after all, each meal had the potential to be her last. Sure, they were sealed in from the zombies. She knew that the same plan had been worked many years ago, but she didn't take anything for granted. If these things wanted them badly enough, they could probably find a way inside.

After dinner, they turned out the lights in the common room. They took one last look out into the night. The sea of undead continued to churn as they paced back and forth like a crowd at a music festival. The numbers certainly hadn't thinned since the night before. Grace hoped for a different view at dawn.

CHAPTER 16

Day Two Lockdown

My first thoughts today were of Charlie. I half expected him to be lying next to me when I woke up. I cried when he wasn't there. Roy saw me and let me be. He understands. I don't know if his father survived the last outbreak. He didn't say one way or the other, but I never asked. I have a feeling he's hiding more than he lets on. If I had lived through what he did at such a young age, I'd probably keep some things hidden, too...

Day two was a bright, sunny day. A beautiful day under any other circumstances. The walking dead continued to saunter around in droves, a gross juxtaposition against an otherwise glorious wooded setting.

While Grace was writing in her journal, Roy walked up next to her and held out a deck of cards.

"You play?" he asked.

Grace set down her pencil and looked up at

263

him, incredulously. "Seriously? You wanna play a game?"

Roy quickly appeared taken aback. "We've got nothing but time on our hands in here. Time to pray for our survival… time to hope those creatures *don't* find a way in… time to think about who we've lost because of all this… or, we could spend it by trying to take our minds off of it."

Grace immediately felt ashamed for throwing Roy's idea in his face. She set down her journal and got up from the chair, and followed Roy to a table.

Grace and Roy passed the time by talking about their lives outside of the hut. They talked about home, the things they had done before the outbreak. Roy talked about how he'd inherited ownership of the camp store. He also talked about how his father had told him about the undead sometime after the last outbreak.

"He said to me, 'Roy, you can't tell anyone about what happened.'"

"Did he say why?" Grace asked.

"He said, 'It's a secret.' He said, 'Nobody knows about this other than us locals, and if outsiders find out, they'd never come back.' It's a story that was passed down to me, passed down to him, and so on and so on, going back centuries."

Grace studied his hands after he spoke. He

didn't fidget a bit. He'd accepted this explanation a long time ago and never looked back, never questioned it.

"Don't you find that a bit strange, though?" Grace asked.

"What's that?"

"All these years, this *energy,* or whatever you want to call it, has been here. Yet nobody but the locals has ever known about it?"

"Is that so hard to believe?" he asked.

"Well, yes, it is," she said. "You'd think that, at some point, the secret would get out."

Roy finally shifted positions in his chair. She'd struck a nerve.

"Something happened," she insisted. "What was it?"

Roy laid his cards down. He rubbed his hand through his reddish-gray hair, scratched his beard under his chin. There *was* something.

"Please tell me," Grace said.

Roy looked her in the eye.

"If you really want to know, I'll tell you," he said. "But remember, once you know, you can't *un*know it."

Grace was confused, but she didn't show it. She simply stared back into his lifeless eyes.

"I want to know," she said.

"All right then." Roy sat back in his chair and folded his arms. "People are smart these days. Some yahoo goes around telling you that he saw the dead come back to life, you gonna believe him? No, of course you're not. So, these days it isn't such a big deal."

"What isn't such a big deal?" she asked.

Roy's eyes went to the floor. His face was full of shame.

"Letting them go," he said softly.

"Letting who go?" Grace asked. "I don't understand."

Roy turned his head up again, looked her in the eyes.

"Letting *you* go, letting *them* go, back in the fifties," he said. "Someone claims to be Jesus Christ and sets up camp in the Midwest, he might get a hundred people to follow him, but to the rest of the world, he's a crazy person."

"Right. So?" she said.

"So," Roy continued, "two, three hundred years ago, people weren't that smart. In seventeenth-century Salem, Mass, if some girl ran home and told her family, '*I saw Anne place a curse on Margaret!*' Anne was a goner. Similarly, if someone ran back home and told his family, '*Hey, there's a bunch of dead people eating the living up in the mountains!*' people would have

266

believed him. As much as people *don't* believe these days, they believed even *more* back then, so...we kept 'em quiet."

"How?" Grace asked.

The words came slowly. Softly. "By doing what we had to do."

Grace was silent. She watched as Roy's eyes reddened at first, then filled slowly with tears.

"We did what we had to," he repeated. He wiped a tear away, his hand shaking, and looked off to the side.

Grace didn't want to believe it. She couldn't and wouldn't believe it. There was no way it happened like that, not even in those days. She began shaking her head.

"No," she said. "It can't be."

"Oh, it sure can," Roy said, meeting her eyes again. "And it was."

"They were...killed?" she asked.

"Last thing we—" he cut himself off, "—*they* needed was for people to believe that the dead were coming back to life up here. So, they were...handled."

"How could they get away with it?" she asked.

"They got away with it because they all signed an agreement. If any of the ones who did the 'handling and disposal' had talked, they'd have been killed."

Grace stared at him in horror.

"And I'll tell you what," he said. "Nobody ever talked."

Grace rested in her chair. She didn't speak as she tried to let the information sink in. It was too much to take. She knew then that she should have backed out when Roy had given her the chance. She didn't want to know any of this. She wished she'd never asked. She wanted to erase this entire conversation from her memory. She wanted to erase the entire trip, to have Charlie back, to be at home, living their boring lives together, expecting a child, maybe two.

But now she sat in the hut, across from Roy at a shitty picnic table playing a hand of cards that was merely a buffer between now and the time she'd be able to leave this place and never look back. She suddenly felt empty inside, hollow, and in a weird way attached to this place and its terrible history. She knew then that the scars of knowing what happened here hundreds of years ago would run deeper than any others she'd sustained during this trip.

Roy stood from the table. Grace didn't even acknowledge his walking away. She simply sat there, motionless, pinned down in her chair by the weight of nearly four hundred years of murderous secrecy. Roy was right: There was no unknowing it. She would

carry the burden of this knowledge for the rest of her
life.

CHAPTER 17

Day Three Lockdown

I couldn't sleep last night. My mind was busy imagining the killings of innocent people hundreds of years ago. I wish he hadn't told me. I wish I hadn't been such a brat. It's my own fault. I should have just let it go. He warned me. I know better than to pry into things I shouldn't. I just can't stop thinking about how many lives were pointlessly taken. I wonder if they kept records of every time someone was..."disposed" of. I wish Charlie was here. I wish I was home. I wish there weren't hundreds of fucking DEAD PEOPLE STALKING ME OUTSIDE THE HUT!!! I need to move on. I don't know how much longer I'll be stuck here, but it's only the third day. Here's hoping there are fewer days ahead of me.

"Hey there," Roy said, his tone apologetic. He'd startled her. She didn't even notice him approach, as she was curled up in a chair writing in her journal.

"Hi," she said, her voice somber.

He looked down at the floor, his hands in his pockets and his feet nervously kicking at the ground like the school nerd about to ask the head cheerleader to prom.

"I'm sorry about yesterday," he said. "I shouldn't have told you. It's my fault."

Grace sighed and put down the journal.

"It's not your fault," she said. "I pushed the issue. I've been pushing it ever since I woke up here. I shouldn't have."

"I just don't want you to have the impression that—"

"Roy," she cut him off. "You weren't there. It happened a long, long time ago." Roy nodded, his eyes red and swollen. "You didn't do any of those things. You're not those people. And I still trust that you're doing the right thing by making us wait it out. Okay?"

He nodded again vigorously, fighting back more tears.

"Thank you," he said.

She waited as he took a few deep breaths, rubbed his eyes. She noticed that behind him, one of the double doors to the kitchen was propped open.

"What's up?" she asked.

"We need food. The deli meat is gone. I have to open the freezer."

271

Grace felt her heart tick a couple extra beats.

"Right now?" she asked.

"Well, it's daylight," Roy said. "Just like you preferred."

Grace knew they'd eventually have to get into the freezer. It was likely that Bruce and Cheryl were frozen by now. They'd been in there nearly four days. She wasn't sure how long the human body could sustain that kind of cold, nor did she know how long an undead could sustain it, but she was certain that neither Bruce nor Cheryl was a threat at the moment.

"Okay," she said. "Let's give it a shot."

They walked into the kitchen together. Roy passed by a knife block. He reached and pulled out a carving knife.

"You're going to open the door," he said, handing her the key. "When you do, I'll take out whatever charges our way."

Grace nodded. Together they counted to three. On three, Grace yanked the door open. Roy braced himself, lunging in a warrior stance, uncertain of what would happen. After a few seconds, he stood up straight, and stared into the freezer.

"What is it?" Grace asked.

"I think I see your friends."

Grace poked her head around the door. There, huddled in the back corner of the freezer, were Bruce and Cheryl. She recognized Bruce's face. He looked like a porcelain doll. He sat on the cold floor with Cheryl stuck in his frozen clutches. The broken mop handle was no longer in Cheryl's skull; Grace assumed Bruce had removed it.

"I don't know anything about these things being frozen," Roy said. "No idea if they can come back or not. We might want to consider getting rid of them."

"It should be fine," Grace said. "He was still alive, and I killed her after she'd turned."

Roy thought about this for a moment. "We should probably get them out of the hut at some point."

Grace shook her head. "Tomorrow. Let's just get something we can make for dinner.

They both entered the freezer and pulled out steak, fish, pork, chicken, and frozen vegetables.

That night, they dined on prime rib, steamed broccoli, and corn. Grace had even found a bottle of Cabernet that, surprisingly enough, complemented the steak nicely. They ate until they were full, careful to eat all that they took so as not to let anything go to waste.

Later, while Grace was getting ready for bed, she saw Roy standing by the large window. She stepped over to his side.

"Numbers dropping yet?" she asked.

Roy squinted out into the night. "You know what, I think they are."

Grace felt her heart leap with excitement. "Really?"

"Yeah, I think so. Take a look for yourself."

Grace looked out into the night, allowed a moment for her eyes to adjust. She closed her eyes for a few seconds. She told herself not to be swayed by Roy's opinion. *What do you REALLY see?* she asked herself before opening her eyes.

She scanned the crowd and watched the lines of undead shift back and forth. She looked beyond the large group and out toward the lake. There was a small, bare patch of grass on the eastern side of the lake. It had been occupied by the undead the day before.

She almost jumped up and down. The immediate crowd hadn't thinned out, but farther back, the crowd wasn't as deep. The undead were...dying.

"I don't believe it!" she said.

"I know. I thought the same thing," Roy replied.

"The crowd doesn't extend back as deep as it did before!" Grace wasn't aware that she'd raised her voice.

"I know it's exciting," Roy said, "but you'll want

to keep it down a bit."

"Shit, sorry," she said, finally realizing how loud she was.

Roy chuckled, "It's okay. It's good to find something to be happy about, huh?"

"Damn, you bet your ass!" she said.

They laughed a bit more before finally going to bed. They took turns pointing out more areas outside that had previously been occupied by the undead. Grace began to feel hopeful for the first time in days. The decrease in numbers of the undead was only a small victory, but it was something to hold on to. She was certain that the numbers would continue dropping from this point on. Grace thought about Charlie and how happy he would be now that it seemed like there was a chance she was going to make it out of there alive. She wasn't aware that she fell asleep with a smile on her face.

CHAPTER 18

Day Four Lockdown

The undead are finally dying off! God, that doesn't make any sense when I read it back. Still, I can't believe it. I feel like we're actually going to make it. I know it's just a small number, but if the numbers continue dropping, the undead might be gone in a few days. Who knows how many more might disappear in another day or two! Or three! I badly wish that Charlie was with here. I know he wanted me to get off this mountain alive. I feel like it's actually going to happen. It's his spirit that keeps me going. I'm hopeful I'll be able to fulfill his last wish.

Bruce's and Cheryl's bodies proved to be more difficult to remove than expected. Cheryl's wounds alone had bled out so much, both their bodies stuck to the floor and walls of the freezer. Roy used the broken mop to dig around them, chipping away at frozen, blood-soaked hair and skin. Grace used a steel spatula to loosen up frozen blood that had fused them to the floor.

At one point, Grace had been working on one of Bruce's arms, which had frozen to one of the steel racks. Grace had been attempting to loosen the arm when her foot slipped on the icy floor, sending her tumbling toward the dead bodies. When she collided with Bruce, she felt his arm break off at the shoulder.

Grace turned to Roy, who'd stopped what he was doing. She raised an eyebrow, asking him wordlessly if he was thinking what she was thinking. Roy nodded thoughtfully. If they could break up the bodies into pieces, it would be easier to dispose of them both.

Roy set the broken mop handle down on the floor and grabbed onto a couple racks to steady himself. He checked his footing to make sure he wasn't going to slip. Then, with sheer brute force, he raised one leg and brought it down on Cheryl's left arm. The arm separated and hung there. After a few more heavy stomps of Roy's boot, Cheryl's arm came loose, but the fabric of her sleeves held together. Roy grabbed her hand and pulled the arm out. He examined it for a moment.

"I suppose this will make them lighter to move," he said. "The clothing won't weigh much, even if it is frozen."

They both continued to dismember the bodies as much as possible. In the end, they were able to take both of Cheryl's arms, one of Bruce's, and both of Cheryl's legs. Bruce's legs were frozen under Cheryl. Blood and moisture had all but left him fused to Cheryl's torso.

Roy wiped sweat away from his forehead. He turned toward the freezer door, which was open.

"I don't want to waste any time in here letting them thaw," Roy said. "Go take a look down the hallway, see if we can throw them outside right now."

Grace quickly stepped out of the kitchen, walked through the common room and down the main hallway. Even during the day, it was dark in the halls since all the doors were closed, but the main door had a window which let in a fair amount of light.

She reached the door and peered outside. The undead paced around aimlessly. If she and Roy opened the door quickly and shoved Bruce's and Cheryl's bodies outside, the undead might be too stunned to react before they closed the door. It was worth a shot.

She ran back to the kitchen. Roy was already dragging the ice-stiffened bodies out into the common room.

"How's it look?" Roy asked.

"I think if we're fast enough, they'll never know

what happened," she said. "By the time they figure it out, we'll be closed and locked up again."

"Good," he said, struggling to move the frozen mass of death. "Help me drag this mess down the hallway. We'll take care of the arms and legs after."

Dragging both bodies down the hallway wasn't half the chore that chipping them out of the freezer had been, but it wasn't easy, either. Two frozen-together bodies moved like a square across a flat surface. A three-hundred-pound square. Their bodies were solid, so getting a grip was easy, but sliding them across the carpeted floor in the hallway was a challenge.

When they reached the door, they were both breathing hard.

"Are you ready?" Grace panted.

"Give it a minute," Roy said, heaving deeply. "Let's catch our breath a bit before we do this.

Grace stood and looked out the window. The undead continued to walk back and forth just outside. The idea was to slam open the door and knock over several of them in the process. At the same time, Roy would push the bodies down the steps. It would be easy.

"All right," Roy said, his breathing slowing down. "Let's do this."

Grace pressed her weight against the door and

gripped the handle with both hands. Roy shimmied the two bodies up as close as possible, giving Grace enough room to throw the door open. He got to his knees and placed his right hand on the back of Bruce's neck, his left hand behind his back. What was left of Cheryl's corpse lay in a heap in front of him.

"When I say 'now,' open the door," Roy said. She nodded.

He wiped the sweat off his forehead, took a deep breath.

"Now!"

Grace forced open the door. She'd expected to slam into an undead, but there were none. The door simply swung open all the way, and the handle slipped from her hand and slammed loudly against the side of the hut. Several of the undead nearby stopped and turned immediately upon hearing the disturbance.

Roy leaned into the frozen bodies, pushing with every bit of leverage he had. His right hand, greased up by his own sweat, slid up Bruce's neck toward the back of his head, snapping it cleanly off his neck. Roy fell forward, propelled by his own force. He tumbled over the two bodies and halfway down the steps. A dozen of the undead ran to the door. Awkwardly, Roy pushed himself backward, up the steps and into the doorway. Grace watched as he tried to back into the hut while simultaneously attempting to push the bodies out the door. She reached out and pulled on the frozen bodies to help.

"Don't worry about me! Get the door!" Roy shouted.

Grace let go of the bodies and reached back for the door. She pulled it around, closing it against the bodies that were now half outside. *Fuck it,* she thought. She let go of the door and it whipped open, slamming against the hut a second time. Again she gripped onto Bruce's arm. She pulled the frozen mass out over the step while Roy pushed from behind.

An undead suddenly approached the door. He gnashed and clawed at Roy, tried to pull him outside. Roy fought him off with his one free hand while still pushing the frozen bodies out the door. The undead grabbed his arm. Roy tried again to shake it free, but this time it held on tight.

"Get him off me!" Roy shouted.

Grace let go of the frozen mass and came around to Roy's left. She kicked repeatedly at the zombie's hand, but its grip was like a vice. Roy was now sitting down completely, pulling his arm against the zombie's grasp and pushing against Bruce and Cheryl. Miraculously, the leverage was enough to force the frozen bodies out the door and down the steps.

Grace held on to the door jam and continued

kicking at the zombie's arms, but it held on.

Then, without warning, a second zombie, a woman, came from the right. She wasted no time bypassing the struggle completely and lunged for Roy's exposed arm. He howled in agony as her yellowed, jagged teeth sank into his arm. She shook her head viciously and removed a patch of skin the size of a credit card. Blood sprayed onto the faces of Grace, Roy, and the two zombies. Unable to see, the first zombie let go of Roy's arm. Grace ran around to the other side of the door way and shoved a foot into the female zombie's face. As the undead woman stumbled backward, Grace reached out for the door handle, swung it closed, and locked it.

Grace fell to the floor and backed into the corner. The terror was over for the moment but her adrenaline was racing. Her eyes were wide as she stared at Roy's wound. Roy squeezed his eyes closed, grimacing from the pain. Instinctively, Grace got up and ran down the hallway and into the kitchen. She grabbed a towel off of one of the counters and ran back down the hall toward Roy.

"Let me see it," she said.

"Don't bother," Roy said through gritted teeth.

"Give it to me!" Grace shouted.

Roy complied and let her wrap his arm. The blood quickly soaked through the white towel, turning it cranberry in color.

"It's pointless," Roy said, still out of breath.

"I don't care!" Grace yelled again stubbornly. "I don't fucking care!" Tears now formed in her eyes.

When she finished wrapping Roy's arm, she stepped back and watched as he held the towel against the wound. The blood had now soaked through so much that it started to stream down his hand and fingers. Grace was sobbing.

"It's all right," Roy said without looking. "It's only a flesh wound." Now he looked up at her with a small grin.

"I'm so sorry," she said. Her voice stuttered as she sobbed. "It's my fault."

Using his good arm, Roy put his hand on the ground and propped himself up on one knee.

"It's nobody's fault," he said, standing up straight. "It was a good idea. Just poor execution." His face showed the look of defeat, but also of acceptance.

"Roy, you're gonna—"

He waved a dismissive hand. "I know what's going to happen," he said. "Let's go find a few fresh towels and we'll talk about this later."

They walked back to the kitchen in silence. Grace felt horrible. If only she hadn't let go of the door. If only she'd seen the other one coming. She could have saved him. She should have done something. But what *could* she have done?

Grace replayed the whole incident over and over throughout the rest of the day. She openly talked through different scenarios that would have resulted in more favorable outcomes, but Roy wasn't in the mood for listening. He'd already accepted his fate. Grace, however, was still talking about strategies, schemes they could have employed that would have kept them both out of harm's way. She simply wouldn't let go.

After an hour of listening to Grace's hindsight planning, Roy talked her into a game of poker in order to take her mind off of it, but it was of no use. She stared at the red-soaked towel (he'd gone through a dozen at this point) on his arm as he shuffled. Even when he dropped and picked up cards, her eyes followed the wound on his arm. They decided to call it quits after the third time she'd ended up with seven cards during a game of five-card draw.

She crawled up onto a chair, tucked her knees to her chest, and stared out the window. Roy kept himself busy by cleaning the wound, redressing it, and pacing around the hut. He checked the doors every now and then just to make sure they were still locked. They didn't say a word to each other until after nightfall.

Roy prepared dinner while Grace sat curled up in her chair over by the window. She didn't notice he'd set the table. She didn't even notice when he walked up next to her.

"Dinner's ready," he said.

She jerked her head, snapping out of the trance she'd been in all afternoon.

"You okay?" he asked.

She regarded him with disheartened eyes and only shrugged.

"Yeah," Roy said plainly. "It's been a tough day."

Grace was shocked by Roy's carefree demeanor. It was like he hadn't just been bitten by a zombie earlier, like his death sentence hadn't just been written hours ago.

She leaned over the arm of the chair. "Aren't you scared?" she asked.

"What's to be scared about?"

Is he for real??? "You're gonna turn!" she said. She pointed toward the window. "You're going to become one of them."

"Yeah, but not for a little while just yet."

She looked at him curiously.

"How do you know?" she asked.

"It all depends on the severity of the wound," he said. "This one is barely a scratch."

285

Grace's eyes wandered around as she recalled the mess that was Charlie's neck and shoulder after Rose had attacked him.

"I'm guessing your husband probably looked worse?" Roy asked.

She shuddered when the image of Charlie, lying on the floor, blood pulsing out in quick bursts, flashed in her memory.

"Well, the more serious the wound, the quicker the uh—'virus,' enters the person's body, kills them, and ultimately, reanimates them. If the wound is less severe, the virus *still* gets into the body. The process just takes longer."

Grace was appalled. "Are you sure?"

Roy nodded. "I've seen it happen," he said. "I've seen a man turn from human to—" this time he motioned toward the window, "—that. It ain't pretty, but it doesn't happen in a matter of minutes, not usually." He wanted to stop there, but Grace was still staring back at him with her eyebrows arched, prompting him to continue. "Here you go again, wantin' to know things you do *not* want to know."

"It can't be any worse than what you've already told me," she said.

Roy sighed. "Well, first there's gonna be some nausea. Then the nausea is going to turn into severe pain. I'll probably start throwing up blood sometime after—"

"Okay, okay," Grace said, putting her hands up in surrender. "You're right, that's enough. Let's just stick with nausea and go from there."

Grace put her feet down and sat forward in the chair, her elbows resting on her knees. She closed her eyes and shook her head in an effort to eliminate the visual of Roy vomiting blood.

"Ultimately," Roy continued, "the body has to die first. As I said, it's like a virus. Once the living tissue is destroyed and the soul leaves the body, the body itself can reanimate."

Grace stared blankly, her head resting in her palms. "It's still just so unfucking believable."

"I know," Roy said. "But as they say...it is what it is.'"

Grace looked up at him with a raised eyebrow. It was a bullshit reason, but she knew it was true. *It's just what happens,* she thought as she stared into his knowing eyes.

"Well, come get it while it's still hot," Roy said, turning away from Grace.

He walked over to the steel table they'd been using for meals. Grace slowly got up from the chair. Her muscles ached as she labored across the room, as she hadn't eaten all day. Her body had sustained more physical and emotional strain than she'd realized.

She sat across from Roy, who'd already begun to eat. She watched as he hungrily fed one forkful after another into his mouth.

"You've got quite the appetite," she said.

Roy looked up at her solemnly. He set his fork down and finished chewing a large bite of food before speaking.

"All kidding aside, this is my last meal," he said. "And time is not on my side."

Grace understood. In fact, she felt stupid for making such a comment. She'd only been trying to make small talk, but she was aware she'd chosen the wrong words. Roy looked at her sternly for a few seconds before he put his head back down and continued eating.

"I—I'm sorry, I just—"

Roy waved his hand. "No need," he said between bites. "I still wouldn't trade your company for solitude."

He looked back up at her while he was still chewing. He winked at her. Grace shot back a half smile, still feeling guilty about the comment, but relieved that he hadn't taken offense.

They dined quietly after that, both of them enjoying the meal, ham steaks and cut green beans. Grace would later write about this in her journal as being, "surprisingly peaceful and humbling."

After dinner they both took to their "posts," as Grace now called it: looking out the window at the thinning horde of zombies. The number had dwindled considerably since last night. Grace was sure there were now half as many as there had been when she'd first looked out the window four nights ago.

Grace and Roy stood there for hours, much longer than any of the previous nights. They shared idle talk, but nothing of substance or significance. Roy had asked what she was going to do once she got off the mountain. Grace told him that she would get in her car, head south toward home, and never look back. He asked her what she would tell Charlie's family. She told him she hadn't even thought that far ahead yet.

Amid the small talk, Grace wondered how long Roy would stay before he...checked out. It hadn't even occurred to her what his plan might be. *Is he going to shoot himself? Is he going to leave the hut? I hope he doesn't expect me to do it.* While these thoughts swirled around her head, she was sure that Roy was simply drawing out whatever time he had left as a human being, spending as much time with another living companion for as long as his living body would allow. And the truth was, she was happy to be by his side until the end.

It might have been about three a.m.——Grace had lost track of the time——when she saw the first signs. Roy's breathing had gotten a bit heavier and faster. He'd begun exhaling from his mouth, much like an expectant mother practicing Lamaze. He held his stomach, as if in pain.

"How ya doing?" she asked, afraid of the answer.

He turned to her. Even in the low light she could see that his face had turned dreadfully pale. Beads of sweat accumulated on his forehead.

"I think it's time for me to go," he said between breaths.

Grace had known that this moment was coming. She'd known it since hours earlier when the zombie had bitten his arm, but she couldn't hold back the tears once again.

Roy put a hand on her shoulder. "It's going to be all right," he said. "You're going to be okay, and that's what's important. It's what your husband would have wanted, right?"

She couldn't even nod or shake her head. Her body simply convulsed as she sobbed harder. Roy leaned in and wrapped her with his arms.

"It's all right now, child," he said, his voice soft and calming. She cried hard against his shoulder. "You'll be fine. You just have to stick it out here for as long as it takes, okay?" She nodded her head against him. He rubbed a soothing hand along her back as her cries receded to sobs, and then to whimpers. He released his hug and held on to both her shoulders.

"Look at me," he said.

Grace looked up. She could barely see through the tears.

"It's gonna be lonely, but you keep a good head about ya and you'll be fine, you understand?"

Her eyes dropped down to the floor as she nodded.

"Okay then. You gonna walk me out?" he asked, this time with another of his trademark half-smiles.

She nodded again slowly.

They walked down the hallway, toward the main entrance. Roy held onto his stomach as his insides burned and churned. He coughed into his hand several times. He wouldn't say it or show it, but Grace knew he was coughing blood when he started wiping his hand against his pant leg.

When they got to the end of the hallway, Roy peered out the window in the door to assess the zombie activity.

"Okay, there aren't too many now," he said. "We should be able to do this, no problem."

Grace was still fighting back sobs as she turned to him.

"Don't you need something?" she asked. "Aren't they going to come at you?"

"They're not going to hurt me," he said with pity. "By now, they'll already know I'm one of them."

Grace squeezed her eyes tight, and curled her lips, fighting back another waterfall.

"Now, I'm going to walk out the door," Roy said. "You just have to close it behind me. Do it quick, but don't slam the door, okay?"

Grace wiped her eyes. "Yes," she said.

"All right partner, I guess this is it." Roy held out his hand. "Thanks for not thinking I was some crazy old man." He smiled.

Grace half chuckled as she shook his hand.

"Thank you for saving my life," she said.

She pulled the revolver she'd found in Bruce and Cheryl's room from her waistband and handed it to Roy. It was loaded with only one bullet. Grace kept the rest.

"Leave it where I can find it," she said.

Roy took the gun.

"Don't worry," he said, motioning toward the door. "They're not going to touch it."

After one final look out the window, he opened the door quietly and walked down the steps. When he had cleared the door, Grace pulled it closed quickly, allowing it to latch quietly.

She watched from the door as the other zombies observed the newcomer walking among them. Roy stumbled forward, holding the gun with one hand, his stomach with the other. Grace looked on as Roy continued merging with the surrounding zombie traffic. He headed toward the back of the horde, opposite the hut and closer to the lake, where there were fewer of the undead.

Grace came away from the door and walked back down the hall toward the common room. She resumed her post, watching from the huge windows. The night sky was clear; the stars lit up the lake and the surrounding grounds. She was sure she'd be able to make out Roy in the well-lit night, but with his slow gait and awkward limp, he blended right in with the undead. She'd completely lost him. She was sure he'd made it beyond the horde at this point though. She scanned the lake and the trails; there were a few stragglers here and there. But she couldn't tell which was Roy.

Then, a spark of light and a loud crack off in the distance. Grace saw the figure by the water's edge. It fell to its knees and slumped forward. It lay completely still. Grace watched it lie there.

When the sun came up, she was still watching.

CHAPTER 19

Day Five Lockdown

Roy, my friend, died early this morning. He died trying to protect me. Actually, it might be more accurate to say he died the previous day, just after he was bitten by the zombie. Because it was at that moment he knew his life was over. I knew it, too. He stayed with me, though, and I with him, right up 'til the end. I gave him the gun so he could go quickly. He talked at dinner about how he didn't want to come back as one of them, so I told him about the gun I'd found in Bruce and Cheryl's room. He said he'd walk out past the horde, somewhere out in the open, to draw attention away from the hut, and do it there. I saw him. He was way out there, but I'm sure it was him. The shot was loud and the light from the gun, although brief, was bright enough for me to see.

I didn't sleep at all last night. After Roy died, he fell forward, and I could barely make out his figure as anything more than a tiny, darkened mass off in the distance. I saw some of the zombies walking back toward the lake. It's very surreal.

It's like they're drawn to it. I'm not sure what it means, if anything. Maybe nothing. Either way, it's eerie as hell. They seemed to congregate, to meet about something. Who knows—maybe they know I'm still inside, and they're just trying to figure out a way to get to me.

I've now seen two men die trying to protect me. One was the man I love, the other a man I'd come to call a friend. Both were kind and caring. Both were caught in the wrong place at the wrong time. Which makes me wonder: Why did I make it? How have I been able to survive? Is it simply because I was under the protection of another? Am I smarter? Just lucky? Maybe with nobody left but myself, I'll be the one attacked. Then again, as long as I keep the doors locked, I shouldn't have to worry about that.

Grace sat in her chair, staring out the large common room windows at the grounds and the lake. The zombies were certainly dying out now. The once enormous sea of the living dead was now drying up. The numbers had been cut by more than half; about a third of them remained, pacing around the hut in hopes of catching the last of the living. Grace wasn't about to give them the satisfaction.

She jogged laps up and down both halls to pass the time. She jogged from the main door, down the hallway, through the common room, down the second hallway to the non-functional door, and back.

She wasn't able to keep time, so she counted the number of laps. She decided to count off a hundred laps, thinking that would pass at least an hour of time.

In the beginning, she would look out the large windows between laps every time she passed by the common room. She didn't honestly expect to see fewer and fewer of them; she just felt she needed to keep a constant eye on the problem. Granted, it wasn't a "problem" until it became one, and that was what she was watching out for.

After the first twenty laps, she gave up watching the windows and concentrated on her breathing. She stared straight ahead, down the empty corridors. As she ran, her mind raced. She began to wonder what might happen if a zombie broke down one of the doors to the rooms. She imagined the undead piling in through a window, breaking down a bedroom door, right in her running path. She'd have no chance to survive. This vision didn't stop her, but it heightened her awareness enough that she slowed her pace. She didn't want to be running at too fast a speed just in case the unexpected should happen.

At fifty laps, she'd broken a sweat. She was certainly fit, but with the lack of fresh air circulating inside the hut, the air grew stale. Her breathing was slightly more strained than she was used to. She was accustomed to jogging outside daily in the fresh, ocean air. Charlie would jog with her. He had been able to keep up with her before his knee injury. After, he would hang back and jog at his own pace. He'd had the stamina to go the distance; he just didn't have the equipment to move at the same speed.

At seventy-five laps, she had to start pushing herself. She wasn't able to take in air as deeply as before. Breaths were shorter now, much like her stride, which she'd slowed down even more in order to extend the duration of her run. Her chest began to burn with that familiar flame as she reached down as deep as she could for each breath.

At eighty laps, she wondered what she was going to do with the rest of her day. She hadn't bathed in almost a week and she was aware of her own stench. She couldn't use the bathhouse; she'd certainly be killed. Perhaps she could bathe herself in the industrial-size sink in the kitchen. That would consume all of five minutes.

At ninety laps, she'd wished she had more energy to go on. She would have loved to run another hundred laps, but it seemed as if the air had been all but sucked out of the hut. She was straining for each breath. She could rest up and do another hundred laps in the afternoon.

At ninety-five laps, she was happy to be almost finished. In fact, she thought about quitting at lap ninety-five, but she knew quitting wasn't in her. She would finish this race. Much like her survival in the hut, she'd come this far; she might as well go the distance.

One hundred laps.

She finished where she'd started, at the main entrance. She leaned over and supported herself by putting her hands on her knees. She coughed a few times as her lungs begged for fresh air. When she regained a bit of her wind, she walked back down the hall with her arms up, her hands on top of her head, forcing her lungs to expand as she gasped for as much air as she could. She felt a sense of pride in completing her jog, an otherwise meaningless task.

She came into the common room with her hands and fingers still locked on top of her head. She looked out the common room windows.

She dropped to the floor immediately.

What the hell was that?

Had she really just seen what she thought she'd seen? Her mind raced as her eyes scattered across the floor in front of her.

What the fuck is going on outside?

She stayed close to the floor and spider-crawled to a sofa nearby. She slowly got up on one knee and raised her head just enough to see over the large window sill.

They weren't moving. The zombies had stopped and were completely still. The march of the dead had halted for the moment as they turned and faced the hut.

All of them.

The worst part was, they weren't scattered across the lawn and around the lake like they had been before. They now gathered around the hut. Sure, there weren't nearly as many as before, but before they had been pacing aimlessly. Those that remained now stood perfectly still, their dead, grey eyes fixed on the hut.

Fixed on her.

What does that mean? Grace asked herself. *Did they discover a way inside?*

"What do you want?" she asked, barely above a whisper.

She ducked back down and crawled toward the kitchen. The only window in there was the one on the back door. The idea of being surrounded by the undead was unnerving, but she had to see. She had to know what she was dealing with.

She pushed open one of the big, steel kitchen doors. She looked behind her as she did, toward the windows. She couldn't see them. Which meant they couldn't see her either.

She crawled through the doorway, into the

kitchen, and when she was clear of the door, she let it close slowly behind her and stood up. She inched her way through the galley, toward the back door.

As she approached the back of the kitchen, she steeled herself against the wall, scooting her feet sideways as she crept toward the door. In her mind, she envisioned hundreds of them, pawing at the back of the hut, staring into the kitchen through the small hole in the door. She took a deep breath before checking the backyard.

There were none back there. A sigh of relief. Then, a horrifying realization.

They *saw* her.

There weren't any behind the hut. They didn't need to be back there. Because they knew exactly where she was. They'd probably watched as she ran up and down the halls. For how long, she didn't know.

She walked back out of the kitchen, into the common room. She stood still as she scanned the faces of her predators. There was no reason to duck and hide now. They saw her and she saw them. And the undead simply stared back, motionless, blood dripping from every orifice as they hungrily watched her. She wanted them to keep moving, but she also wanted them *not* to move, to simply disappear. She willed them to turn and go about their routine.

And then it happened.

Without warning, the horde charged the hut.

The sound of slapping, clawing, beating, growling—they were trying to get inside. The noise was deafening, like listening the crowd at a baseball game. Hands and feet, arms and legs, heads and shoulders—they attacked the hut with endless ferocity.

Grace sank into a fetal position and wrapped her arms over her head. She screamed.

"*STOP IT!*"

But the noise continued.

She was sure the doors to the rooms would implode at any second. She was certain they'd busted through the windows.

"*STOP!*" she screamed again.

But there was no stopping. The beating continued. Grace cried so hard that she could no longer hear the din of the zombies pounding against the hut. She could only hear the ringing in her ears. She scratched at her head repeatedly. Strands of hair came away from her scalp as her mind finally let go. The zombies had surely broken in by now. She envisioned the undead pouring in through the windows and crashing through the doors. Soon they would spill into the hallways and into the common room. She would be dead within seconds. Grace expected to feel the presence of the undead surrounding her at any moment. She had given up, simply stopped caring. She wanted to be at peace. For once. Just for once...

And then, just as quickly as it had begun, it stopped.

Her eyes burned from the tears that had flowed. Mucous collected around her nose and mouth. She opened her hands. She looked down and saw strands of dark hair stuck to her sweaty palms. There was also blood from scratching and pulling so hard at her head. She curled her fingers inward. Her nails were full of hair and flecks of scalp.

But the ringing was gone.

The noise was also gone. She realized it was silent again. She looked up at the windows. There were no hands slapping at the glass, no arms or shoulders. She slowly rose from her knees, just enough to see the ground outside.

They were there. Milling around and shuffling like they had before.

What the fuck? she thought. Not wanting to be seen by them again, she crouched down and crawled through the common room, back to her chair. She climbed up, curled in between the armrests, and tucked her feet under her. She rested her head against the back of the chair and gazed outside. Had that really just happened? What was that all about? She watched lazily as the horde pulsed back and forth outside. She suddenly felt something next to her hip. It was the journal. She picked it up and flipped open to her last entry. She glanced at the words she'd written earlier that morning.

Maybe the attack on the hut had something to do with Roy's death? Maybe it was a way of telling her she was next?

Grace flipped the pages backward, to the beginning of the journal. There was writing inside the cover:

"This journal belongs to Caitlin Madison."

Grace's heart skipped a beat. *You've got to be kidding me,* she thought. She hadn't bothered to read what had been written by the journal's previous owner. She wasn't sure she wanted to, even now. All she had was time though. Time and curiosity...

CHAPTER 20

My first journal entry, 8/23/2011

>   *My parents are taking me camping! It's my first time! I can't wait to go sleeping in a tent in the woods! They've been promising me for years that they'd take me camping and now I finally get to go! I don't know what to take. Daddy says I don't need to take anything because there will be no power in the woods. NO POWER! So, since I won't be able to update my friends on Facebook, Mom gave me a journal. She said I should write everything down that I would normally type on Facebook. Then when I get home, I'll be able to type everything I wrote onto the computer. Seems really old-fashioned to me, but since there's no internet and no TV in the woods, I guess this will be fine.*

Grace smiled at the innocence that leapt off the page. She tried to remember what it was like to be Caitlin's age. Internet hadn't even been around. Even cell phones had been rare. Grace imagined what her journal would have said when she was eleven years old. With no internet and only about thirty channels to surf (twenty of which were useless and only about six that got decent reception), surely it would have been Barbie dolls and Easy-Bake Ovens.

When she was finished reminiscing, she continued on to Caitlin's next entry:

Second entry, 8/24/2011

This is such a long car ride. I didn't know we were going camping ON THE MOON! Actually, it's just New Hampshire, but it's still far. Daddy says we're almost there. He said, 'Another 15 minutes.' He said that about 15 minutes ago. I'm starting to think this might not be so much fun. I'm going to try to sleep in the car a little. I'll write more when I wake up.

OMG!!! The mountain is SOOOOO BIG! I can't believe I'm going to climb that thing! Daddy says it will take over a day! He says we have to start really early in the morning and then stay overnight at a 'hut.' Mom told me that a hut is a place where hikers can go to rest and eat. Sounds neat. I wonder who we'll meet there.

Oh, the man at the store, his name is Roy. He's funny-looking. He has a big beard. You can only see his mouth when he talks.

A short laugh escaped Grace's lips as she remembered seeing Roy's "wreath-beard" for the first time. She'd had no idea at the time that this same man would eventually save her life, and then save her life again by giving his own.

She continued reading.

8/25/2011

We just had breakfast and we're about to leave. It's still kinda dark out, but Daddy said this is how early we have to leave if we want to make it before the sun goes back down.

I had a weird dream last night too. I dreamed of a man who was hiking down the mountain. He looked sick. I remember feeling scared in my dream. Mom says it's just because I'm nervous. I told her I'm not nervous. She told me, 'It's your first time hiking, Caitlin, and it's a big mountain. You're just nervous, that's all.' I don't think she's right, but whatever.

Grace remembered her dream the night before the climb. Charlie had dismissed it much like Caitlin's mother had. Grace found it very peculiar that she and Caitlin would have such a similar dream. In hindsight, her dream now felt like a premonition. Grace had heard a story about a woman who had de-boarded a plane minutes before takeoff, claiming she "saw" something happen to the plane in a vision. Hours later, the plane crashed during a horrible storm. All the passengers had died.

Grace tried to shake the feeling of dread inside her. Had she predicted this? Impossible. *Purely coincidence,* she told herself.

She looked up from the journal. She hadn't noticed the sun had gone down. She set the journal down on the arm of the chair and stood so she could see outside.

The horde had thinned out even more. Even better, the ones that were left had continued their endless mope along the grounds. Grace was sure she only had to hold on a few more days. She wouldn't jog anymore. No sense in drawing any further unwanted attention to herself.

After eating a quick meal, she turned out the few lights she'd had on, curled up on her mattress, and shut her eyes. She wanted to continue reading Caitlin's journal, but she was exhausted from not having slept the night before. She would pick up reading in the morning. For now, she needed to rest.

There was no guarantee the zombies would stay reticent, and Grace wanted to have some strength just in case she found herself squaring off against any of the undead.

CHAPTER 21

Grace felt as if she'd no sooner closed her eyes when she opened them the next morning. Bright, blinding sunlight cascaded in through the large windows and into common room. Her eyelids were sore as she blinked rapidly, allowing only a fraction of light into her pupils. She had slept long and hard. She didn't realize how long she'd slept until she looked at the clock on the wall.

It was 12:31 p.m.

She was groggy. She hadn't slept like that since her college days. She rolled and stumbled off the mattress on achy legs and shuffled into the kitchen.

She reached into the fridge and removed a gallon of milk. She drank nonstop for several seconds before pulling the container away, taking a long, deep breath. She walked over to the back door and checked the backyard.

No zombies.

Grace nodded to herself, relieved to find none

309

of the undead mulling around back there. She gulped another mouthful of milk and put the container back in the fridge.

Back in the common room, the light was less harsh now that she'd had a few minutes to wake up. Her legs were less achy, and her head was alert and awake. She took a moment to look out onto the grounds.

She felt a charge of electricity run through her. There were a dozen zombies outside, maybe two dozen at most. A wave of guarded relief swept through her. It was almost over. She was going to outlast them. She was going to survive. She could feel it.

Grace moved over to the chair where Caitlin's journal had sat overnight. She eased her body onto the soft, velvety cushion, opened the journal, and began to read.

OMG! THAT WAS SOOOO LONG! I can't believe how far we hiked. I am SOO out of breath. It's beautiful though. Daddy took pictures of all of us in front of a huge waterfall. Then, when we got up a little higher, he pointed out over a cliff, toward some mountains. Then he told me, 'Those mountains are in Vermont!' You can see so far from up here! Mom says we're so high up that God can hear prayers from here.

Grace put the book down. She buried her face in her hands as she cried. She couldn't stop thinking about how unfair this life had been for Caitlin. Granted, life had dealt Grace and Charlie unfair hands as well, but she and Charlie were already in their thirties. Caitlin had died at age eleven. She would never graduate high school. She'd never have a chance to attend college or have a career. She'd never be able to have a first kiss or make love for the first time. She'd never have a child of her own. Her life had ended so abruptly.

Grace threw the journal across the room. She didn't want to read any more of it. The words were a painful reminder of the horror Caitlin had never seen coming. She wished she had been able to consume Caitlin's pain and suffering so that she wouldn't have had to bear it. But Grace knew she couldn't. Caitlin had suffered a great deal.

Charlie had suffered, too. Right up until she had brought the axe down.

Again and again.

And again.

The pain of knowing how much Caitlin had suffered, considerable as it was, was nothing in comparison to the loss of the man she loved.

CHAPTER 22

The days began to run into each other. Grace couldn't remember if it was Day 6 or 7 or 10 or 15 of the lockdown; she'd officially lost count. She tried to remember how many times she'd seen the sun rise and set but eventually lost interest in how long she'd been there. At one time, she *had* been interested in how much longer she'd have to stay, but even the prospect of leaving had become less appealing. Even though she remained alive, she had lost her life on this trip.

She'd lost it more than once.

She positioned her chair in front of the big, bay window, looked out over the grounds and at the lake. She sank into the chair so she wouldn't have to see the horde of undead trudging endlessly. But she could still see the tops of their heads bobbing slowly. She was pretty sure the numbers had continued to drop, as the heads had become fewer and fewer.

She scribbled drawings in the back of the

journal to stay busy. Now and again she tried a game of solitaire, but even that became dull after only a few hands. Her only company came in the form of Caitlin's journal. She hadn't wanted to continue reading, but when she read the journal, it was as if Caitlin was reading aloud to her.

Reluctantly, she picked up the journal and flipped it open to where she'd last left off.

We just ate lunch at the hut. I had chicken soup. It was OK. The hut is really cool! It's big and it has a lot of rooms. There are a lot of people here. They all seem nice. They're just like us. They are hiking the mountain too. Some got here today and are hiking to the top tomorrow. There are other people who just came down from the top today and are sleeping at the hut tonight and going back down tomorrow. It's so cool! Mom asked me if I was bored because I didn't have a computer. I'm not bored, so I told her I'm having fun. I can't wait to see the top of the mountain. Daddy says, as high as we were today, we're going to be even higher tomorrow! He said there are mountains even higher than this one!!!

Before dinner, Daddy, Mom, and I walked around the lake for a while. It's so pretty. There are a lot of beautiful flowers around the lake. I wanted to pick some, but Daddy said we have to leave them be. He said we have to 'leave no trace.' I guess that means we can't leave garbage and stuff behind. And we can't break anything like tree branches or step on plants and stuff. Geez!! There are a lot of rules for being outside.

After we ate dinner, we went outside for the showers. That's so weird!!! You have to shower outside here. There are a lot of showers though so it's not like people have to wait in a long line. We're getting ready to hear some scary stories soon. The lady named Terry said that they're going to take turns tonight telling ghost stories or something. Daddy says if I get too scared we can go back to our room. I said I won't get scared. I think it will be fun.

We just got back from story time. I am so scared. That woman told a story about dead people who come back to life. At first, I wasn't scared, because it sounded really corny. But then she said some things about how the first settlers had died and then came back to life and killed the people who were still alive! Daddy says it's just a story. Mom says so too. But she was really scary. Terry, I mean. She's big. She takes care of the hut. She was nicer before. Now she's just trying to scare people. I don't like her. I have to go to sleep now. I'm afraid I'm going to have bad dreams tonight. I hope I don't.

I'm in the ladies bathroom. It's really dark still. A bad man came into our room so my mom told me to run and hide. He came in and fought with Dad. I think he bit Dad in the arm. That's when Mom told me to run and hide. I felt

314

something scratch my leg when I ran past the bad man. I think he scratched me. It hurt when it happened but it doesn't hurt now. It's still—

A woman named Grace just came into the bathroom. I was trying to be quiet but she heard me crying. She said she wanted to help me. I'm scared. I don't know if she really wants to help me. What if she wants to hurt me? My leg itches now. It itches where the bad man scratched me. I feel sick too. I don't want to tell Grace I feel sick because then she might not help me.

She just left. I hope she comes back. She said she is getting her husband. I hope he's OK and not like the bad man. My tummy really hurts now. I feel like I am going to throw up. My leg hurts a lot now too. I wish Mom was here. She said she would come get me when it was safe.

I just threw up and there was blood. I'm going to go and find Grace. I think she—

Grace let the journal fall from her hand. It fell to the floor, landing on its cover with a *slap*. Her eyes went to the sky outside. It was dark and the stars were out. She was crouched so far down into the chair that she couldn't even see the tops of the zombies' heads anymore. She only stared up and out at the night sky. All but one of the stars were twinkling. Grace knew it was a planet. She fixed her eyes on it while all the stars around it flickered in her peripheral vision—a million strobes pulsating, quivering, enhancing the unblinking planet at the center of her vision.

She stared at the planet in the middle of the stars long after she'd fallen asleep.

CHAPTER 23

Grace opened her eyes. A noise had disturbed her sleep. She sat up on the mattress and tried to determine the direction from which the noise had come. Again, the noise intruded the silence, startling Grace. It came directly across from where she lay in bed. Someone was knocking on one of the large windows. Grace pulled the sheets away and stood from the mattress. She looked toward the windows.

Her eyes were wide as she saw Charlie there. He was knocking on the window. He was wearing the same clothes as he wore the last time Grace had seem him. His neck was nearly destroyed and his head was completely a mess, due to the multiple strikes from the ice axe, but somehow, he was right there, standing outside. His mouth was moving. Grace could tell he was trying to say something, but she could barely hear him from the other side of the glass.

"Charlie!" Grace yelled. "Are you okay?"

Charlie continued knocking. His mouth also

continued to move but Grace still couldn't hear him. She could barely make out sounds. He was definitely trying to tell her something.

"What is it?" she asked desperately.

She closed the distance between herself and the windows. Charlie's voice was a little louder now. A little clearer. He was asking her a question.

"Are you in there?" Charlie asked.

Grace was confused. He was staring right at her.

"I'm right here, baby! Can't you see me?"

"Are you in there?" Charlie repeated.

Grace banged her palm against the window. "I'm here, Charlie!!! I'm right here! What's wrong?"

But Charlie continued knocking. Grace couldn't understand what was happening. She slammed both hands against the glass and called out for Charlie. But it was no use. Charlie only stood there, knocking at the window.

Grace woke and immediately sat up in bed. Disoriented, she looked around.

Charlie.

She jumped from the bed and ran to the window.

There was nobody outside. It was only a dream. Charlie was not coming back to her.

A knocking sound from down the main hallway drew her attention from the window. She walked cautiously through the common room and into the hall. She squinted as she tried to identify where the knocking had come from. Her eyes were sore again, likely from all the crying she'd done the previous day. Grace thought of Caitlin's journal. Reading Caitlin's words was the last thing she'd done prior to going to sleep. She couldn't help but continue to feel sad for the little girl.

Another knock. This time it was more of a pounding. Grace turned her head toward the main door. There was a person knocking at the entrance to the hut.

She took a few tentative steps into the hall. She could see a face in the window in the door at the other end. The person's eyes lit up upon seeing Grace. It was a man. He waved. His mouth was moving but from this distance his voice was a mere mumble.

Without concern for her safety and without considering the zombies outside, Grace moved toward the door. The man outside had turned to his right. He was saying something. There was somebody else with him, but Grace couldn't see who it was or how many people there were.

She reached the door and looked out the window. There was a man and a woman.

"Hi!" the man said, his voice raised. "Can we

come in?"

Grace regarded him skeptically. His face glistened with a thin layer of sweat.

"Who are you?" she asked softly. Her throat was dry and her voice cracked.

The man turned toward the woman outside.

"This is Shelly and I'm Robert," he said. "Can we come inside?"

Grace turned toward Shelly. She looked spooked by something, uncomfortable about being there.

"What are you doing here?" Grace asked, turning back to Robert. It was a full-on inquisition.

"We found a dead body over by the lake," Robert said. "Are you okay?"

Poor, sweet Roy, she thought. He'd taken himself out for the greater good. It occurred to her she'd never thanked him for it. Then again, how do you thank someone for shooting himself in the head?

"Hello!" Robert pounded on the window in the door. Grace jumped as she came out of her trance. She collected herself. Something about Robert and Shelly didn't seem right.

"What time is it?" Grace asked.

Robert looked at his watch. "7:30."

Grace pinched her eyebrows.

"How are you just getting here at 7:30 in the

morning?"

"We're night hikers," Robert said.

"What?"

"We hike at night. We left at midnight."

"From the campground?" Grace asked.

"Campground's closed," Robert said. "We parked up the road a bit, near a trailhead."

Grace nodded as if this made sense.

"Who else is with you?" she asked.

"Like I said, it's just me and my girlfriend, Shelly," he said.

Grace turned to Shelly. She'd been awfully quiet this whole time. She was tall for a girl. She had blonde hair, tied back in a tight ponytail. Her skin was milky white and perfect, except for her rosy, flushed cheeks. Certainly a nice change from the dead, gray-skinned people Grace had grown accustomed to seeing. The two of them looked young, probably in their early twenties. Robert himself had quite the physique, his chest muscles prominently on display even through his fleece jacket. A Red Sox cap covered his shaggy brown hair.

She looked over Robert's shoulder, past Shelly, and off into the woods. Grace tried to remember the last time she'd seen one of the undead. It had been several days since she'd even bothered to look out the windows. Was it possible they were finally gone?

All of them?

She casually unlocked the door and opened it.

"Thank you," Robert said as he stepped in easily. Shelly smiled apologetically as she walked past Grace. The two of them looked up and down the walls and doors of the hut. Grace's head was still in a fog. *How did these people get here? Didn't they see any zombies?*

"Where is everybody?" Robert asked. He seemed a little too anxious for information.

Grace's eyes were still on the ground, unfocused.

"Hello?" Robert said again, snapping his fingers. Shelly grabbed his arm; a silent urge for him to calm down.

Grace blinked, jerked her head.

"There's nobody here," she said.

Robert and Shelly exchanged a nervous glance.

"Well, we need to call someone about that dead body," Robert insisted.

"Phone's out," Grace said dryly.

"You're kidding," Robert said.

Grace slowly shook her head. Her face was blank, expressionless.

"Well what are we going to do?" Robert asked.

"I'm sure you'll think of something," Grace said. At that, she turned toward the door.

"Wait," Robert started toward her.

"Where are you going?"

"The place is all yours," she said. "I was just leaving."

"What?!" Robert huffed like a child throwing a tantrum. "Why are *you* leaving?"

Grace stopped walking and turned to Robert. Her eyes were cold as she stared into his.

"I'm leaving because I made a promise to someone very important to me."

Robert cocked his head, confused, but he didn't say anything. He couldn't. He didn't know what that meant. He tried to think of something to say just as Shelly spoke up.

"We found a gun outside." Shelly had finally found her voice. Grace saw Robert's shoulders slump forward immediately following those words. "It was down by the lake," she added.

"Were there any bullets left in it?" Grace asked.

"No," Shelly asked. Again, Robert displayed his annoyance as he swung his arms up and down at his sides.

"Okay," Grace said. Her gaze again went to the floor as she tried to think. "I guess he only required one bullet."

"Who did?" Robert asked.

"Never mind," Grace said.

323

"Anyway, you might want to consider reloading it. There are some more bullets by the chair facing the big windows in the common room."

Grace walked to the front door, pushed it open, and walked down the steps. She swore she heard Robert's voice trailing off as she stepped out onto the lawn.

For the first time in more days than she could remember, the morning sun warmed Grace's skin and clothes. She walked across the grounds toward the lake. She stopped at the water's edge. She was amazed at how many there had been. Yet, as she stared into the crystal clear water, she saw no trace of them. She turned back to the hut and stared. It had been home for as long as she had been there. Now, it was hell; Grace would be damned if she ever found herself locked inside again.

She started toward the spot where she'd seen Roy shoot himself. The body lay face-down. There was blood and meat that had turned black and moldy on the ground. Flies had long since laid their eggs on the rotting flesh; maggots now infested the carcass.

When she came within ten feet of the body, she stopped. She thought of the life that had once occupied the form that now lay still in front of her. She wondered if Roy had had any family left. Perhaps an uncle, a cousin. She realized then that she'd never asked. She'd simply taken him for a loner. Surely he'd had friends, though. Someone would miss him. Grace would miss him—that much she knew.

Eventually, it was the shirt that tipped her off. Roy had been wearing a red flannel shirt. The body on the ground wore a tan-colored shirt. The person's hair was black also, not Roy's reddish-brown. More importantly, and even though the body was face-down, Grace could tell the person did not have a beard.

This body was not Roy.

Where the hell is Roy?

Grace's heart quickened as she looked around. She suddenly felt claustrophobic as panic began to settle in. She spun and stared back at the hut. She could see nobody; neither Robert nor Shelly passed by the large windows. Grace turned again and scanned the far edge the lake.

She saw him immediately. He was crouched by the water's edge, feeding on something. Grace recognized the red-flannel shirt, even from a hundred yards away.

Roy hadn't shot himself. At least not in the head. He'd turned into one of them. He'd probably eaten the body that now lay on the ground in front of Grace. That only meant on thing.

There would be more.

Without drawing attention to herself, Grace turned and walked quietly toward the trail. She had a long way down and she'd need more than just a head start on him.

When she could no longer see the lake or Roy, Grace broke into a sprint.

Shelly watched through binoculars as Grace disappeared into the woods.

"She's out," Shelly said. "Call it in."

Robert removed the walkie-talkie from under his shirt. He brought it to his mouth.

"Team 2, this is Team 1. We've got one down and one survivor, a woman. She's coming your way. Be advised. Over."

There was a hiss and a crackle.

"Is she clean or dirty? Over."

"She's clean," Robert said into the talkie. "She just left the hut. She's heading back to the campground. But Roy's down. He's dirty, by the lake. Over."

"We'll take care of the girl. Over."

"How's my perimeter?" Robert asked.

"Perimeter is set, five-mile radius. Over."

"Good. Keep your eyes open. You know the drill. Over and out."

Shelly stared at Robert as he calmly replaced the

talkie on his hip. She was amazed and disgusted by his callousness.

"Don't you feel anything?" Shelly asked.

Robert looked up, stunned.

"What should I feel?"

Shelly placed her hands on her hips.

"Didn't you hear what she said? That poor woman probably lost someone close to her."

Robert shrugged his shoulders.

"Hey, this is the gig," he said.

"I know," Shelly said. "And I didn't ask for it. I just wish sometimes that we didn't have to do that."

"Hey, that was always Roy's problem," Robert snapped. "He cared too much. He couldn't do one simple job like take care of the girl. Christ, he couldn't even pull the trigger on himself! And now look at him." He pointed out the window. "He's a fuckin' deadie."

Shelly stared at the ground, moping.

"Hey, don't start that shit," Robert said. "We've got a long day ahead of us and we haven't even seen the summit yet. Let's get moving."

Shelly removed an empty garbage bag from her pack. She shook it open and began searching the common room for anything that might raise suspicion. She searched inside and underneath the furniture.

She started with the large pieces—the sofas and recliners. When she finished, she stood up and made a quick scan of the room. There was an object under one of the picnic tables on the other side of the common room that caught her eye. She walked across the room and bent down to look at the item.

It was the journal.

She picked it up and quickly leafed through the pages, not stopping to read anything. She noticed a picture that looked like it had been drawn by a child. She also noticed Roy's name a couple of times as she flipped through the book.

Without spending much time, she tossed the journal into the trash bag and moved on to the kitchen. Robert was right—they had a long day ahead of them.

ACKNOWLEDGMENTS

I personally wish to acknowledge the assistance of the following people during the writing of this book: Bernard Loubier, Matt Loubier, Bernie Loubier, Matt "Deuce" Forcier, Christine Forcier, Stephanie Calderon, Kenny Barton, Tyler Loubier, Wendy Loubier, and Nick Rose. Your guidance has been invaluable.

Thanks to Michael and J.Anna Aloisi, and everybody at AuthorMike Ink Publishing for this opportunity, and for taking a chance on me. If Michael had told me 15 years ago we'd both be where we are now, I probably would have smashed a frying pan over his head. Thanks buddy.

This book would still be in dire need of assistance without the wonderful and precise efforts of its editor, Meredith Dias. You are amazing.

Special thanks to Mom and Dad: You never let me believe I was ordinary (even when I tried to be). And while I still haven't quite figured out how to thank you for that, I won't stop trying.

And to Jess, my bride: Sometimes I don't know how you put up with me, but thank you. I'm sorry for keeping you awake all those nights as I sat up in bed next to you, tapping away at my keyboard for hours (sometimes into the next morning). You've been incredibly patient with me through this entire journey. Thank you for entertaining such a crazy idea.

Lastly, but certainly not least, if you're reading this now, that means there's a good chance you've probably read this book. I especially cannot thank you enough, and I hope you enjoyed the last 300-and-something pages. Or, perhaps you simply flipped through to the acknowledgements page to see if you recognized any of the above names. In either case, and from the bottom of my dark and twisted heart, thank you.

CPSIA information can be obtained at www.ICGtesting.com
Printed in the USA
LVOW091105100911

245705LV00001B/1/P